Benjamin Squirrell
and the
Hadleigh Workhouse

A NOVEL BY

PETER HOLLAND

GW00690541

Brigand
London

Brigand Press,
All contact: info@brigand.london

Cover design
www.scottpearce.co.uk

British Library Cataloguing-in-Publication Data
A catalogue record for this book is
available from the British Library
Printed and Bound in Great Britain by CPI
Group (UK) Ltd, Croydon CR0 4YY

ISBN: 978-1-912978-30-4

Author's notes

Benjamin Squirrell and the Hadleigh Workhouse is Peter Holland's fourth novel, set in 1793. In February 2020, Peter gave a talk at Hadleigh library about the parish workhouse, the subject of his dissertation for an MA in early modern history (1500-1800). He was delighted with an audience of over sixty and the talk seemed to go well. During the discussion that followed he explained his studies had led him to become an aspiring author of historical fiction, and several members of the audience suggested his next novel should be about Hadleigh's workhouse. Just over a month later, Covid19 arrived and he set about this challenge, a welcome distraction from the worsening situation of a world-wide pandemic. He started writing in April and by November the first draft was complete.

Some characters were real; in 1793 George Watson was the minister of St Mary's, and the town surgeon was George Parsons, his name changed to John to avoid clashing with that of the reverend. However, the characterisation of them is fiction, and it is possible the workhouse master was a kind, benevolent man, and the minister and doctor were not. This is what writers of fiction do.

Benjamin Squirrell is a young Hadleigh man, who along with his parents, Peter has had the pleasure to meet over the last four years. When thinking of who the protagonists would be, his name stood out and Ben agreed to its use. Other characters in the book are based on more wonderful local people, but Peter will leave them to recognise themselves. One of his regrets is not having the literary skill to write dialogue with an accurate use of the beautiful Suffolk dialect, which one can imagine being rich and alive in the town in 1793. Perhaps he might try in a sequel.

Acknowledgements

I have been most fortunate to have received help and encouragement from a number of friends and family. Local residents Amy Smithen Bennett and Rebecca Taylor listened patiently to my ramblings about the idea of the novel on Saturday mornings along Hadleigh's disused railway track. My gratitude grew when they agreed to be readers of instalments as I wrote the book through the summer and autumn, appreciating their kind words and encouragement. Dave Bryan, Chris Douglas and Philip Tew continue to support me with patience and advice, and I was delighted to find another reader, Susan Howorth, who has known me longer than anyone. Finally, thanks go to Scott Pearce, without whom this is unlikely to have been possible.

Dedication

To the real Daisy Tappin (1921-2000)

Contents

1 Benton End Farm

An army of flies seemed to hang in suspension above the
surface of the river, drawing the children towards the riverbank
for a curious, closer inspection. Sarah held the hand of the
youngest, eight-year-old Amy, lest she tumble down the bank
into the River Brett. There was no danger of drowning at this
point in the river's course at this time of year. Just half a mile
downstream from Hadleigh, where the Brett gently meandered
past a group of cottages and a farm, collectively known as
Benton End, Sarah's concern was the chastisement she and
Amy might face from Mr Ward if they returned to town in wet
clothes at the end of their day of labour.

The nine children had been relieved to deposit the bale
of hay in the meadow under the long overhanging branches of a
large willow tree, and as soon as they put it down three horses
casually traipsed towards them. A wooden pallet was used to
transport the bale, which must have weighed close to 300 lbs.
The two eldest, sixteen-year-old Sarah, and seventeen-year-old
Benjamin, supervised the group, instructing them where to
take hold of the load, and despite their number, it remained a
difficult task. Thankfully, the journey was just 100 yards from
John Humphries' barn, from where the farmer watched without
offering help, only a few words and gestures to focus their
attention.

'Come on, I haven't got all day, and do not pay Daniel
Ward good money for you to tarry!' Humphries snarled raising
his stick. The bale was carefully lifted, with Ben, Sarah,
Arthur and George taking most of the weight at the corners of
the pallet, the other five children filling the spaces in between.

'Take care Amy, do not stand beneath the pallet, lest
we lose our grip and it falls on to you,' Ben said kindly to
the youngest, who in her effort to help lowered her shoulder
beneath the load. The pallet was slowly carried down the gentle
slope from Benton End Farm, across the Colchester Road,
towards the river. Standing on the riverbank, they could see
more clearly that the mass of flies was not suspended, rather it

was moving up and down, as if dancing, or performing a ritual.

'What are they doing?' Amy asked, still holding Sarah's hand, feeling comfort and security from contact with the older girl.

'They are mayflies, Amy, and they do this for just a short time each year,' Sarah replied.

'What is it they do?' Amy asked, and Sarah realised it might be the first time Amy had witnessed this sight.

'Well, they are dancing, looking for a partner, to mate and produce a family,' Sarah said.

'And then what happens to them? Because I have not seen them before,' Amy asked with curiosity.

'Some people say they fly away to become fairies, Amy. Other people say, after laying their eggs, they die.'

'I think I prefer the first story,' Amy said looking up at Sarah.

'Me too,' Sarah replied with a smile.

As eight of the children had stood admiring the mayflies' choreography, Ben had run back to the farm to collect the basket they had carried with them that morning.

'We should rest a while,' he said on his return.

'Should we eat now, Ben?' Sarah asked.

'Yes, but perhaps we should move along, leaving the horses in the shade of the willow with their bale. Otherwise, they may take a fancy to our victuals,' he replied with a smile to his friend. Just to their right were the remains of a building, with some large stones and rotting wood.

'What was here?' Arthur asked.

'There was once a water mill here,' Ben replied.

'To make flour?' Arthur said.

'No, not here, Arthur. The flour mills are the bigger ones in town. It was probably a mill used for grinding corn or perhaps fulling,' Ben said as the children looked at him, and he knew further explanation would be required. 'Fulling is part of the woollen cloth process, where the wool from the sheep is made more durable. The water from the Brett was diverted here to turn the mill wheel, which powered a mechanism to beat the cloth. Or it may have been a small corn grinding mill.'

His audience listened in silence as he attempted to explain the feat of engineering, but Ben could see from their faces that more detail might be difficult to comprehend, so he led them towards the riverbank.

Inside the basket was a linen parcel, tied with string, as well as two clay containers, their spouts sealed with corks from old wine bottles. They all gathered as Ben and Sarah opened the linen parcel to reveal two loaves and a slab of cheese, and uncorking the containers freed the unmistakeable aroma of a weak ale. A knife was taken from the basket to cut the loaves and cheese, which was passed hand to hand amongst the children, followed by the clay containers, each member of the group taking a draught from the same spout. For some minutes no words were spoken as each of them felt pleasure in being free from lock and key, and commands from the adults who controlled their lives. They were sat on a riverbank in the early summer sunshine, watching the miracle of thousands of mayflies competing for mates. Freshly baked bread, Suffolk cheese and local ale added to their contentment, and for a short while they could forget the reality of their condition. Looking at the seven younger children sitting between her and Ben, Sarah glanced up to see him doing the same and smiled. Seeing Sarah smile in his direction gave Benjamin Squirrell a warm feeling, as he could not deny he had come to admire her. Sitting in her company, he knew they could not stay on the riverbank for long but could not resist the temptation to remain until called. They did not have to wait long.

'You lot, you have eaten and tarried long enough. I have paid for your labour, not your pleasure. Look lively or face the consequences!' Humphries called from the road and turned to return the short distance to his barn.

'Come on, we must return to work,' Ben said, rising to his feet and led the children back up the gentle slope across the road to the farm.

Alongside the farm was the imposing Benton End House, a tall building that stood like a fortress, guarding the town from invaders who might approach from the south along the Colchester road. Ben wondered who might live in such a huge house, which looked larger than the building in which he dwelt with seventy others. To the rear of the house a wall separated Benton End's famous gardens from the farm fields on which he and the others were to toil. Evidently a great man named Adam Buddle, learned in the art of botany, had lived there 100 years earlier, and as a consequence the gardens were rich with rare and exotic plants and flowers. But they were not there to admire or learn about nature as John Humphries was waiting for them and did not look pleased.

'I said you could stop to eat, not take repose! Before you finish for the day, I want that north field planted, half turnips, half potatoes, so the good people of Hadleigh will have food for the winter.'

'Yes, sir,' Ben replied, knowing Humphries was a man to avoid vexing, having seen him set about boys, and even girls, who were under his charge for a day of work. 'We will set to immediately, sir.'

'Go on, then,' Humphries replied, 'and be sure to do it with care, or Ward will be informed, and the payment reduced.'

The children followed Ben as he marched briskly towards the field behind the barn to begin the afternoon's labour. 'At least he has not raised his stick,' Ben thought, but he did not look behind to where Sarah had waited to ensure none of the younger children should incur the farmer's ire. As she was last to walk past him, Humphries moved across her, causing her to stop, and casually raised his hand to touch her breast. Sarah froze with revulsion, embarrassment, and a feeling of shame, but could not think of anything to say and looked down at the ground.

'Sorry, miss,' Humphries said with a smirk, 'you had better get along,' and stepped back, allowing her to continue.

'Come on, Sarah,' Amy said, turning round on hearing Humphries' voice, but ignorant of what caused Sarah to pause.

'Yes, Amy,' Sarah replied, relieved to hear the little girl's concern, and hurried after the others, as if nothing had happened.

They worked for five hours until the field was planted, and after an inspection by the farmer, they were dismissed.

Ben led the group out of the farm past Benton End House that towered above them, making their way back to Hadleigh along Benton Street. It had been a day of tiring labour, particularly the afternoon of bending to plant, but they had been outside in the sunshine all day. He looked over at Sarah, who seemed quiet.

'Are you well, Sarah?'

'Yes, Ben. Thank you. I am weary from our toil.'

'Ah, yes. We should all sleep well tonight,' he replied.

Sarah tried, unsuccessfully, to smile. Her thoughts were of farmer Humphries and his hand on her. 'Why did he do that?' she thought, feeling an overwhelming sadness.

The walk along Benton Street in the late-afternoon sunshine returned the children to a rare feeling of well-being and temporary freedom they had enjoyed earlier sitting by the Brett watching mayflies. As they proceeded along Benton Street, to their left groups of cottages, varying in age, hid their view of the Brett. Where gaps appeared, they could see the river beyond the meadows along its banks. To their right, more cottages lined the road, behind which the land climbed steeply to the Priory woods.

Their return to Hadleigh was interrupted as a collection of swallows wove between the small buildings, over a herd of cows and along the river, before rising vertically towards the heavens. The audience of nine stood in amazement at the acrobatic performance, as the swallows disappeared from view, reappearing from the direction of Benton End to deliver another display.

'What birds are they, Ben?' asked Arthur, one of the younger boys in the group.

'I think they are swallows, Arthur. Although they could be swifts. It is hard to tell when they fly so fast,' Ben replied.

'What is the difference between them?' Amy asked. All nine gazed up to the sky, squinting as they tried to focus on the birds, listening for any knowledge Ben might share.

'Well, I think swallows have a slightly longer tail, and may be lighter in colour.'

'Are they like the mayflies, Ben?' Amy asked, 'because

I do not think they are always here.'

Amy's reasoning caused Sarah to smile, for a moment forgetting the incident earlier at the farm, and she looked admiringly to their tutor to listen to his reply.

'Swallows are like mayflies as creatures that appear at the beginning of summer, Amy, but I do not think they die the next day or become fairies. People say they fly here from distant lands to the south, where it is warm during the winter. They stay here through the summer, fly away when the days turn cold, then return again the following year.'

All of the children were looking at Ben as he explained another mystery of nature. It was different to the teaching they received in the 'house, which was less interesting, focusing on learning their letters and numbers.

'I think I should like to be a swallow,' Amy said, envying the freedom of the bird to leave England when the cold came.

'Or a swift!' Arthur added with a smile.

'Aye, a swallow or a swift would be a fine life,' Ben replied, understanding their sentiments, which reminded him of the time. 'We had best be getting back, lest Mr Ward is displeased.' With that the lesson was ended and they continued towards town.

Five minutes later they reached the end of Benton Street, where it became Hadleigh High Street, leading straight into the town. At the point where the road name changed was a junction with the Ipswich Road, which climbed the hill out of Hadleigh towards Suffolk's largest town, just ten miles away.

'Let's cross the river over the footbridge by the mill, then back across Toppesfield Bridge,' Ben said, leading them down to the left, off the main road. The children willingly followed him, happy to enjoy the river for a few more minutes before being fed and kept inside for the night. He led them down the steep Tinker's Lane, along a narrow path between two vegetable gardens, and over the little footbridge that was no more than ropes and pieces of wood, just where the river was at its narrowest after the great engineering feat of the mill wheel. They could have forded the Brett where Tinkers Lane crossed as there had not been rain for some time and the river was low, but this was more fun.

'Don't fall in,' Arthur called as he shook the side ropes, causing an unstable vibration through the pieces of wood along which they stepped carefully. But none of the children were afraid, with even Amy shrieking with delight and shared laughter.

Four minutes later they were crossing the river again over Toppesfield Bridge, a more solid structure than the footbridge by the mill; wide enough for carts and carriages to cross in opposite directions, built from stone with three arches more than 400 years earlier. The town side of the bridge became Duke Street leading 200 yards back to the high street, but a short way along this thoroughfare they turned left along a path to Market Street and the Ram Inn. Turning right just past the hostelry was a path leading to their destination, the back of the Hadleigh Guildhall. There sitting outside on the steps to the back door sat Daniel Ward smoking tobacco from a clay pipe, watching as the children had turned onto the path.

'At last, there you are. Why have you come from the direction of the bridge, and not the high street?' he barked.

'We came via the mill, sir,' Ben replied, fearful of what might follow, but thankfully there were no blows as punishment for their diversion.

'Well, get in. Mistress Yates has supper ready and the others are hungry,' and Ward gestured for them to enter the building through the small door. His face was a blank mask until Sarah passed; she was met with a grin which she did not acknowledge and lowered her head to avoid his stare. However, it was witnessed by Ben who noticed her discomfort. 'Good,' Ward said. The door was closed and bolted, and Hadleigh's workhouse doors were secured by the master.

Inside, the nine children joined sixty-three other souls at a collection of tables in the main downstairs room of the guildhall. A supper of vegetable broth with traces of game, and a thick slice of bread was prepared by Tess Yates, mistress of the workhouse and three of the older women inmates, whose primary role was feeding the other sixty-nine paupers. An hour later all seventy-two inmates were in their beds and another day was over.

2 Parish Vestry

The Reverend George Watson and Eleanor, his fourteen-year-old daughter, stood under the portico at the entrance to his church, peering up towards the sky.

'It is raining, father. Shall we go home until it ceases?'

'I think it is just a brief summer shower, Eleanor. Look, there is blue sky following the gloom.' Sure enough the clouds that brought the heavy shower were moving on, giving the impression of being pursued by sunshine.

It was only thirty or so footsteps from the entrance of St Mary's to the Deanery, their home, at the south end of the church. However, the reverend wanted to walk round to the north side to call in on his friend, John Parsons, the town surgeon, to talk about a matter for their next vestry meeting. Eleanor was friends with the doctor's daughter, Alice, making the visit a pleasant occasion for her too. So, instead of returning to the Deanery, they took a few minutes to sit on the stone seating of the portico, looking across the small graveyard that lined the east side of the church, and the impressive guildhall barely forty yards away, just beyond the headstones. St Mary's was an equally imposing church, larger than might be expected for a town the size of Hadleigh. It was believed to date back more than 700 years to the time of Guthrum, the local lord who made peace with Alfred, but the old Anglo Saxon edifice was rebuilt by Norman lords after the Conquest, and then by English merchants and tradesmen in the fifteenth-century. Like the wide high street, St Mary's was testament to the wealth created by the woollen cloth industry, trade and wealth that had diminished over the preceding century, but the church and high street remained.

As forecast by her father, the rain ceased after a few minutes, replaced by bright sunshine, giving the grass between the graves a sparkling sheen. Eleanor smiled and looked up at her father, whose thoughts were elsewhere.

'It has stopped raining, father. Shall we continue?' she asked, eager to see her friend.

'Yes, of course, my child,' George replied, his thoughts returning to the present.

They walked along the path that separated the east side of the church from the graveyard, with a view to turning left along Church Walk. As they got to the top end of the church, seven adults and five children walked across their path, causing them to stop.

'Watch yourselves,' a man shouted with authority from the rear of the line. 'Reverend Watson does not want you walking across his feet, or those of his daughter.'

George Watson recognised the voice of Daniel Ward. He also knew some of the weary faces from his regular visits to their place of abode, as well as coming into closer contact with them and others when offering the holy sacrament of communion each Sunday. Eleanor did not recognise individuals but knew who they were as a collective. She was well aware that behind the impressive Tudor frontage of the guildhall lived many unfortunate souls.

'Thank you, sir,' and, 'Thank you, Reverend Watson,' several said as they passed, nodding respectfully, even touching a forelock. The last of the inmates was followed by Daniel Ward.

'Good day to you, Reverend, and to you, Miss Eleanor.'

'Good day to you, Daniel. Have they toiled all morning?'

'Aye, Reverend. They have worked the fields by the river, just the other side of Pound Lane,' Ward replied. He sensed his superior's concern and did not care to explain himself, so he said no more and followed his charges along the path at the side of the guildhall towards the entrance at the rear.

Eleanor was struck by the sight of the children, whose coarse linen workhouse uniforms were wet, suggesting they had not taken shelter during the rain. Further evidence was their wet hair, matted to their heads and faces, producing a look of destitution. But she knew these children were not destitute.

'Father, will they change into dry clothes once inside the guildhall?' she asked as they disappeared from view.

'I am sure they will, Eleanor,' he replied, more through hope than certainty. 'That is something else I might raise at the vestry meeting,' he thought as they proceeded the short distance along Church Walk to John Parsons' house.

The church vestry had been added to the north end of the church back when the woollen cloth industry was still profitable. Beyond, another graveyard lined the west side of the church, where the stones were in shadow most of the day due to the height of St Mary's and a number of large trees. Church Walk ran parallel with the high street just fifty yards to the north, visible at the end of several dusty paths between the houses. Two houses dominating Church Walk were the Red House, with its two great Tudor chimneys, then Church House fifty yards further along, which whilst being as big as its neighbour, had a more modest appearance, partly hidden by a well-kept hedge. As they walked past the Red House, someone was visible behind the hedge of the house ahead.

'Alice!' Eleanor called and a broad smile spread across her face. She looked up at her father, who returned a gracious look and nodded, signalling his daughter permission to run the short distance to the gap in the hedge at the entrance to Church House. Inside, greetings were exchanged, and the two girls were free to spend time together in and around the building, providing they left their fathers to speak privately in John Parsons' study. Church House had been closely connected to St Mary's for over 200 years, and Reverend George Watson found it ironic that he was able to sit securely above a priest hole, built at the time of the Tudors to hide his predecessors, who could be burnt at the stake for heresy.

'For what reason do I owe the pleasure of your visit, George? Not that you need a reason to come to my humble abode,' the doctor asked as he poured tea.

'There are a couple of matters that I wish to raise at the vestry meeting this evening, John, to which I thought I would make you privy beforehand,' the Reverend George Watson replied. In the privacy of the doctor's study the two men talked for almost an hour, until it was time for their daughters to return to their studies.

The Deanery Tower, popularly known as 'Pykenham's Folly', had stood for 300 years. It was an impressive but strange, anomalous structure, dominating the south end of the area where St Mary's stood on one side, the guildhall on the other. Archdeacon William Pykenham had it built as a gatehouse to what was hoped would be a palatial home, but completed in 1495, nothing else was constructed as the Archdeacon died in 1497. Almost 300 years later his monumental gatehouse looked out of place, the palace he had hoped to build never realised, but perhaps to call it his 'folly' was ungenerous of the churchman who also built twelve almshouses on George Street, providing security for up to twenty-four elderly poor for three centuries. However, Pykenham's Tower was not left to ruin, as it formed a welcome extension to the Deanery, housing amongst other things a fine library. It was in this room that Reverend Watson invited the five other vestry officials for their meeting that evening.

'Good evening, gentlemen. Thank you for coming here for our gathering,' Reverend Watson said. 'Would you care for a glass of wine?' His convivial greeting and start to the meeting was met with nods and smiles by the other attendees. The library in the tower attached to the Deanery was not large but comfortably accommodated six men sat around the circular table, and the shelves of books provided a learned environment in which to conduct vestry business. Six glasses of red wine were poured, each man carefully lifting the small, delicate crystal to his lips. As well as the town surgeon, the other vestry officials were John Brownwigg, churchwarden and Hadleigh man of substance. Samuel Hancock, churchwarden, assessor of land taxes and rates, and owner of several small businesses. Edward Grady, assessor of land taxes and rates and owner of the Falcon ale house. And lastly, Daniel Ward, the master of the workhouse, who coming from Ipswich was not a local man, and unlike the others, he was in paid employment to fulfil his duties in ensuring the parish delivered the poor relief it was obliged to provide by law.

Once greetings were exchanged and wine sipped,

Reverend Watson opened the meeting with a prayer, followed by the usual format.

'Doctor Parsons has agreed to minute the meeting, and so we shall get straight down to business. Mr Ward could you inform us of the current numbers of souls inhabiting the workhouse. Have there been any changes since our last meeting one month ago?'

'Well, Reverend, I can report there are currently seventy-two inmates residing inside that place across the way. A month ago, there were seventy-three, but two left, one eight-year-old boy having the good fortune to be offered an apprenticeship, and one elderly spinster being placed in one of Pykenham's almshouses. In the same month we have received a new inmate, a sixteen-year-old girl.' Daniel Ward spoke plainly and dispassionately.

'Thank you, Mr Ward. May I ask if the spinster has been given a whole almshouse to herself?' John Brownwigg asked indignantly, as the one roomed terraced homes were intended for two occupants.

'No, Mr Brownwigg, she will share with another elderly woman recently widowed,' Ward replied.

'May I ask if the two women know each other?' the reverend asked.

'I cannot say, Reverend. Does it matter?' Ward replied, rather curtly.

'No, of course. I am sure the lady is pleased to find herself in a secure place with the company of another of similar circumstance,' Watson said.

John Parsons could sense the difference between the two men, so offered some support for his friend by asking, 'And who is the girl who has recently arrived, and what is her circumstance?'

'The girl is Sarah Taylor. Her mother receives outdoor relief, but they were not coping, so the eldest child has been admitted to the workhouse,' Ward replied, knowing either the reverend or the doctor would question this arrangement.

'Could we not have increased the outdoor relief to the mother, to allow the family to stay together?' Reverend Watson asked, but Ward was prepared.

'That family has received increases in outdoor relief twice in the last year, Reverend. Is it fair to other families who seem to manage? Besides, coming to the 'house gives the girl an opportunity to contribute. She is young and strong, so can work, instead of being idle in her subsidised home.' He was ready with a strong economic argument, which was met with agreeing nods from three of the others, outnumbering the reverend and the doctor.

'Very well, thank you for this information, Mr Ward. Let us move on to financial matters. Mr Grady and Mr Hancock, could you report on income you have collected for the parish,' George Watson asked.

'Well, sir, I mean Reverend,' Edward Grady said, 'Mr Hancock and I divided the assessing and collection of land tax from farmers and poor rates from households, he collecting from the farmers, whilst I visited and collected from the other.'

'Very good, Mr Grady. That sounds like a sensible and time-saving arrangement. What is the outcome of your endeavour?'

'I can report that the parish has collected eighteen pounds nine shillings six pence in land tax from forty-three farmers this month, sirs, which is slightly more than the previous month. This gives us a total of fifty-one pounds eight shillings four pence for the last quarter, sirs,' Samuel Hancock said, and the others nodded, indicating their approval.

'This compares to the poor rate I collected from households, which came to thirty-two pounds two shillings nine pence for the last month, also an increase on the previous month. For the last quarter the total poor rate collection is ninety-four pounds fifteen shillings seven pence,' Edward Grady added, and again there were approving nods as Doctor Parsons recorded the figures.

'Thank you, gentlemen,' Reverend Watson said, turning back to Ward. 'Would you report the figures for the indoor and outdoor relief, Mr Ward?'

'Yes, Reverend. Would you like the figures for the workhouse first, or those for outdoor relief?'

'Whichever one you have to hand, Mr Ward.'

'Outdoor relief was provided last month for twenty-three families, which totalled 108 souls, at a cost of thirty-five pounds seven shillings five pence, and one hundred and twelve pounds three shillings six pence for the quarter.' The other five listened carefully and Dr Parsons continued to record the figures. 'In the workhouse, expenditure was twenty-four pounds three shillings ten pence for the month, and ninety-six pounds seventeen shillings four pence for the quarter. Workhouse income for the month was twenty-three pounds four shillings eight pence, and sixty-eight pounds thirteen shillings two pence for the quarter.' Ward was succinct, no need for explaining, just the figures, which the doctor computed. In fact, all six men had made their own columns of money coming in, and money leaving the parish coffers. After a minute or two, Doctor Parsons spoke.

'If we are looking at the last quarter, which gives a wider view of the parish accounts, I believe the totals are as follows: Income from land taxes of fifty-one pounds eight shillings four pence, poor rates of ninety-four pounds fifteen shillings seven pence, and the workhouse of sixty-eight pounds thirteen shillings two pence, comes to a total of two hundred and fourteen pounds seventeen shillings one penny. Expenditure of ninety-six pounds seventeen shillings four pence for indoor relief in the workhouse, and one hundred and twelve pounds three shillings six pence for outdoor relief, comes to a total of two hundred and nine pounds and ten pence. Therefore, I am pleased to declare the parish poor relief system has shown a surplus of five pounds sixteen shillings three pence for the last quarter.' The others looked at their lists as the doctor spoke, and eventually they all looked up.

'Are we in agreement, gentlemen?' Reverend Watson asked, to be met with a collection of 'Aye,' and 'Yes, Reverend,' replies. 'Excellent, gentlemen. May I thank the three of you for your continued and conscientious service to the parish in our efforts to fulfil our obligations and do God's work,' the reverend added.

'Amen,' the other five concluded.

'If that is all, Reverend, I would like to seek further refreshment in the Ram,' Daniel Ward said with a smile, 'and anyone else is welcome to join me,' and lifted himself from the chair.

'Ah, there are a couple of points I would like to raise, if you could just delay your appointment at the Ram a few more minutes, Mr Ward,' George Watson said, causing the workhouse master's smile to disappear as he sat back in the chair.

'Of course, what is it, Reverend?' Ward asked looking around the table.

'Well, it is a sensitive matter, Mr Ward, and I do not wish to offend you by questioning your judgement.' Reverend Watson paused, casting a glance towards his friend and ally, Dr Parsons. There was quiet for a few seconds as he considered his words before continuing. 'Some of us are becoming concerned that the children in the workhouse seem to be continually used as a source of labour for farmers and manufacturers, when they might be receiving schooling and doing light work inside the workhouse.'

Ward looked directly at Watson, 'They work to contribute towards paying their cost to the good people of the parish, who have to pay for the poor through land taxes and rates, Reverend.' Ward could barely conceal his contempt. 'Would you have us increase those taxes and rates so the younger paupers can be schooled all day? I think those people who pay for the workhouse may say otherwise.' Ward answered him with a strong argument; the money to fund poor relief had to come from somewhere, so Reverend Watson left that matter for another day, but could ask a second question about the welfare of the children.

'Very well, Mr Ward. May I ask if the children have a change of clothes? This concern became apparent this morning when I saw them returning from working in the fields in the rain. They looked most pitiful, understandably tired from their labour, but so wet they might suffer an ague. If illness takes hold in the close confines of the workhouse, we may have fewer able to work. Do you agree, Doctor Parsons?' the reverend said, looking to his friend for some support.

'Indeed, there is increasing knowledge from physicians suggesting mild infections of the lungs and chest can lead to more serious disease, particularly if the patient suffers from cold and damp living conditions. But I think we have always known this. Were we not all chided by our mothers, "you will catch your death," when we were young?' Doctor Parsons offered hope for Reverend Watson, and Ward realised this was a persuasive argument, particularly if the children became ill when he needed them to work.

'I believe there are dry linen undershirts that can be worn if work teams return wet,' the master relented.

'Very good, Mr Ward,' the reverend replied, 'could you let me know if more clothing is required. I am sure we can find the funds to procure them if necessary. Particularly in light of the surplus this quarter.'

'Yes, reverend. I will enquire with Mistress Yates,' Ward said, wanting to get to the Ram and a pint of ale.

There was no more vestry business to be conducted, so Reverend Watson concluded proceedings with thanks to the vestry officials and to God. Ten minutes later, after polite goodnights were exchanged, Edward Grady, Samuel Hancock and Daniel Ward were sat at a booth in the Ram Inn. They had looked about carefully to see if there might be others who could overhear, but it was almost deserted except for a few old men at the other end of the room. Nonetheless, after purchasing three pints of ale, they spoke in hushed voices.

'The priest is a botherer, who does not understand the complexity and economic reality of poor relief,' Ward said before taking a draught of ale, some of the liquid escaping his mouth and dripping from his chin onto the table.

'Aye, it is plain to see he irritates you, Daniel. But be patient, it is his vocation to fret over the poor. Besides, keeping him satisfied with the work we do, is to our gain. So, if a few linen shirts, or even an extra hour of lessons, are required to keep him happy, we should comply with his requests.' Edward Grady was circumspect. There was no need to take risks by drawing unwanted attention over the welfare of the inmates.

They needed to look at their position without prejudice or emotion.

Sam Hancock nodded in agreement with Edward Grady, adding, 'Aye, let the good reverend have some clothes for the paupers, and we can continue in our enterprise unhindered. Speaking of which, how have we done this month, Dan?'

'We continue to prosper, Sam,' Ward replied, 'the difference between what we declared this evening for land tax revenue and what we collected, was eighteen shillings nine pence. For poor rates it was sixteen shillings six pence, and for workhouse labour it was thirteen shillings six pence. If my arithmetic is correct, that is a total of two pounds eight shillings nine pence, which shared three ways comes to sixteen shillings three pence each. Do you agree?' he asked his two partners. They thought for a few seconds, nodded and smiled.

'Aye, that sounds about right, Dan,' Samuel said.

'Good work,' Edward concurred.

'Right then,' Ward said, pulling his cloth cap to the edge of the table. He calmly reached into his purse and produced two small cloth bundles, each tied with string. Placing them under his cap, he pushed it back to the middle of the table. First Edward moved his cap to the middle, alongside Ward's, which he lifted moving one of the small packages from under the cap to his and moved it back to his lap. The same manoeuvre was repeated by Samuel and their business was concluded. Each man smiled with satisfaction, enjoyed another pint of ale and departed for the night, their spoils being more than a God-fearing soul might earn through honest labour in one week.

3 Sarah

Sarah remembered the day two months earlier when Daniel Ward came to their cottage. The man was blunt and he intimidated her mother.

'Mrs Taylor, it is too costly to the parish for your family to remain in this house,' Daniel Ward had said. Margaret Taylor stood aghast, hearing words she had dreaded.

'Sir, Mr Ward, what does that mean?' she asked, when in truth, she knew already.

'It means, Mrs Taylor, the five of you can no longer stay here, unless you can contribute towards the cost of your habitation, food and fuel,' he replied.

The mother of four put an arm round the shoulders of her two middle children, whilst her eldest, Sarah, placed her arms around the youngest, Alice, just ten years old.

'Sir, where will we go?' the distraught mother asked, as tears fell down her cheeks.

'Madam, you know where you will go. The parish has been bound by law for over 200 years, since the reign of Elizabeth, to provide a place of habitation for its poor, and that place is the workhouse.'

Margaret, like everyone in England, knew this, but she was hoping beyond hope that there might be an alternative. Perhaps a smaller house, less costly for the parish ratepayers. After a few moments to fully comprehend his meaning, she released her hold on her children and sank to her knees, her head almost touching the master's boots.

'Sir, I beg of you, is there another place, a smaller cottage? We could cope with just one room.'

'There are no other homes I know of that are vacant at this time, madam. It is not the responsibility of the parish to provide houses. We provide those things to keep you alive, but paying the rent is beyond our obligation. If the rent cannot be paid, then we will place you in the workhouse. There is no other alternative. The parish can place in this cottage a more deserving family than yours; one that can pay some of the costs. Such a family would be less of a burden on the men who pay their rates to provide relief for the likes of you.' Ward spat out the last four words to make his disdain plain.

Margaret Taylor could not see the contempt in his face. She was crouched low, ashamed and humiliated, embarrassed that the children should see her condition. Ward looked up from the wretched woman at his feet and focused on the four children. 'Perhaps there is a solution that could see you remain here.'

'Yes, sir,' the mother said, looking up, wiping tears with her apron. 'Thank you, sir. What is it?' She gathered herself, stood up and placed a hand on the shoulders of the two middle children, listening to hear the solution that might save them.

'Your liability to the parish could be lessened if one or two of you came to the workhouse to earn money to contribute towards the cost of your family to the parish. You must understand this is not an arrangement that is offered to every family.' They listened in silence to their possible salvation and pondered its meaning.

'Would we come to the workhouse each day, sir?' the mother asked. 'How many of us would be required?'

'You did not hear me clearly, Mrs Taylor, or did you misunderstand? I said one or two, and they would be required to reside in the workhouse until you no longer required poor relief as a family. At such point you would be self-sufficient and no longer a liability to this parish.' He was getting irritated by the pathetic woman. Again, there was quiet as the family realised its meaning.

'Sir, you would have me give over one, or two of my children?'

'You are not "giving" them, madam, they would be working to support their family, which is beyond your means.' His voice was becoming stern. 'You can take it or leave it. I have other things to attend to. I can be back tomorrow with men to see the house is cleared.' That was his final word, but he hoped she would accept the offer, which might help him pursue another enterprise for his pleasure.

Margaret was quiet, trying to consider the possibilities. The youngest children going to that place was too painful. She had heard stories of boys and girls suffering cruelly and rarely seeing the light of day. 'Perhaps I should go, leaving Sarah to care for her brothers and sister?' she thought.

'Mother, I will go,' Sarah announced. 'It might be for just a short while and I can do more work than my brothers and sister. Besides, they need you, their mother, here.' Margaret looked at Sarah, and wanted to protest, to say 'no', but her throat was dry, and she realised it was the only option to ensure they did not all go to that place the next day. For a moment she was quiet.

'Would that be satisfactory, sir?' Margaret asked.

'I said one or two, but if the girl works hard and obeys orders from Mistress Yates and myself, then she may be enough to ensure your family can remain here.'

'Yes, sir. I will, sir,' the girl said.

'Very well, I expect to see you tomorrow morning when St Mary's strikes seven.' With that, Daniel Ward turned and walked out of the cottage.

So it was that she came to reside in the workhouse, alongside seventy or more others, ranging in age from an infant there with its mother, to a woman of eighty, unable to be housed in one of the town's almshouses. After the initial shock of the reality of being kept under lock and key, Sarah found she adapted to the strict regime of life inside the guildhall without difficulty. Breakfast, some sort of lunch, and supper were served every day, and the inmates who prepared it tried to make each meal as nutritious as possible. She realised this alone made the workhouse attractive to a homeless beggar, as well as each inmate having their own bed in one of four large rooms for adult men, women, boys, and girls. At the age of sixteen she was one of the eldest in this last bedroom, not yet considered an adult woman. Lights out was at sunset in summer, and they rose from their beds at 6.00am when St Mary's bell struck six times. The work was more tedious than it was tiring, and providing she kept her head down, she was safe from being chided or punished. Perhaps the best part of her new life was making friends and providing comfort to the younger paupers, like Amy, an orphan of eight years. There was even schooling, at which she was one of the most learned, having been taught her letters and numbers when she was younger. In fact, she was asked to assist the teacher in passing on her knowledge to the children, something she enjoyed, even encouraging her to aspire to one day becoming a respectable teacher in Hadleigh, or a surrounding village or town. However, Sarah's relatively tranquil existence in the workhouse lasted only a month.

***

'Foul, disgusting girl!' the master shouted. 'Mistress Yates, help me put this miscreant into the box.' He was grappling with Lucy Draper, who was lashing out with fist and nails, drawing a line of blood on Daniel Ward's cheek. Lucy was not a small girl and was strong having lived on a farm before finding herself in this place through no fault of her own, due to unfortunate family circumstances when her father died a few years earlier. With long dark hair and eyebrows, which made her alluring to men, she had the physique of a young woman not to be trifled with. Ward had admired her for some time, but it was only after some ale in the George tavern on the high street earlier that day that he found the confidence to try his luck. But the ale had clouded his judgement, as master or not, she was unwilling to tolerate his groping advance. Only once he was assisted by Tess Yates did they manage to force Lucy to the floor, watched in shock and horror by an assortment of inmates. No one had witnessed his failed attempt to molest her, made aware only by her screams and the ensuing furore. As Tess Yates sat on Lucy's legs, the girl was pinioned by Ward gripping her wrists and holding her arms tight behind her back, causing her to scream with pain.

'Squirrell!' Ward said seeing Benjamin looking on, 'bring the manacles from my office. Hurry boy!'

Whether he thought their treatment of Lucy was severe was irrelevant, Ben had to follow the order, or face Ward's wrath as well. He fetched the shackles as instructed, with padlock and key attached, passed them to the master, who quickly employed them with their intended purpose. The result was Lucy's incapacitation, making further struggle futile. But Ward did not intend to leave her with any doubt about her position and once Tess lifted herself off Lucy's stricken body, he grabbed hold of the girl's long black hair, hauling her to her feet. He continued to exert control by wrenching her hair back so forcefully her face was lifted to stare at the ceiling. The manacles had been applied tightly so they pressed hard into her flesh and wrists, causing her further discomfort. She could have kicked him, but she knew her resistance was over.

'You all saw it. This girl has committed a serious assault against an officer of the parish,' he shouted so the gathered throng could bear witness. 'She may well find herself before a justice of the peace for her violent action, but until that is decided, she will spend a week in the box. Mistress Yates, if you would be so good to assist me…'

Lucy was led to the back of the guildhall, where a room was used for storing anything not being used, from piles of unprocessed wool to the spinning wheels used to manufacture cloth. Any protest by Lucy was prevented by Ward pulling her hair so tight her mouth was wide open, unable to form words. Everyone knew of the box and where it was located; at the back of the storeroom was a square wooden panel in the floor, measuring three feet by three feet. Beneath the wooden panel was a hole in the floor, which had been dug many years earlier for the purpose of providing a subterranean cell. Some said it was a hole used to hide catholic priests at the time of the last Edward and Elizabeth. It was six feet in depth, with nothing at the bottom, except for a bucket for a prisoner's waste. Tess Yates lifted open the wooden panel with some sadness, as she had seen what time in the box could do to a young person. She was of a mind that lashes would be more kind than isolation in a tiny space in complete darkness, interrupted just once a day for removal of the waste bucket and passing food and water down to the unfortunate occupant. When Ward announced a week in the box for Lucy, Tess was taken aback. 'Was he serious? Would the girl survive a week?' she thought. But it was not her position to question or undermine the master, her superior, particularly when he was enraged. 'If he's kept her in there for three days, I will appeal to him to show clemency as we need her to work on picking the rope that was ordered yesterday,' Tess thought, but before then she had to assist Ward in getting the girl safely into the box. With a compliant prisoner, this could be achieved by lowering them carefully, lest they injure themselves in the six feet drop to the bottom of the hole. However, with a young strong woman with Lucy's spirit they were not guaranteed co-operation. Ward stood Lucy at the edge of the hole into which, one way or another, she would be placed, maintaining control through his tight grip on her hair and the manacles behind her back.

'Sit down, girl,' he said quietly in her ear, so no one else other than Tess Yates could hear. Lucy had no choice but to comply, lowering herself to the floor, so she was sat with her legs hung over the edge of the hole. Keeping a tight grip on her hair with one hand, he leaned forward for one last comment before she began her sentence. 'Just remember this, next time you decide to defy me.' With his other hand he turned the key in the padlock of the manacles, which fell with the chains to the floor behind Lucy and he used his boot to push her forward into the hole. Lucy had half expected to be pushed into the hole and managed to move her arms forward and bend her knees, avoiding serious injury from the fall, apart from a collection of scratches and bruises. Without further word, Ward placed the panel back into position and used the padlock from the manacles to secure the bolt. With his heartbeat falling and satisfied he had maintained his authority in front of the inmates, he turned and left, leaving Tess Yates to pause with some sadness. Her thoughts were with the girl below, alone in the hole in darkness.

The incident with Lucy left a darker cloud than normal over the workhouse. Anyone who had not witnessed it was soon made aware through whispers later as nightfall came and the inmates prepared for bed. After a day or two, Daniel Ward's mood improved, to the relief of the inmates and Tess Yates, who had tended to Lucy, taking food, emptying the waste bucket, and speaking to her for a couple of minutes each day. After the third day, Tess spoke to her superior.

'The girl has been in the box for three nights. Shall we get her out to start working and paying her way?' She thought an appeal on the grounds of commerce and profit might be more persuasive than compassion, and she was correct.

'Yes, Tess, I think you are right, we could use her right now, as more farmers are asking for labourers, and we have that order for oakum to fulfil. Very well, get her out.'

***

Three days later Tess Yates was off duty for the night, returning to her family home in nearby Polstead. Like the master she was entitled to two nights away from the workhouse each month, which could be taken as two single nights, or as two together. It was left to the pair of them to agree the rota to their mutual benefit. Supper had been served and cleared away under the supervision of Gracie Carter in the absence of Tess. Gracie was one of the stronger women, like Lucy Draper, unafraid of anyone. Her striking red hair made her stand out in a crowd, leading some to liken her to Elizabeth and her father Henry from two centuries ago. 'It was during Elizabeth's reign that part of this place became a poorhouse. She had red hair like her father, the last Henry,' Tess Yates would tell inmates. 'Perhaps Gracie is a distant relative of the Tudors?'

If Gracie was listening, she would usually reply with some levity, 'Aye, but it must be my misfortune to be descended from one of his bastards for me to have ended up in here.' Her no-nonsense attitude to life made her popular with the other inmates, particularly the women, who found her presence offered some security. Following so soon after the incident six days earlier, Gracie was mindful of Lucy's vulnerability with Tess being away, so she asked her to assist her, Daisy and Evy with supper and clearing away, keeping her close and away from Ward. She knew that despite his authority, the master would not attempt another improper advance if Lucy was with her. When it was time for lights out, Gracie kept Lucy at her side until they were in their beds in the adult women's room.

In the girls' bedroom they were also getting ready to

sleep. Sarah was one of the eldest girls and enjoyed providing some comfort and security to the younger ones like Amy, sometimes telling them stories their mothers might have told before the lights were extinguished for the night. As the youngest girls gathered around Sarah for such a tale, the bedroom door opened.

'Sarah Taylor,' Daniel Ward announced. All of the girls looked round, startled by the presence of the master in their room.

'Yes, sir,' Sarah replied, surprised, concerned there was a problem.

'I am told you are good with your letters, and I need some assistance with a document. Put the girls to bed and come to my office.'

'Yes, sir,' she replied. It was an odd request, but it did not occur to her to think he could have asked one of the men, boys, or adult women. She was mindful of not wanting to cause him displeasure after the incident with Lucy, and remembered her promise made in front of her mother to obey orders. 'Shall I come with you now, sir?'

'Get the girls to bed, then come,' Ward said and left the room. Sarah followed the master's instructions and five minutes later knocked on the door of the workhouse office. She had been inside the room just once before, the day she reported to the workhouse some five weeks earlier. Ward opened the door.

'Come in, girl,' he said quietly, not wishing to wake any of the other inmates, particularly adults like Gracie Carter, who were in the rooms down the corridor. Sarah was wearing her nightgown, a long faded white linen dress, which reached to just below her knees, covered by her work tunic. She was barefoot, and Ward felt slightly aroused by the sight of pale white lower legs, ankles and feet. 'I need your help with these papers, Sarah,' he said gesturing to the small pile on the desk against the wall below the small window, which like all the workhouse windows had three iron bars the other side of the glass. As Sarah walked past the master, she could smell alcohol on his breath, and noticed an uncorked bottle of port on the

26

table. She looked down at the papers, asking innocently, 'Shall I read them, sir?'

'Yes, Sarah, I would like you to read them, and for you to tell me what you think they mean. But first let me provide you with some fortitude for the task. Here, taste a drop of port,' and he poured two glasses.

'Sir, I do not drink fortified wines, they are too strong for my head. I am unaccustomed to such liquor.'

'In normal circumstances that may be so, but this is not such a time. I insist, and it will help you with the task you face.'

Sarah felt compelled to do as he instructed and carefully put the glass to her lips, sipping the contents, which was strong but also mildly sweet. Placing the glass back on the table, she stood facing him and, as she was about to begin the task of reading the papers, he moved closer. Just twelve inches from her face, she could smell his sweat.

'I need you to do me a favour, girl,' and as he spoke, he placed his hand on her breast.

'Sir!' she exclaimed with horror, but before she could say or do any more, the same hand moved to cover her mouth, his other hand forcing her arm behind her back, twisting it so she felt some pain and could not move away. With control of her body, he pulled her close and she felt his foul breath as he spoke.

'Listen, missy, you and your family owe me. You will pleasure me, or yours and their circumstances will change for the worse.' Sarah began to cry, unable to speak or escape, moving her head sideways to show she was not compliant with his wishes. 'Do you understand, girl? I will be satisfied. If not you, perhaps one of the younger girls, or your sister if I choose to bring your family here.' She closed her eyes, realising there was no choice, nodding her head as tears continued to fall.

Ten minutes later, Sarah climbed into her bed, trying to avoid waking the others, but Amy was not asleep. 'I was concerned for you Sarah, are you well?' The little girl whispered from the next bed, reaching across with her hand.

'Thank you, Amy,' she replied and reached over to hold

her hand.

Sarah's tears had ceased to fall when she left Ward's office. Lying in her bed, she felt numb and cold from her ordeal, which stopped short of Ward taking her honour, but still left her feeling violated. She wished she could feel the security of her mother's embrace, but the warmth and kindness of a small girl was the only comfort available to her. 'Thank you, little angel,' Sarah said, holding Amy's hand until their eyes closed and they both slept.

4 Feoffments

Four days later a work team of five stopped to eat some victuals, having toiled all morning on the twenty-five acres of land the other side of Pound Lane. Daniel Ward had escorted them along Church Walk to the patchwork of small fields by the river used for the purpose of growing a wide variety of vegetables and some fruit. There he handed them over to James Pike, a local farmer with more land just outside Hadleigh, which he had given over to growing wheat and barley. Despite having more acreage outside the town, Pike could not turn down the opportunity when six acres of rich fertile soil came up for lease. 'Soil so close to the river benefits from occasional flooding, making it more productive and highly sought after,' he told to his wife when she questioned his decision the previous year. The inmates stood in silence as the master spoke to the farmer ten yards away, unable to hear, but could see a small pouch passed from Pike to Ward. They all guessed it contained coins, payment to the workhouse for their labour, and without addressing the team of five, Ward returned in the direction of the guildhall, to continue his duties. Before they had set out, he had made it clear to them they had better work hard for Mr Pike, who was paying a valuable contribution towards their cost to the parish. The farmer explained their tasks, weeding, turning the soil, adding manure, planting seeds, which would all produce a second summer crop to follow their efforts from February, and apart from Sarah, the work team had performed the same role twelve to fifteen weeks earlier, so it did not require too much instruction. They were happy enough to be there working outside, as Pike was a fair employer. When St Mary's struck twelve times, he said they should pause to eat and rest, even adding some meat pie, left over from his family's table the previous night, a welcome supplement to the rations provided by Tess Yates.

  The work team consisted of two adults, Gracie Carter and Martin Lyndon, and three younger inmates; Lucy Draper, Ben Squirrell, and Sarah Taylor. Following the whining of

Reverend Watson at the vestry meeting, Ward decided to provide a few extra hours a week of learning for the youngest children, even going to the trouble of arranging the lessons through a contact, so the schoolmaster could come to the guildhall for that purpose, for which he was thanked by Watson and Doctor Parsons.

'I will be back before St Mary's bell is struck again, so eat and rest until I return,' James Pike said, and walked off in the direction of the Angel tavern. He had paid for the job, not their time, so was more concerned it was done right. Whether it took six hours, or eight, was of no consequence, and his experience was labour was more productive when refreshed, much like a beast pulling a plough.

'Thank you, sir,' Martin said, respectfully touching his cap, and along with the others he sat down at the edge of the field beside the Brett. Like Gracie, Martin was one of the prominent inmates in the workhouse, having found himself there after losing all his money, and more, from playing the dice at the back of the George. His only immediate option to the workhouse was the debtors' prison in Ipswich, a less attractive proposition. So, until he could settle his financial liabilities, he would stay there in the guildhall, where he became established as the strongest inmate, his muscular body testament to his early years as the son of a blacksmith. 'Perhaps I should take up that offer to go abroad to soldier for the East India Company,' he had thought several times when considering his predicament. The recruiter had promised the Company would clear his debt and deduct it from his wages, which promised to be generous. However, for now he would reside with seventy others in the guildhall and labour as instructed.

'Mr Pike is a kindly master,' Ben said.

'Aye, he is one of the better ones. We have been fortunate today,' Martin replied.

Ben enjoyed the company of the older and stronger man who, along with Gracie, provided younger inmates with a sense of security. Being much younger and less muscular, Ben admired the chiselled face and body of the older man that resembled a sculpture he once saw in a book.

'How much do you think Mr Pike paid Mr Ward for our labour?' Lucy asked as the food prepared by Tess Yates and the farmer's leftover pie was divided five ways.

'I cannot say, Lucy, but I doubt if all of it will find its way into the workhouse coffers,' Martin replied, glancing back across the field, lest anyone might hear.

'What do you mean, Martin?' Ben asked. Martin looked around again to see if anyone was within hearing.

'Ward is a nasty man, as Lucy found out just a while ago. I think he is also a greedy man, and when he collects money for our toil, or rates and land taxes, he must find it tempting to dip his nose in the trough.'

'Definitely,' Gracie added, 'he's a dark stain on the soul of Hadleigh,' and glanced at her young friend, Lucy.

'That must be wrong, I mean, it must be unlawful,' Ben said indignantly. 'How does he get away with such abuse of his position?' he asked, looking to Martin, his elder, for explanation.

'That is a good question, Benjamin Squirrell, and yes, it is indeed unlawful. Proving it would be difficult though, because they are all in it together,' Martin replied.

'Who?' Ben asked. Martin looked round a third time in the space of barely a minute, and then at Gracie, who nodded her consent.

'The men with power in Hadleigh, Ben,' Martin said. 'The vestry officials, who collect the rates, payments by farmers like Pike and the manufacturers who use us as cheap labour. Ward charges them less than they would pay men and women they might employ directly. They do not care if Ward takes a shilling of the seven shillings they paid, if the same work would have cost them nine shillings employing free labourers.'

Ben, Lucy and Sarah listened carefully.

'But the vestry is receiving less than was paid. Reverend Watson and Doctor Parsons would be displeased,' the young man said.

'Yes, if it could be proven, Ben,' Gracie said, 'but

that is unlikely if the farmers and manufacturers agree with the figures provided by Ward. And the vestry is happy in its ignorance if Ward keeps providing a steady income to pay for the workhouse and outdoor poor relief.'

'Those men who employ us cheaply through Ward are often trustees of the feoffments, or brothers and cousins of such men. Their honesty and moral behaviour is assumed, taken for granted, Ben,' Martin added to support Gracie's point.

Lucy and Sarah had sat quietly listening to Gracie and Martin, feeling sickened by revelations of the master's corruption and greed, then more so when 'moral behaviour' was mentioned. Lucy was seething with anger and hatred for the man who ten days earlier had tried to molest her, then locking her in the box. However, her rage would have been uncontrollable if she had been aware of the fate Sarah suffered a week later. The younger girl sat in silence, listening but showing no emotion, as if feelings were a luxury no longer afforded to her. Ben had noticed the change in her demeanour in the last few days, thinking her melancholy must be due to her missing her mother, sister and brothers. He had resolved to try to raise her spirits, but just then he was intrigued to learn more form Gracie and Martin.

'What are the feoffments?' Ben asked. Martin looked at Gracie, to see if she might explain.

'They are charities, Ben, established long ago to help people in Hadleigh,' Gracie offered.

'Why call them feoffments and not charities?' the young man asked. Gracie paused, looking back at Martin for clarification.

'Reverend Watson told me it's an ancient word that goes back 700 years to the Conquest, when William and his lords shared the land of England in return for money and a pledge of allegiance. That was part of what is known as feudalism. Here in Hadleigh the two feoffment charities raise money by leasing land and properties they have come to own over the centuries. Then they use the money to do good deeds,' Martin explained.

'What good deeds would they be?' Lucy asked, mindful of their predicament.

'Reverend Watson told me the Market Feoffment looks after the marketplace and the guildhall, which I suppose includes the likes of us,' Martin said.

'I thought the vestry owned the workhouse,' Lucy replied.

'The church vestry organises the 'house for the parish, but it does not own the guildhall building. Reverend Watson says the vestry pays the Market Feoffment ten pounds rent every year.'

'What of the other feoffment,' Lucy asked.

'The Grand Feoffment looks after almshouses for the elderly poor,' Gracie said.

'How many almshouses are there, Gracie?' Ben asked.

'Well, there are the twelve Pykenham almshouses on George Street, and the six Raven almshouses on Benton Street, which can accommodate thirty-six old souls who would otherwise be with us in the 'house. But there may be more. Reverend Watson said the Grand Feoffment buys cottages when it builds up funds, in which poor families can be housed,' Martin said.

'How does he know all this about the feoffments?' Ben asked curiously.

'He's a trustee on the board of both feoffments.'

'What are they, trustees?' Lucy asked.

'They are the men who are custodians of those charities, Lucy. They watch over the work and finances, to see they are working correctly,' Martin replied.

For a few moments there was quiet, as the three younger members and Gracie thought about what Martin had shared with them. Lucy was angry that if there are men like the reverend who should be keeping a watchful eye on the charities and the workhouse, how could they not see what Ward was doing. Ben was curious to understand how the two charities and the workhouse might work together, for better, or perhaps for worse. Then there was Sarah, who had listened but whose attention was sparked by Martin's comments about the Grand

Feoffment providing cottages for poor families. 'Perhaps mother could be considered for such a home, and we could be free of Daniel Ward,' she thought.

'Who are the other trustees?' Ben asked.

'I do not know who they all are, Ben. But I do know that along with the reverend, other men who are trustees in the two feoffments and vestry officials are Doctor Parsons, John Brownwigg, Edward Grady, Samuel Hancock, and… Daniel Ward. There are other men who are trustees of the two feoffments, and there may be men who are vestry officials and may be a trustee of one of the feoffments, so they can work together to help the poor,' Martin replied.

'Or they can work together to exploit us for their gain,' Ben said, referring to Martin's earlier comment, and the others considered his meaning. Lucy and Sarah both felt saddened to hear Ward was a man of such importance in Hadleigh, particularly the younger girl, who for a minute thought the Grand Feoffment might offer hope.

Tess Yates' ration of food, and the Pike family left-over pie, were washed down with a shared quart of weak ale, the clay jug passed amongst them as they relaxed beside the Brett. Pike would not return for a while yet, so Martin and Gracie both laid down to enjoy a rare opportunity to rest their eyes in the middle of the day, while Lucy and Sarah sat gazing across the river, their focus on nothing in particular. Ben sat and observed, noticing the difference between the two girls. Whereas Lucy looked angry, her steely face framed by her dark hair, Sarah looked lost, tormented by her thoughts. As Ben looked at her, a tear seemed to creep from the corner of her eye and she bowed her head hiding her face, her hair a curtain against intruding eyes. Ben felt drawn to her, wishing he could put an arm around her shoulder to comfort her, but that might not be welcomed, and he did not wish to upset the girl he had come to admire.

'I will try to keep an eye on her and be her friend if she would allow,' he thought, but for the moment he had to be content with just sitting there in her company as the time passed and one o'clock approached.

'Gracie, Martin, it is time to return to work. Here comes Mr Pike,' Ben said, giving them both a gentle kick, pulling them out of their slumber. As he did so, St Mary's bell was struck once.

'I trust you have eaten and rested, but I now require you to continue with your work,' James Pike said, as he walked across the grass from Pound Lane.

'Thank you, sir, we are indeed replenished and refreshed. Our thanks to Mrs Pike for that fine pie,' Martin said, having risen to his feet. Within minutes the five inmates were continuing with the task of tending to James Pike's six acres of vegetables, which they completed in the late afternoon sunshine.

5 Rope Picking

St Mary's bell was struck six times and the inmates inside the guildhall stirred from their slumber in the four cramped bedrooms. Changing from nightshirts into their uniforms they filed along the corridor to the eating room by the kitchen, where Tess Yates and her three assistants were already preparing breakfast for over seventy souls. Each day was the same, with porridge made from oats grown near Kersey, just three miles away, and a splash of milk. Whilst it might be less sumptuous than they might dream of, the simple meal was healthy and filled their stomachs at the start of each day. As they ate in silence, Daniel Ward walked along the middle between the tables to where Tess was wiping her hands on her apron.

'I have changed the work rota for today, Mistress Yates, as we have received a delivery of rope that requires picking for a customer in Ipswich,' Ward announced loud and clear before reaching the end where Tess stood. His desired effect was to inform the inmates of what lay before them that day. He referred to the task of picking apart old rope until it was no more than fine fibres called oakum, which was sold to ship builders who mixed it with tar to produce a caulk used in sealing gaps between wooden planks. That day some of Hadleigh's workhouse inmates would be employed as thousands were in workhouses and prisons throughout England. It was far from backbreaking but was intensely tedious and damaging to hands and fingers, which became calloused and cracked. 'A work team of about fifteen able-bodied inmates are needed in the fields at the top of George Street, and we also have bone crushing, spinning and washing to be done here in the 'house. So, listen for your names and we shall set you to your tasks,' the master continued once alongside Tess, turning to address his listening audience.

Spinning and laundry work was invariably allocated to women and girls, whereas the farm work and bone crushing was generally given to men and boys. Rope picking was usually done by older men and women, who were less mobile and could perform the duty by being seated most of the day. Bone crushing involved old bones being chopped, split and grinded down to tiny pieces to be used as fertilizer. Once the farm work team was dispatched in the direction of George Street, with a warning not to tarry, Ward supervised the inmates set to rope picking and bone crushing, while Tess Yates instructed those spinning and washing.

Tess liked these days when the guildhall was alive with industry and there was a busy hum about the place. Many workhouse masters insisted on silence amongst inmates as they toiled, which Ward would sometimes demand, depending on his mood, but Tess preferred to allow conversation providing they were working. As the women and girls formed two lines to either spin yarn or wash bedding and clothes, Tess realised several younger girls had been assigned to rope picking with the elderly, which struck her as odd. Sarah, Amy and twelve-year-old Alice had been told by Ward to go to the room where piles of rope waited for processing into oakum.

'Are the younger females better employed washing and learning spinning, Master Ward?' she asked before they were dispatched for the day.

'Normally, I would use them so, Mistress Yates, but today this order from Ipswich is a priority and requires more hands,' he replied.

It was an unusual use of the girls, but she followed his reasoning based on commercial necessity, and required no further discussion. However, she did feel some concern for the youngest, Amy, and her small soft hands.

Within ten minutes of the master's announcement at breakfast the four work teams in the guildhall were setting about their tasks, and the able-bodied team of fifteen men, which included Ben, was making its way up George Street to work the land of a local farmer. Sarah, Alice and Amy sat down amongst the eleven elderly men and women on two long benches, with piles of rope laid out in front of them.

'Doesn't seem right,' Daisy Tappin said in a hushed tone to Evy Swinburn, 'the poor mite's hands will be in shreds

37

by lunchtime.'

'Aye, this is no work for a small girl,' Evy replied quietly, 'Ward could have set her to learning to spin yarn.'

'What happened to their schooling? The young 'uns should be learning their letters and numbers,' Daisy added, carefully looking to see no one could overhear her criticism of the regime.

'Here, missy, come and sit between me and Daisy,' Evy said with a raised but kindly voice. Sarah looked up and smiled, welcoming the offer to Amy, and guided her to the space on the bench between the two older women.

'And why don't you two sit here, either side of us,' Daisy said with a smile to Sarah and Alice. 'We can show you how to go about the work.'

'Thank you, Ma'am,' Sarah said, again appreciating the care shown by the old woman.

'Thank you for your manners and courtesy, young lady, but please call me Daisy, and this is Evy.'

With eight women on one bench and six men on the other, the task of picking apart the old rope was begun. Each piece of worn rope had been cut to a strip of twelve inches, allowing it to rest on the inmates' laps as their fingers unwound and picked it apart until it was just a fine fibre, which was then deposited at their feet. This allowed the supervisor to see how much oakum each worker produced. If it was a place of paid employment, the workers would be paid for each pound in weight of the fine, light fibre. But that was not the case in the guildhall, where each pile was simply a measure of the inmates' work ethic and output, which if lacking could result in the master's displeasure and chastisement. Daisy was mindful of this as they worked through the first hour. Amy and the other two girls carefully watched and copied her and Evy, and eventually mastered the simple skill. But their progress was understandably slow, evident from the tiny piles of fibre at their feet.

'Well done, Amy, you will be an expert rope picker soon enough,' Daisy said, giving the little girl a gentle hug with one arm around her shoulder.

'Thank you, Daisy.' The kindness of the old woman drew a smile from Amy, who did not mind the work with Daisy and Evy either side of her.

Evy looked over to Daisy, catching her eye, then nodded towards the tiny pile of fibre at Amy's feet with a look of concern, which Daisy understood. What will the master's reaction be to Amy and the other girls producing piles of oakum much smaller than the expected quota? They knew he could not be relied on to be understanding of their novice status and soft hands. Glancing down at the little girl's hands they could see them turning red with soreness, and soon enough small tears would appear on her palms and fingers. It was tedious, but the effect on their hands was the most injurious aspect of the work.

'Here, Amy, let me assist you so we keep Mr Ward satisfied,' Daisy said, and the kind old lady leaned forward to move some of the fibres from her pile over to Amy's. Looking to her right, she could see whilst Sarah had produced more fibre than Amy, it was still 'light,' so she moved a small amount to her pile too.

'Thank you, Daisy,' Sarah said, 'but I would not wish you to suffer at my expense.'

'Do not worry, Sarah, Daisy Tappin can toil faster,' she replied with a smile.

Evy nodded her approval, adding, 'We can help each other, girls,' and she repeated Daisy's actions, pushing some of her pile over to Amy's, and then some to her left onto Alice's pile.

After two hours mid-morning approached, and Daniel Ward returned to check on their progress and the quiet conversations ceased. He cast his eyes along the two benches at the men and their piles of oakum, then the women, pausing at Sarah, who felt his stare and looked down at her pile. Daisy noticed but was not surprised as she knew he was contemptible and his lustful look at the young girl was no more than she would expect of 'the pig,' as he was referred to amongst the elderly women.

'I see you have made some progress, but the piles of

fibre are unequal, which will be accounted for, one way or another,' Ward announced. The precise consequence of lower production was uncertain, but the threat was clear. He did not need to say more, so turned and left to check on the progress of the other work teams, leaving the rope pickers to continue with their manufacture of oakum.

They had all understood the menace in Ward's words, causing a quiet atmosphere to descend on the fourteen rope pickers. One of the older men, Harry, looked over to the women after giving the situation some thought, and spoke quietly across to the women's bench.

'Daisy, let us share the fruits of our labour. We can continue with our toil and the small girl can stop at intervals to distribute the fibre, so the piles are roughly equal. I fear his actions if small piles suggest any of us slackened,' Harry said glancing at Amy. The others understood and nodded, resulting in the fourteen continuing, but at intervals as the piles of fibre grew, Amy would stop, taking a few minutes to distribute fibres from one pile to another. As a result, the fourteen piles of oakum were roughly equal. Amy would return to the bench, where Daisy smiled and winked, and the little girl continued with her modest contribution to the collective effort of breaking down thick rope into fine fibre.

Ward had made his way to the other room to check the team of nine men crushing bones. Unlike rope picking, these able-bodied men faced a more physical task, working their way through a pile of bones supplied by local slaughter men and butchers, as well as those of dead horses and dogs. Each man was armed with a mallet, ramrod and a flat piece of stone, which were powered by his muscle to break the bones down into tiny pieces. This final product would be swept into sacks and finally into a sealed barrel, then sold to farmers as fertilizer. After inspecting their work, Ward left them, as there was no point in constantly standing over them, and it was tedious for him. It was mid-afternoon and he knew he would not be missed if he disappeared to his office to take a nap. Martin Lyndon watched him as he left them.

'Lazy bastard,' the strong man spat, before picking up

his mallet, another bone and continuing with his work.

Mid-afternoon passed and late afternoon brought the work teams closer to the end of the day's labour. In the room with the older women and her two friends, Amy was on her knees shuffling oakum fibres humming as Daisy and Evy smiled. Hearing the cheerful sound as he approached, Ward paused outside before entering, which allowed him to observe the scene without anyone noticing. Seeing the small girl moving oakum between the piles, he soon realised what the work team had been doing. Whether it resulted in more or less oakum being produced for his Ipswich customer did not concern him. More important was the affront he felt to his position as master, which turned to anger as he considered their attempted deceit. As he entered the room the girl kneeling at the piles of fibre was unaware of his presence, unlike the other thirteen inmates sat on the benches.

'So, you've taken it upon yourselves to produce equal piles of oakum,' Ward said, startling the little girl, who turned to face him, still kneeling. 'There is good reason for separate piles for each worker, and that is to identify those who are slackers, like you,' and with that he grabbed roughly the arm of Amy, pulled her to her feet and pushed her across the piles of fibres towards the bench, where she fell heavily with a scream at the feet of Daisy and Evy.

'You treat her most harshly, Ward,' Daisy exclaimed as she rose to her feet to assist Amy, who lay stunned with cuts to her arms and legs.

'Ward? You do speak with impertinence, old woman. When you speak to me, you will call me sir, or Mr Ward. Do you understand me?' and with that he raised the stick he carried for the purpose of discipline and brought it across her head. Daisy fell where she stood alongside Amy, and there was a collective gasp amongst the other twelve inmates. Harry was enraged and moved to stand up, but his friend gripped his arm to dissuade him, knowing it would only result in him also being subjected to Ward's anger. 'Does anyone else need persuading of how to behave here in this place?' he shouted, as Daisy laid still with blood seeping from her mouth. For a

moment there was quiet, a stand-off, as Ward stood one side
of the piles of fibre, the old woman and young girl lying on
the floor, the other twelve inmates seated. Harry was seething
with anger, but remained seated, waiting for Ward to leave so
he could assist Daisy. Whilst on the other bench, Sarah felt
fear course through her body, and trembled as she witnessed
the violence unleashed by the man she already feared for a
different reason.

'Get these piles into the sacks, now!' the master
screamed as he left the room.

Evy, Harry and the others quickly moved to help Amy
and Daisy to the benches, where they were checked for injury.
Some water was brought to clean the scratches to Amy's arms
and legs, which made her wince, but she assured them she was
largely unhurt.

'I am well, do not worry, Miss Evy,' she said with a
smile.

Daisy was stunned by the blow from Ward's stick, and
an inspection of her mouth suggested she had lost one of her
few remaining teeth. Rinsing her mouth cleansed it of blood
and she too was able to utter reassuring words of defiance.

'He's a swine, that man, so he is.'

Evy gave her friend a hug, and they all sat for some
moments gathering their thoughts, until Harry spoke.

'You two ladies stay seated, lest you feel light-headed,
and we can gather the fibres into the sacks.' Approving nods
and words showed agreement with Harry's suggestion, and the
unhurt twelve completed the task of the rope picking team.

Gathering all of the oakum was important as Ward
would return to ensure none of the valuable fibre was wasted,
and finally the eight sacks were filled, tied with string and left
against the wall by the door. Upon completion they all returned
to the two benches where they had spent the day and waited for
his return. Evy put her right arm around the shoulder of Amy,
and Sarah did the same to Daisy. No one spoke, still shaken by
Ward's brutality. Instead, they rested in silence, each thinking
about what they witnessed in the small room and their lives
in the guildhall. Finally, the quiet was broken by the youngest

voice.

'What do you think Mistress Yates will prepare for our supper this evening, Evy?' Amy said, looking up at the old lady to her left, at the same time moving her right hand to gently clutch Daisy's.

'Ooh, I hope it's something nice,' Evy replied, looking down at Amy and smiling.

Amy simply returned the smile, enjoying the comfort provided by the two older women, something she missed and could remember from her early years before she became an orphan. When the master threw her to the floor, she was hurt and laid still for fear of antagonising him further, a tactic she had learnt was best employed with bullies, so she had not seen his treatment of Daisy. The cuts and bruising to her arms and legs stung, she could withstand such pain, but the cruelty shown to the old woman would have caused a sadness worse than the physical injury.

After a short while Ward returned. He was calmer, announcing as if nothing had happened and his handling of Amy and Daisy was normal, 'Well now, let me see how you have fared.' He looked at the eight sacks of oakum and then at the fourteen seated rope pickers. 'I see you have made some effort to tidy the sacks and floor. Those sacks must now be taken to the storeroom where they can be placed into the barrels until they are collected for transportation to Ipswich. This task requires only two of you, Harry and George, the rest of you can return to your rooms to wash yourselves before supper.' As the two older men waited, the other twelve filed out of the room, but after the first few had exited Ward called out. 'The floor is unswept, and we can't waste good oakum. Sarah, fetch a broom!'

For the others it was nothing to cause alarm, but Sarah felt a chilling terror on hearing his command. Her effort to look as if it was of no concern was unconvincing and standing next to her when they all paused to listen, Daisy could see fear in the girl's face.

'Yes, sir,' Sarah replied, and as she brought the broom Daisy followed her.

'Sarah, is there something that scares you?' the old woman asked.

'No, Daisy, I will be fine,' Sarah said bowing her head so Daisy could not see her face.

'You men get these sacks to the storeroom and place them in the two barrels you will find empty. Then join the others in getting yourselves clean,' Ward said.

'Yes, Mr Ward,' Harry replied, as he and George took a sack with each hand and made their way to the storeroom.

Sarah had returned with a broom and proceeded to gather the remaining fibres of oakum but was interrupted. 'Just wait, girl. There's no point starting until all the sacks have been removed. Just stand there and let me have a look at you,' Ward said with a grin. There was nothing she could do, so she stood holding the broom as fear overcame her.

Harry and George returned to collect the four remaining sacks without even looking at Ward or Sarah, both relieved to be finished with rope picking work for the day.

'Very well, you can sweep the floor now, girl.'

As she swept the fibres towards one pile in the middle of the floor, Ward stood glaring at Sarah. She could not see his stare, fixing her gaze towards the floor trying to avoid contact with his eyes, but she felt his eyes piercing through her. Then, after a minute or two of her final task of the day, she was unaware of his movement behind her until his hand came over her shoulder and covered her mouth, preventing her from making any sound. At the same time, his other hand came around her waist and pulled her firmly against his body. She was unable to move, her body rigid with fear. For a moment he just held her tight and she could feel his foul breath and smell his sweat, familiar from the evening in his office.

'Don't forget, you owe me, girl,' the master said quietly in her ear, and as he spoke his left hand moved down from her waist groping her through the layers of her workhouse uniform. Unlike the ordeal in his office, this humiliation lasted only moments, but Sarah's tears fell. Then it stopped, as suddenly as it had started, and Ward stepped back.

'Go on, join the others and get cleaned!' he said with

44

venom.

Sarah picked up the broom she had dropped and left the room. In a distraught state on leaving, as she passed along the corridor, she had not noticed someone who hid in the shadow of another doorway. Moments later, Ward followed her to resume his duties. After he had passed the same doorway, a small figure emerged from the dark. Daisy's jaw still ached from Ward's blow an hour or so earlier, but now she felt an emotion stronger than the pain; anger and hatred having witnessed his violation of Sarah.

'Damn you, Daniel Ward,' she whispered looking at the small pile of fibres that remained on the floor inside the rope picking room.

6 Commerce

John Brownwigg was one of five men who sat as a trustee of the Grand and Market Feoffments, as well as a member of the town vestry, the other four being Reverend Watson, Dr Parsons, Edward Grady and Daniel Ward. His difference to them lay in his reason for supporting the three institutions. John Brownwigg, in his fifth decade, was a man of commerce; the owner of two mills, a cloth manufactury, a farm and an ale house. He was widely recognised as one of the wealthiest men in Hadleigh, but unlike men of comparable wealth, his family was considered 'new money,' starting from his grandfather and consolidated by his father. They believed in an industrious work ethic and being clever with money, investing and expanding their enterprises at the right time. It followed this that his involvement in three noble institutions to help the poor was purely political, allowing him to keep an eye on, and influence, decisions that might affect Brownwigg family interests. As a result, he attended meetings he would prefer to miss, but this sacrifice was made palatable by knowing he could profit whenever it suited by using workhouse labour.

Ben walked across Toppesfield Bridge, stopping to look over the side at a pair of swans and three cygnets that disappeared from view, moving under the bridge's central arch as they swam upstream. Looking up, Ben saw the large white wooden building of three floors that housed the mill, just 100 yards downstream. Turning left on to Tinkers Lane, Ben followed the riverbank to his destination for the day.

At that place the River Brett was used for the purpose of turning the great wheel, by a channel under the building that straddled its course, where the water collected, with some of the river flowing into the adjacent mill pool. Just past the mill the water from the mill pool and wheel channel converged to continue as the River Brett to its confluence with the River Stour and eventually into the sea. Ben stopped to look down into the mill pool, where the water was calm and huge water lilies grew, where he could see small fish appearing as they swam out from the under the shelter of the lilies. 'If there are small fish here, perhaps there will be larger ones too? Could it be a good place to fish?' he thought, standing for a few moments, watching the little fish darting in and out of their lily refuge. 'Do they know the herons cannot see them if they stay beneath the lily leaves?' he wondered, and again found himself in awe of nature. But his study of water lilies and fish was short-lived, interrupted by a loud call.

'Boy! I have not paid for you to stand gawping at the river. Get yourself over here, before I send you back.'

John Brownwigg knew that Ben, identifiable by his workhouse uniform, was the boy he was expecting. In fact, he was the boy he had requested of Daniel Ward, having been impressed with his work before.

'I do not want one who is too small and weak, nor one older and worn out. Send that lad who came with the group of children that worked for me two weeks ago. He acted as a supervisor of the group. Do you remember the boy?' Brownwigg asked.

'Aye, I know the boy you refer to, Mr Brownwigg. I will send him along to start work as St Mary's strikes seven times.' Ward replied, and as a result Ben was told to report to Mr Brownwigg at Toppesfield Mill as he ate his porridge breakfast.

'Yes, sir,' Ben replied looking up towards the mill, from where the voice came. He marched the last thirty yards to the mill entrance at a brisk pace lest Mr Brownwigg was displeased. His employer for the day stood in the doorway and watched Ben approach.

'Good, we do not want anyone who is unpunctual. Remind me of your name, boy.'

'Benjamin Squirrell, sir.'

'Very well, Benjamin Squirrell, follow me,' and Brownwigg led him into the mill. Inside the building was dominated by the huge wheel turned by the water that flowed beneath. Accompanied by the sound of the great volumes of water gushing against the paddles, the noise amplified as it bounced off the walls. 'Wait here while I get the miller,'

Brownwigg said with a raised voice to ensure he was heard above the din, and climbed the narrow stairs to the first floor. Minutes later, he returned followed by a man wearing an apron.

'So, who is this?' the man said with a smile, immediately putting Ben at ease.

'Benjamin Squirrell, this is Mr Crabb, the master of Toppesfield Mill,' Brownwigg said.

'Good morning, sir,' Ben said respectfully.

'Good morning to you, Benjamin Squirrell. Welcome to Toppesfield Mill. I will show you how the mill works and explain your work for the day.'

'Yes, sir. Thank you, sir.'

As Steven Crabb was about to begin Ben's induction, he was interrupted by John Brownwigg.

'I will be on my way, Mr Crabb, as I have other matters to which I must attend. Please put the boy to work as I have paid the master ten pence for his labour for the day.'

'Yes, indeed I will, Mr Brownwigg. We have a page of orders for flour that the boy can help us meet.'

'Very well, Mr Crabb. I will leave to allow you to get on with your trade and bid you good day. Work hard, Benjamin Squirrell, and perhaps you will make something of your life.'

'Yes, sir,' Ben replied but the man of commerce had already turned and was making his way to the door and out onto Tinkers Lane. Ben and Mr Crabb watched him leave, then the miller spoke.

'Well, Mr Brownwigg is a busy man, and we will probably be more industrious without his presence, Benjamin. Or should I call you Ben?' the miller said with a smile.

'Yes, sir. Ben, sir.'

'You are a polite young man, Ben, but there is no need to keep calling me sir. You may call me Steven in here.'

'Yes, sir, I mean, Steven,' Ben said with a smile.

'Excellent, Ben. Listen carefully as I show you around the mill and introduce you to the others.'

Ben was introduced to Peter and Will, both young men of a similar age to him, who were up on the top floor when he first entered the mill. To Ben's relief his colleagues for the day were cheerful and friendly, which was always a concern when workhouse inmates came into contact with folk outside. Some could be condescending and cruel in their attitude and comments, looking down on those at the bottom of Hadleigh society. However, the three men Ben was working with for the day held no such prejudice, and he quickly felt safe and welcome.

Like most people, Ben had never understood why a mill was such a tall building. Only after being inside listening to Steven and witnessing its operation, did he fully grasp the reason for its height. Everyone knew there was a great wheel turned by the flowing river, but only after seeing the mechanism inside was it all clear. The water wheel was on the bottom floor and as it rotated its shaft connected to a pit wheel, which was also vertical, so the water was turning both. The pit wheel had teeth around its rim, which on turning connected to the teeth of a horizontal wheel or gear, which turned the main shaft of the mill. Above this wheel was a second larger horizontal gear wheel, whose rim teeth connected to and turned another shaft, or spindle, that rose through the ceiling to the next floor level. On this floor the spindle turned the top of two grinding stones, while the bottom grinding stone remained still. From the top floor, grain was poured through a chute or tube down to the middle floor and into the middle of the grinding stones that turned it into flour. The grain brought to the mill from nearby farms was hauled to the top floor with the use of pulleys, where it was stored before being poured down the chute into the grinding stones below. As the grain was ground down to a fine flour it fell out from between the grinding stones, was gathered and poured through a small narrow chute to the ground floor, where it was bagged.

'And that, Ben, is how a mill works, turning wheat into flour, which we sell to bakers and merchants,' Steven Crabb concluded after showing and explaining in detail each part of the process and mechanism. Ben stood listening carefully at every stage.

With Ben helping Peter and Will on the top floor,

hauling the grain from outside and storing it carefully, the first stage of the process was quickened. Once all the grain that had been lifted to the top floor had been stored, Will went downstairs to the bottom floor to ready the sacks into which the flour would be bagged. Steven was able to attend the bottom two floors, keeping a watchful eye on the main mechanisms, while Ben remained with Peter, and upon the command of Steven, the two boys started to pour the grain into the chute transferring it into the grinding stones. Once this was underway, Ben joined Steven to ensure that the fine white powder used for baking bread gathered without waste, before falling into a smaller chute down to the bottom floor, where Will was waiting to bag the flour. Steven was able to use Ben as an assistant to himself, Peter and Will as and when two pairs of hands were required at the three different stages, resulting in a more efficient process.

Ben did not feel like a workhouse inmate, as he enjoyed the work, the company of the others and learning about milling. So, when Steven called up to Peter to cease supplying grain from the top floor, allowing them to stop for food and drink, it seemed like the morning had passed by without Ben noticing. Peter joined Ben and Will on the bottom floor as they waited for the last batch of grain to move through the grinding stones, emerging as flour, where the three of them worked together bagging it in small sacks.

'Well done, lads. We have toiled to good effect this morning. Now it is time to rest a while and eat,' Steven said, and they walked out of the mill into bright sunlight. While the three youngsters were working, a boy had delivered freshly baked bread that was still warm, made from flour the mill had supplied the previous day. Steven brought a knife, a linen parcel, and a quart pot of weak ale. They sat down beside the mill pool and Ben could not have been more content, eating a delicious lunch of freshly baked bread, Suffolk cheese and ale, watching the small fish below the lilies, and listening to his three 'betters' talk about life outside the place in which he resided. Conscious of the living condition of their new workmate, Steven, Peter and Will were discreet in their conversation, trying to be considerate of his predicament. There was an inevitable curiosity about life in the guildhall, but they tried to be sensitive realising their questions might cause Ben discomfort, particularly as they had come to like him that morning.

'Do you work like this every day, Ben?' Steven asked in a sympathetic tone.

'Yes, sir, I mean Steven. If we are not working for men like Mr Brownwigg outside the guildhall, then we do work inside.'

Peter and Will were curious about the work and listened quietly as Ben explained rope picking and bone crushing, feeling some sadness on hearing how the younger children also laboured. They avoided asking about discipline inside the workhouse, despite having heard stories of cruelty. Peter, in his naivety, was curious about why Mr Brownwigg employed Ben when there were plenty of boys in the town who would work. Steven explained the reason, allowing Ben a rest from answering questions.

'Mr Brownwigg can employ Ben by paying Mr Ward ten pence for the day, whereas he pays you sixteen pence, Peter. He does not need to employ more lads than you and Will at normal times, but occasionally an extra pair of hands are required. He saves six pennies by employing Ben, rather than another one of you.'

'I see,' Peter replied, adding, 'what do you spend your money on, Ben?'

There was a pause before Ben replied.

'I do not receive any of those ten pence. The money goes towards my cost to the parish ratepayers,' and Ben looked down towards the fish beneath the lilies, trying to not dwell on the subject of money.

Peter looked at Steven and Will, embarrassed that they worked with a young man who would receive no payment for his toil. He could not think of what to say, nor could Steven and Will, so the four of them sat in silence with their thoughts.

Resuming their work through the afternoon, Steven was pleased to see the store of large sacks of grain on the top floor gradually diminishing, while the small sacks of flour on the ground floor slowly increased. He also felt justified in his request to John Brownwigg a few days earlier, when he suggested an extra pair of hands would be helpful in meeting a higher number of orders than usual. Brownwigg hated the idea of the business going to one of his competitors so he relented, on the proviso that the extra worker 'paid his way.' Steven knew the price of a 10lb sack of flour and could see by the quantity they were producing that Ben's contribution was far greater than the ten pence he cost for the day, so the mill owner would be pleased with the increase in productivity.

As St Mary's struck three times, Steven told Peter on the top floor to stop feeding grain into the chute.

'Let us rest for a short while and take stock of what we have achieved,' Steven said to the boys. They sat on a bench outside the mill, and he produced another quart pot of weak ale to be shared between them.

'Will we get through all of the sacks of grain before the end of the day?' Ben asked, curious to learn more about the trade of milling.

'Possibly, Ben. We will see. Providing we have enough 10lb sacks of flour to meet the orders, and some more for any that may arrive tomorrow, Mr Brownwigg will be satisfied with our labour. Before St Mary's strikes six times, we will cease production and tidy the mill on each floor,' Steven replied.

'Does Mr Brownwigg like a tidy mill?' Ben asked.

Steven smiled, replying, 'Mr Brownwigg likes a profit, Ben. Keeping the mill tidy is of more importance to me, the miller, as a miller's enemies include dampness and rats. So, we try to ensure the grain and flour is stored in dry places and there is little or none lying about to attract those hairy buggers with long tails.'

Ben smiled as he listened to the miller, then asked, 'What about at night, when rats are more commonly seen?'

'We have our night watchmen, or should I say night watchwomen,' Peter said with a smile.

'Really? Who are they?' Ben asked.

'Yes, where are they?' Will added.

Steven looked around. 'Well there's one,' he said, pointing over to a wooden store. Then he whistled and called, 'Betsy! Here girl!'

On the roof of the small store sat a large cat, almost entirely black except for a white patch on its chest and four white paws, which it was licking as it sat in the afternoon sun. The cat looked up when Steven whistled and called, but in the nature of cats did not bother to move from its place of comfort. However, below where the cat lay, a small dog appeared from the shadow of the store, where it had chosen to shelter from the sun.

'Here she is. Come, Betsy,' Will said kindly as the white hound with brown patches trotted towards them, its thin tail wagging enthusiastically. She went straight to Will, who had called her, then noticing Ben, approached him cautiously sniffing for his scent. Offering his hand, which she smelt, Betsy judged him to be friendly and sat on her haunches as he stroked her head and neck.

'What about Sally?' Peter said, and on hearing her name, the cat stood up arching her back to stretch. Ben could see that the cat was possibly larger than the dog but, unlike Betsy, she did not feel inclined to join the group, instead lying back down to enjoy some more sunshine. As they moved the quart pot between them, Betsy enjoyed their affectionate petting.

'I did not see them inside as we worked,' Ben said.

'They stay outside during the day, probably sleeping for much of it,' Steven said, 'but at night they are most welcome to inhabit the mill, as between them they make formidable rat catchers, Ben.'

'Ah, I see,' Ben replied. He knew cats make good rat catchers but was uncertain about dogs. 'What breed of dog is she?' he asked.

'Well, she's a mongrel terrier, some of this, and a bit of that. But most importantly she is a fine killer of rats. Between the two of them, they keep the vermin at bay. Don't you, Betsy,' Steven explained as he tickled Betsy's neck.

'They seem to get along,' Ben said.

'Aye, they're like two sisters, so they are. In winter months, I've seen them snuggled together on an old sack for a bed,' Steven replied with a smile.

Resuming work, Steven was able to relax, allowing the three boys to finish what was required and, as he watched them, he pondered how harsh fate could be. There could only be a few years difference between them, three likeable young men, and they all worked hard, but their circumstances were very different. He and his wife were blessed with four daughters, despite hoping for a son, but one never came, and it struck him that were these boys old enough, he could see no reason to object to any of them joining his family as sons-in-law. He had known Peter and Will for several years, each from modest but honest families, both on the way to becoming millers. However, he had never met Ben, and without knowing him he would have assumed the boy to be unsuitable because of where he resided. A sense of shame filled him as he watched the boy helping the other two, smiling and laughing as they toiled together.

'Ten pence, Mr Brownwigg had said earlier at about 7.00am,' Steven thought. 'And he does not see any of those pennies for himself.' In truth, he had never cared for Daniel Ward, who had a reputation in the town for being cruel. There were several stories of him beating inmates for minor infractions, but he recognised the money Brownwigg and others paid for cheap workhouse labour going towards vestry costs as being an economic reality in every workhouse across the country. Steven felt guilty, even though it was none of his doing, and he resolved to treat the boy well.

Once St Mary's bell was struck five times, Steven told the lads to cease the process of turning grain into flour, and to tidy up with brushes and pans that were kept on each floor. Within fifteen minutes the mill was ready to close for the day, with a pile of 10lb sacks of flour stacked neatly, ready for collection early the next morning.

'Well lads, it is time to go home,' Steven said, immediately feeling self-conscious of his choice of words, realising 'home' had a different meaning for Ben. All three looked at Ben with some sadness, knowing he was returning to the guildhall to be locked-up for the night. Peter and Will would stop on their way home for a pint of ale at the George and, despite their desire to invite him, knew it was out of the question for their new friend to join them.

'Ben, I will inform Mr Brownwigg of how productive you have been, and perhaps we will need more help in the future,' Steven said with a hopeful tone.

'That would be most welcome, sir,' Ben replied, slipping back into workhouse language.

'I cannot give you money, Ben, but I have some more of that cheese, which I would like you to have,' Steven said, and handed him a small package of linen, in which was wrapped a thick slab of Suffolk cheese. 'I hope you can enjoy it, without getting into trouble.'

'Thank you, that is most kind,' Ben said with a smile, pleased with the gift as he had never before had any such reward.

Peter and Will shook Ben's hand and echoed Steven's hopes that he would return to work at the mill, and Ben left after goodbyes were said, making his way along Tinkers Lane towards Toppesfield Bridge. He knew the master would be expecting him, so he could not tarry too long, but he couldn't resist pausing on the bridge to try the cheese, so opened the package and broke off a large piece. 'I might as well,' he thought, 'if Ward discovers I have it, he will confiscate it from me.' After sampling the delicious treat, he wrapped the remaining cheese and placed it under his shirt. Then he continued making his way back to the guildhall feeling happy with the day, having worked with three good men and learnt a lot about the trade of milling.

Much later after supper, when it was time for lights out, Ben climbed into bed and took another piece of cheese from the linen package, which he had hidden under his pillow. Arthur looked at him from the next bed and Ben turned to meet his stare. Reaching back under his pillow, Ben broke off some more cheese and passed it to Arthur, who smiled. The two of them enjoyed the fine Suffolk cheese as they drifted towards sleep, but Ben stayed awake a while longer thinking about something that had stuck in his mind. 'Ten pence. Mr Brownwigg paid ten pence to Ward for my labour.'

7 Rowland Taylor

Sundays were different. The usual morning rise and breakfast were an hour later, allowing inmates to start their day of worship and rest with extra sleep, or whispered conversation with those in beds either side of the one in which they slept. Louder speech was to be avoided for fear of drawing the unwanted chiding of the master and mistress, who could choose to end that period of extra rest on a whim.

Each bed was constructed with the same four pieces of wood, six feet in length, each carefully sawn, six inches in width, and three inches in depth. With three inches between each piece of wood, every inmate had a bed thirty-three inches wide. Laid upon the four strong pieces of wood was a mattress made from tough sail cloth, stuffed with straw, which might occasionally pierce the thick cloth causing a scratch, but usually moulded to the shape of the occupant, producing a comfortable bed inmates were loath to leave.

Before receiving food and attending the Sunday morning service across the graveyard at St Mary's, every inmate had to partake in another weekly ritual. Each of them had to bathe, or more accurately, be bathed. Two lines, male and female, queued in silence to enter the two small rooms where large tin baths were filled with water, which started warm and clean, but changed to cold and dirty as each inmate washed off a week of sweat and dirt. Tess Yates stood in the doorway of the women's bathroom, whilst Daniel Ward did the same for the men. However, they did not undertake the scrubbing of bodies which, if necessary, was performed by one of the older women, like Daisy or Evy, or one of the older men like Harry. When each inmate was signalled to enter the bathroom, their nightshirts were removed and placed on an adjacent stool. Then they stepped into and immersed themselves in the bath. Standing up, they were passed a large bar of soap, which they applied to their bodies and hair, covering as much as they could with the white lather. Any areas of their bodies they could not reach were quickly scrubbed by the elderly attendant. Once completely covered in soapy lather they immersed themselves again to rinse off the soap and accompanying dirt. If required, Daisy, Evy or Harry would use a large ladle to pour more water over their heads and backs. Stepping out of the tin bath, a cloth was used to dry themselves, before putting their nightshirts on and leaving the bathroom, allowing the next inmate to enter.

The order of each queue to the two bathrooms was the same each week, with the youngest first and the oldest last. Fortunately, more hot water was brought from the kitchen, and the filthy water in the baths was emptied and replaced several times, much to the relief of the bathers. For the women the indignity of standing naked in front of an elderly inmate, and within view of Tess Yates, was obviated by the kindness of Daisy and Evy, who averted their gaze when each inmate undressed and avoided looking at their naked bodies from the front. Daisy and Evy treated the younger ones as they might a granddaughter, with considerate words.

'There you are, Amy. The water is nice and clean. Dip your toe, and if it is too hot, I can add some cold water. Let me help you with your hair, young lady.'

'Thank you, Daisy,' the little girl said with a smile, enjoying the attention and help in getting clean.

In truth, the care they showed the young girls was as comforting for the giver as it was for the receiver, providing them with experiences they remembered from past lives. Tess Yates was sensitive to the delicate nature of the weekly ritual and would look out of the room from the doorway, allowing the bather some privacy, which the girls and women appreciated, and showed with a respectful, 'Thank you Miss Yates,' as they left.

In the men's bathroom, Harry would also show discretion and sensitivity, averting his eyes from their nakedness, but with more levity.

'Come on, lad. Get yourself clean. If there is part of you that you cannot reach, I will assist.' As the men's hair was kept short, washing it was straightforward. They were quickly rinsed of any soap and dismissed with a cheery, 'Well done, lad. Get yourself dry and on you go!'

However, the demeanour of the bathroom supervisor was different for the men, as Daniel Ward did not display the same respect for privacy shown by Tess. Instead, he chose to stand and stare at each male as they undressed, bathed and dried themselves. They were aware of this because, as they queued, they could see him looking into the room at the bathers ahead of them. Each one who entered on his command felt his sneering glance adding further indignity to their nakedness. Only a few of the older men, like Martin Lyndon, did not feel uncomfortable under his gaze. Martin, stood naked, unashamedly staring back at the master as he stepped out of the bath, a look of proud defiance requiring no words.

'Move yourself, Lyndon,' was all Ward said as the muscular inmate dried himself, put on his nightshirt and left the bathroom.

On returning to their bedrooms, the inmates removed their nightshirts, replacing them with a clean workhouse uniform, and waited for the next stage of the Sabbath. The daily breakfast of oats and milk was eaten in silence, and an hour later the entire body of the workhouse was led out in single file through the guildhall back door. They walked solemnly along the side path and across the graveyard to St Mary's, where, once inside the church, they were seated at the back on five rows of pews. Each inmate sat and waited with their heads lowered as the rest of the congregation arrived and took their seats, the wealthier, more respectable families of Hadleigh at the front. Once everyone was seated, and the service led by George Watson was started, the inmates looked up to see their betters.

Ben found himself sat next to Sarah, and without speaking he gave her a gentle nudge with his elbow as the service began. She turned her head slightly to see his smile, and for a moment she felt like any other girl sat alongside a boy she admired, and without thought smiled back, before returning her attention to Reverend Watson. Next to her the young man felt elated by the gift of a smile from the pretty girl to whom he felt increasingly drawn. Ben tried to concentrate on the words coming from Reverend Watson's mouth, but found his attention distracted by Sarah, who had done nothing improper. He wanted to hold her hand, fantasising he might one day court her, perhaps be referred to as her 'young man.' However, he knew such a move of his hand was too dangerous in more than one way. She might be scared, or even repulsed, by so bold a contact, and there was the consequence they would face if they were seen. So, he kept facing the front, smitten by the smile Sarah bestowed on him

After church it was customary for the workhouse inmates to have some time to contemplate the messages from the Bible delivered in the service. They knew this meant they could enjoy some freedom with conditions they would be wise to observe. The alehouses were closed on the Sabbath until later in the day, so there was no opportunity for drunkenness. Similarly, any licentiousness was to be avoided and was difficult to achieve in the small town on a Sunday morning when many families were out and about. Every one of the inmates was expected back inside the guildhall by the time St Mary's bell was struck twice.

Outside the church some of the inmates chose to stay in the immediate area where they felt safe from taunts over their condition. Young men in every town could be cruel in their treatment of paupers, forgetting how precarious life could be, and that they too could be only two months of rent arrears away from the workhouse. So, if possible, they were to be avoided, and Reverend Watson and Doctor Parsons were always visible after the Sunday service, providing some protection. If it were sunny the churchman would encourage Bible study, providing copies of the good book, and the doctor would listen to inmates if they were feeling afflicted by malady or injury. Should the weather be inclement they were welcome to sit and read their bibles inside St Mary's.

Ben wanted to speak to Sarah, even though he was not sure what to say and when he looked over towards her, he caught her eye. Again, he was pleased to see her smile and started to walk over to where she stood. But as he did, he was called by Arthur.

'Ben, come on, we are going to catch fish.'

The younger boys had planned to fish with their primitive rods, lines, hooks and worms, an activity they had looked forward to all week, and Tess Yates had said she would welcome some fish being added to a vegetable stew. Ben's heart sank, even though he normally loved fishing, as he thought he might sit and talk to Sarah. But he could not disappoint the younger boys, who looked up to him as an older brother. He looked over to Sarah, who smiled and waved.

'Go on, the boys will be disappointed if you do not help them. We can talk for a while before the bell strikes twice, unless you are catching so many fish, you cannot stop,' Sarah called with an even bigger smile.

Ben felt relieved that she said they might still talk before returning to the guildhall, so with a shrug of his shoulders and a friendly wave, he said, 'See you in an hour,' and made his way to the river with Arthur.

In bright sunlight Sarah paused on the path that wound between the graves on the patch of land between the guildhall and St Mary's, looking down at the white stones marking the last resting place of the dead. Some were solitary, usually with the name of a man, whilst others listed the names of two, sometimes three members of the same family. She wondered who they were? Families like Pegg and Petfield, whose gravestones stood tall, proudly recording the lives of respectable people with wealth. She glanced up at the guildhall, with its fine Tudor frontage, a celebration of the wealth of the town, much of it provided by the former woollen cloth industry that had largely disappeared. But behind that frontage lived her fellow inmates, who if they died would not be buried in that patch of land just yards from where they lived, worked and slept. Sarah's short stay in the workhouse had not yet seen her witness the death of an inmate, but she was aware that some, usually the old or the very young, became ill and died. Sometimes there were tragic accidents, she was told. It saddened her to think those Christians residing in the guildhall, who attended church each Sunday, would not be buried here amongst the fine white gravestones; they would be laid to rest in spare patches of ground to the south and west of the church, in paupers' graves. It was still consecrated ground, but the only marker might be a wooden cross that would eventually rot leaving no record of who laid beneath the soil. If there were several paupers to be buried, they would share the same grave.

'If I took my life, would it be such a sin?' she thought, but what scared her more than displeasing God, was the thought that her family might not know where she was buried. 'How many months or years would pass before a wooden cross with my name would disappear, leaving no trace?'

In the immediate area where she stood the most recent addition to the white gravestones was Sarah Pegg, whose inscription stated she had died just two years earlier, 13th February 1791. Sarah wondered who she was and where she lived? Perhaps in a tall brick house like the Red House on Church Walk? Another stone listed John May, who died in 1762, and was joined by his mother, Jane May, in 1778. That stone and what it said about the May family seemed curious to Sarah. 'Did he die before finding a wife and raising a family? Or did his father die before the son made his fortune, enabling him to glory in an impressive white stone?' she thought. 'It must have been sad for Jane May, living those further sixteen years without husband or son.'

Alone with her thoughts, she looked towards the south where she saw Pykenham's Tower and the Deanery, and her mind wandered to her grandmother's tales of their family's distinguished past.

'We Taylors may not be as wealthy as some folk nowadays, but we have descended from one of Hadleigh's finest men,' nana would begin. When Sarah first heard the story of her family's lofty origins, she would sit wide-eyed, listening carefully. That was eight years ago when she was younger, and over the following years she learnt to listen politely, so that by the time nana died three years ago the words were etched in her mind.

'Rowland Taylor was the Dean of this parish and several others in these parts, Sarah. He lived in the Deanery

with Pykenham's Tower attached to it, housing his fine library.'
Nana would recount Rowland Taylor's story from almost 250
years earlier, when he was the Rector of St Mary's.

'Not only was he a great man of the cloth, Sarah. He
was also a great man of the people. The year before he died,
he was angry at the way so many poor in Hadleigh lived,
particularly the old and infirm. One evening he called on one of
the wealthy woollen cloth merchants, John Raven, and ordered
old man Raven to accompany him to see the hovels in which
his workers lived. Raven and his son, also named John, were so
moved by what they saw that they bought land down towards
the end of Benton Street, where they built the almshouses
that still stand today,' nana would say, explaining in detail
their ancestor's career and demise. 'Like so many, Rowland
Taylor had been born a Catholic before Luther's protests led to
the Reformation. Also like so many others, he embraced the
reforms and Henry's new Church of England. During the reign
of the boy king, Edward, Taylor rose to prominence within the
Protestant church. However, following the death of the young
king before his sixteenth birthday, England's next monarch was
Mary, who had stayed true to Catholicism. Queen Mary tried
to persuade the people of England to return to the old church,
but too many were unwilling, and that was when she became
most cruel. Do you know what she did, Sarah?'

'No, nana,' was the reply, even in the later years when
Sarah was familiar with the story, she knew how much her
nana enjoyed retelling.

'She lost patience trying to persuade and waiting for
reformers to return to the old faith…so she started burning
them! Anyone who did not return to the old church, she
burned them at the stake, hundreds of them, and our ancestor
Rowland Taylor was the second man in England to suffer that
awful fate during her reign, in the same year Raven built those
almshouses along Benton Street.'

Sarah would always express horror long after she
knew every line, listening to her grandmother describe how
their ancestor was placed on a horse and taken to common
land just outside Hadleigh, tied to a post and burned until

he was no more than bones and ashes. She knew the story of his death well, but what happened to their family in the intervening centuries was less clear. 'When did we become so modest in our status?' she thought. Whilst her family became impoverished in recent years since the deaths of both her father and grandmother, she was aware that before those traumatic losses her family was not wealthy. What she learnt from her elders was that the Taylor family fell from wealth and respectability sometime in the 1600s, a hundred years or more earlier.

'Perhaps we were on the wrong side during the Civil War?' nana would say, in those last years before her death, when Sarah was growing up and became erudite enough to formulate such an inquisitive question. Whatever the reason, the reality was that her branch of the once esteemed Taylor family was now at the bottom of Hadleigh society, just a step away from them all being condemned to the workhouse and eventually unmarked paupers' graves beyond the deanery.

Standing amongst the gravestones, Sarah found herself sinking into melancholy; her condition and that of her family seemed without hope. She was under the control of the master and tried to block thoughts of him from her mind, but they would not go away. If she ended her life, what would happen to her mother, sister and brothers? Would a pauper's grave be so bad? These thoughts were causing her to despair, so she decided to walk towards the river, where Ben had gone to help the younger boys with their fishing endeavour. 'He is a good person,' and thoughts of the young man she admired for his kindness and knowledge eased the dark cloud that had filled her mind.

Amy had been picking flowers by Pykenham's Tower and saw Sarah approaching.

'Sarah!' she called, 'where are you going? May I join you?'

Hearing the little girl's voice, and seeing her broad smile, provided further relief to Sarah's dark thoughts, and she smiled.

'I am going to watch the boys trying to catch fish,

Amy. Yes, you are most welcome to come with me.'

Without any further encouragement, Amy jumped to her feet and ran over to Sarah, taking hold of her hand. The warmth from physical contact with Amy, and her beaming smile, gave Sarah another reason to not feel complete despair as they walked towards the river to look for the boys.

Behind the deanery and the tower, where 300 years earlier Pykenham had hoped to build a palace, the huge garden stopped fifty yards short of the riverbank, allowing long grass and wildflowers to flourish amongst large trees that formed a small, wooded area. Knowing it was a rare pastime pleasure for the workhouse boys, Reverend Watson allowed them to access the river through an old door in the wall and a path taking them through his garden. Here they were safe from the taunts and stares of other boys, and even enjoyed a stretch of the riverbank that was not fished by others. Under the long lower branches of an oak tree the boys huddled together, busy in their manufacture of fishing rods. At their centre stood Ben holding a collection of long ash tree branches, varying from six to nine feet in length. He placed them all, except for one, on the earthy ground that did not produce long grass being constantly in shadow. Picking up a line of sewing thread that lay on a canvas sack, he tied it to one end of the branch. Besides the lines of thread lay a collection of tiny metal hooks, and Ben carefully tied the other end of the thread to one of the hooks.

'Right, all we need now are some worms. Where is that other sackcloth?' Ben asked.

'Over here,' Arthur said, and behind the huddle he moved closer to the damp earth of the river, where the evening before Arthur laid a sackcloth, having been allowed by Tess Yates to leave the guildhall for ten minutes for that purpose. Experience taught them that placing the sackcloth on moist ground, and leaving it for a day, was likely to produce a crop of worms when the sackcloth was lifted. Sure enough, dozens of worms of different thickness and length squirmed when exposed. Arthur chose one of the larger ones, replaced the cover and handed the doomed invertebrate to Ben, who pushed the hook through the middle of its body, causing it to squirm violently.

'We need to get as close to the water as possible, without scaring the fish, so we very quietly lay on the ground and move the fishing rod, line and bait, and lower the worm into the water. Watch me.'

Walking slowly towards the river, he stopped a few yards short of the bank and laid prostrate, so his head was just ten inches from the edge. Then he gently moved the ash branch forwards, until only two feet of the eight-foot rod remained on land in his grip.

'James, come and hold this rod, which is yours for this hour,' Ben said, and the eleven-year-old crept forward, crawling on his elbows and knees the last few yards lest he disturbed their prey. Ben handed him the long ash branch and crawled back to join the others, where he could continue with their instruction. 'Try to keep in the shadows of the trees, as the fish can see us and scare easily.'

'How will we know if we have caught a fish?' asked Edward, one of the youngest, drawing smiles from the others.

'You will feel the pull on the line, Edward, as the fish tries to escape with the worm. Hold the rod firmly, but don't panic. Then, lift the rod with the hopefully attached fish from the water and onto the riverbank,' Ben replied with a smile.

'What will happen if we are pulled into the water, Ben?' asked Edward.

'You will get wet, Edward,' Ben said with a bigger smile. 'But be careful if you do, as there are large pike in the river, who eat the smaller fish, and they will not be pleased with us taking their supper,' he added with a more serious look, 'and they bite!'

The younger boy looked concerned. 'What would they bite, Ben?'

'Your todger!' Arthur exclaimed, causing Edward further alarm, which was met with some laughter from the others.

'Shush!' James said, looking round, 'I think I saw large fish. You will scare them away!'

They returned to the serious matter of manufacturing

their fishing rods and securing the worms, so that within ten minutes all eight boys were laying along the riverbank waiting patiently. Just as the last of the younger boys was provided with the required equipment, Sarah and Amy walked through the trees to where Ben was fixing his own rod. He got a surprise on their appearance amongst the trees, but it was a most welcome one, evident in his smile.

'Hello, Amy, would you like to try catching fish for our supper?'

Amy smiled and was tempted until she saw the large worm writhing on the end of the thread.

'Oh, perhaps not, but may I watch?' Amy replied.

'Of course, but do not get too close to the water, lest you scare the fish, or worse, fall in!' Ben said.

'We would not want that, would we?' Sarah said. 'Perhaps we can see more if we sit here by the tree.'

Ben looked directly at Sarah and smiled, happy that she was there, and was delighted when she returned the gesture.

Over the following hour or two, the eight boys applied themselves with earnest concentration, all achieving some degree of success. The largest catch was one of the five carp, but there was also bream, chub, roach and tench. Ben explained they should not keep small fish, which should be released back into the river after carefully removing the hook, so they might live and grow to a size worthy of calling food.

Sometime after St Mary's struck once, Edward became very excited by a strong tug on his line, almost pulling the rod out of his hands. Hanging on to the wavering rod, he got to his feet to apply more leverage, determined to not lose his prize.

'Ben! It must be a big one,' he exclaimed, causing the others to look up.

Ben placed his rod down and got to his feet to assist Edward, who was not winning his struggle and was pulled slowly to the edge of the bank. His feet ended where the ground dropped ten inches into the river, and he was leaning over the water, desperately hanging onto his rod. Then, just as Ben was arriving to help him, Edward having leaned too far, lost his balance and fell forward into the Brett.

For a brief moment, Edward disappeared from view, but was soon splashing about trying to get to his feet in the muddy riverbed, which clouded the previously clear water. There was no danger of drowning and he eventually found his footing, standing with the water waist high. Every part of him was wet, causing laughter to erupt amongst the boys. Poor Edward looked for his rod, which had been pulled out to midstream by the unidentifiable large fish on the end of the line having won the struggle with the angler. Like the other six boys, Ben had initially laughed, but then felt sympathy for the younger boy standing forlorn in the Brett.

'Come on, Edward, do not be too disappointed, not even the finest anglers win every battle with the fish,' Ben said, and Edward began to lift his feet out of the muddy riverbed.

'A pike! There's a pike! Make haste, Edward, it is swimming towards you!' Arthur shouted with concern for his friend's safety. The effect was immediate, and Edward scrambled to the bank, lifting his knees to free his feet and splashing his hands through the water.

'Ooh, no, help me, Ben!' the frightened boy exclaimed as he reached the safety of land, and leaning forward Ben grabbed his hand. On land he was met with more mirth from his friends.

'I think that big old pike was after your todger, Edward,' Arthur said, barely able to control his laughter, and as the others gathered round him with smiles and laughter, he realised he was the victim of friendly humour.

'Was it a pike, Ben?' he asked looking up to his elder for some support.

'I did not see it, Edward. There are pike in the river, but thankfully you are just wet,' Ben replied with a sympathetic smile.

The scene was watched with interest by Sarah and Amy, the younger girl blushing at the mention of Edward's private parts. Then they both smiled realising it was all good fun, albeit at the expense of a very wet boy. Like Ben, Sarah felt sympathy for the sorry sight of Edward, but she also found herself feeling admiration for the older boy, who impressed her again with his kindness, something she had witnessed several times before.

Their fishing enterprise was brought to a natural conclusion by Edward's mishap, and as it was a warm sunny day, he was wet, but not yet cold. Ben opened one of the canvas sacks they had brought with them and placed into it about twenty-five fish, their catch for the day. Then, eight happy, satisfied boys accompanied by two girls made their way back through the wooded area and deanery garden towards the guildhall.

It being Sunday lunchtime, they did not have to worry about Mr Ward's possible displeasure at Edward having soaked his clean uniform, which along with his undergarments and boots would have to be dried. Once they were back at the guildhall, Ben went straight to Mistress Yates with the sack of fish and to explain Edward's misfortune. Much to his relief, she was pleased with their contribution to supper and mildly amused by the story, so she gathered some clean clothes for Edward and told Ben to bring her the wet items and boots. Hanging them in the sunshine at the back of the guildhall would ensure they dried a bit before Ward's return, so he should be none the wiser, particularly after an afternoon of supping ale.

The remainder of the afternoon passed uneventfully with most inmates repairing items of clothing and boots, which were always in need of new soles. Whilst he was busy assisting Harry with this task, Ben found himself looking for Sarah at every opportunity when his full attention to leather and nails was not essential.

'Pay attention, lad, lest one of these is banged into your hand,' Harry advised. He liked the young man and would not wish to see him suffer an injury as they applied their imperfect skills as cobblers. 'Your mind seems to be elsewhere today, lad. Are you troubled?'

'Oh, sorry, Harry. No, nothing troubles me. I am just thinking.'

Harry smiled, guessing he might be distracted, and remembered noticing Ben's smile when he was sat next to the girl, Sarah, that very morning in St Mary's.

'Has your head been turned by a pretty girl, Ben?'
Harry asked with a smile, causing Ben to blush, confirming his
suspicion. Ben just smiled and Harry did not feel the need to
ask anything more.

If he could have found an excuse to go across the room
to where the women were sewing, Ben would have found the
young woman filling his thoughts was also finding it hard
to concentrate. Sarah was thinking about the enjoyable hour
or two after church and the young man who supervised the
boys fishing in the river. He was not to know he had lifted
her spirits from her dark thoughts when standing amongst
the gravestones. 'Perhaps life would not be so desperate if it
could be built with a young man like him,' she thought, and
wondered if it was possible for her to feel optimism for the
future.

Supper was fish broth and bread, washed down with a
weak ale, enjoyed by all the inmates. Ben was sat at a different
table to Sarah, but she was facing him so could see his smile
when he looked diagonally through the line of boys facing him
and over the shoulders of the girls facing her. Like him, she
could not resist smiling.

After supper Sunday evening prayers were delivered
by Reverend Watson, who always came over to the guildhall
at the same time each Sabbath, after the bell struck seven
times. Then all inmates were confined to the four bedrooms
before nine o'clock, and a short while later lights out was
declared. Both young people would have been reassured if they
had known that as they lay in their bed waiting for sleep to
overcome them, their thoughts were of each other. For both, the
day had been as enjoyable as any they could remember whilst
living in the guildhall.

8 John Brownwigg

John Brownwigg was keen for the business of the Market Feoffment to conclude. Unlike the Grand Feoffment and the parish vestry, the Market Feoffment trustees were greater in number, consisting of twenty men, whereas the Grand Feoffment trustees numbered only eight, and the vestry just six members. This reflected the interests of those men; the charity with the greatest number was more concerned with commerce like the town market, as well as owning the guildhall. Consequently, whilst some of the trustees of the other two were also present on the Market Feoffment, there were many others whose interests attracted them to only that charity that might be of more obvious commercial self-interest. They were the men John Brownwigg wanted to speak to, who like himself, were looking to connect with like-minded men. He stood up and leaned forward to take hold of the large glass carafe of port, from which he poured the dark red fortified wine into five glasses. With him in the banquet room above the George tavern were Henry Cuthbert, Mark Goodwin, James Ferguson and Thomas Dunningham, who had chosen to remain after the Market Feoffment meeting was concluded.

'Did you find the meeting to be of some benefit, gentlemen?' John Brownwigg asked, before raising the glass to his lips.

'Aye, it was convivial enough,' Henry Cuthbert replied, 'we all seem to be in agreement, regarding the market.'

'Indeed,' Thomas Dunningham added, 'expanding the market by offering three to four more pitches, bringing more trade to the town, can only be to our mutual interest.'

'Agreed,' Mark Goodwin said, 'there is no reason why we should not be attracting folk from villages like Monks Eleigh to our market to buy goods, rather than them go to Lavenham.'

There was a general agreement amongst the five men of business, and this was confirmed with a collective, 'Cheers,' as they all raised their glasses.

'Increased revenue from expanding the market would also pay for employing an extra constable or two on market days,' James Ferguson said, the fifth member of the group making his contribution. 'The good reverend and the town surgeon both seemed concerned about growing rowdiness on market days, but to me it seems a natural consequence of the town thriving.'

'How so, James?' Mark Goodwin asked.

'Well, I think as the market grows and attracts more folk from surrounding villages and hamlets, it inevitably includes lads coming to sup ale and enjoy themselves,' James replied.

'Aye, and when they've had a bellyful, then it's a short step to fists being thrown. It's always been the way with lads from outside town squaring up to the local boys,' Tom Dunningham said, which was met with knowing looks.

'I would wager a pretty girl drawing admiring looks, and a jealous boyfriend, might be another ingredient in such skirmishes,' Henry said.

'The problem is, it be the trade of the priest and doctor to bother about these matters, and I have to listen to their prating in feoffment and vestry meetings.' John Brownwigg said with a sigh. 'One is concerned with immoral behaviour, the other with broken bones.'

'It was always thus, John,' James added, laughing. 'For centuries these boys with a fire in their bellies would have been prime recruits for soldiering. Perhaps we need another war?' He spoke from experience having fought alongside Mark in the American colonies, over a decade ago, where any desire for fighting on their part was satisfied for a lifetime, before they thankfully returned home, defeated but alive.

'James, your memory must be failing you,' Mark said. 'I would not wish war on any of those boys after our experience in the Americas. If you have forgotten the brutal fighting and dead, surely you can remember the cold winters in New York and Massachusetts, as well as the damn mosquitos in the Carolinas in summer. If we were fortunate to avoid American and French musket fire, we were plagued by frostbite and fever.' Mark Goodwin's demeanour changed as he recalled Britain's doomed effort to retain control of the American colonies and having seen many good young men fall.

'Perhaps we are not so far from another war,' John said, 'and this time it will be much closer to home.' The others could guess where he implied the next conflict might be, to where young men wanting to fight would be sent.

'Do you think we will be drawn across the Channel because of revolution in France, John?' Tom asked.

'It may depend on how far it spreads,' John replied. 'When all the trouble started three years ago, when the mob stormed the Bastille, the writing was on the wall. Now we hear they beheaded their King Louis at the beginning of this year. Well, we will see where it goes, but I think it's too close for our King and Parliament.'

'But we decapitated our king over 140 years ago and it did not result in war with France,' Mark said.

'That may be true, but these are different times, Mark,' John said.

'Well, if there is war, I know one thing that will not be in our interests,' Tom Dunningham said, drawing the attention of the other four.

'What would that be, Tom?' Mark asked.

'The price of labour will rise as there will be fewer men available to do a day's work for a day's pay.' Tom's economic erudition was met with nodding heads.

'Aye, it is bad enough now with the supply of labour falling. More and more are leaving to live in the larger towns and cities that continue to grow,' John said. 'Last year I was in London and the place was teeming with folk living cheek by jowl, particularly towards the eastern side of the city.'

'In my cloth manufactury I now pay eighteen to twenty pence a day,' Henry said. 'Soon enough I will be paying a man two shillings for a day's work!'

'At least that is for a skilled job, Henry. I am paying almost the same for a farm labourer,' Tom replied.

All five were employers of men, women and children, across a variety of occupations in Hadleigh and the surrounding parishes. And all five found themselves increasingly facing the same problems regarding a ready supply of good affordable labour. The great changes sweeping through much of England, Scotland and Wales, with young people and sometimes whole families leaving their homes in rural areas in search of greater opportunities in the towns and cities, were as evident in this small corner of Suffolk as they were elsewhere. If a man could lay bricks, shape stone, or mould metal, he could find work almost anywhere as a different kind of revolution to the one in France was occurring across Britain. The manufacture of almost everything was moving from small workshops and private dwellings to larger factories employing dozens or even hundreds under the same roof. It was not a revolution that saw the beheading of kings, rather one of how people lived and worked, a revolution of industry. But those great changes were not in the interests of the men of commerce sitting upstairs in the George Tavern, and as they sipped their port they ruminated on their shared conundrum.

'At least we have the workhouse labour to call on when required,' Mark said, looking at John. 'You have done well to help us gain access to that supply of labour through Mr Ward. For that we are all grateful, John.' The other three joined Mark Goodwin in looking to John Brownwigg and raising their glasses.

'Thank you, gentlemen. I am glad to be of assistance, as our interests are not in competition, but of mutual interest,' John replied as he joined them in raising his glass.

'How many currently reside in the guildhall. John?' Tom asked.

'Just over seventy were reported at the last vestry meeting, Tom, but there may have been more admitted since then, or even one or two leave.'

'Of those seventy, how many would you say are capable of a day's work?' Mark asked.

'It would depend on the nature of the work, Mark. There are a few small children who cannot do much, as well as some aged souls who are nearly ready for the grave, so I would estimate fifty to sixty. I know the aged inmates are skilled at rope picking, but they would not be worth the fee we pay if they were working in the fields,' John explained.

'That is a pertinent point, John. If they are too young, or too old, are they worth the fee the master charges for the day?' Henry asked, and John nodded his head in agreement.

'You are correct, Henry. Mr Ward is very happy to supply labour, but you must take care to ensure they are suitable when you agree a price,' John replied.

'Aye, he provided me with eight to labour in my fields at Polstead, but three were too small to be considered productive,' Mark said.

'Did he ask the same fee for each worker?' asked Henry.

'Aye, he asked, but he did not get, as I said, "Ten pence a day for a man, but I will not pay more than six pence for a child, Mr Ward." Of course, he was not happy with this, and I saw him kick one of the young 'uns as they left at the end of the day. Reward no doubt for the child's poor financial return towards workhouse costs,' Mark explained.

None of them cared for the workhouse master, having seen and heard rumours of his heavy-handed treatment of inmates. But their relationship with Daniel Ward was business, and he was a necessary cog in the provision of affordable labour. However, none of them wanted to see brutal mistreatment of the inmates. Furthermore, they knew it would not go well with the likes of Reverend Watson and Dr Parsons, if stories like the one told by Mark became commonplace. Their supply of cheap labour could be threatened if the 'do-gooders' got involved with their arrangement with Mr Ward.

'In fairness, I can report he provided me with a good lad to work at Toppesfield Mill. The boy did so well, Steven Crabb, the miller, has asked me to get him back,' John said.

'That's good to hear, John. How much did Ward charge you for the day?' Henry asked.

'Ten pence. The problem is, Mr Crabb has since suggested we employ the lad daily, taking him out of the workhouse.'

'That would be good for the boy and the parish ratepayers, John. A workhouse inmate raising himself from parish dependency to self-sufficiency through hard work is a noble story,' Tom said.

'Aye, that is true, Tom, but he would go from costing me ten pence a day to sixteen pence a day,' John replied with a rueful smile, and the others smiled knowlingly.

'We don't want you giving jobs to all the good workers from the workhouse,' John Brownwigg, 'lest we are left with only the aged, the young and the weak to work for us!' Mark said with some levity, which was a thin disguise for their common concern over labour supply.

'Mr Ward supplied me with twelve labourers two weeks ago, when my fields needed some extra hands after losing two families to London. I realised if I did not get a full team of workers up on those fifteen acres, I was in danger of losing the crop,' Tom said.

'How did they work, and how much did he charge?' Mark asked.

'Overall, I would say they were satisfactory. Seven were strong men and women. I reckon three were average, and the last two were weak, but those two were able to assist with carrying tools and moving bags of harvested potatoes and turnips. He asked for twelve pence per worker per day, and as I employed them for two days, I paid him 288 pence, or one pound and four shillings,' Tom replied.

'That is a nice return for the vestry. Mr Ward is good value for his annual salary of fifty-five pounds,' Henry said raising his eyebrows. 'My simple arithmetic suggests that if he had thirty of the inmates out working each day, at that rate you paid, Tom, he must be collecting about thirty shillings each day, which would be about nine pounds each week.' Henry's computation was not lost on the others, who appreciated his inference that the master was handling substantial sums of money on behalf of the vestry and the parish ratepayers.

'Indeed,' Mark added, 'which would come to between £450 and £500 per annum, if they worked six days each week for a whole year. A tidy sum!'

'Add to that the money he collects from parish ratepayers, and we see Mr Ward must be handling considerable amounts of money on a weekly and monthly basis...' Tom said, reinforcing the points made by his colleagues. None of them wanted to make allegations, but they were all thinking along the same lines. John Brownwigg understood their inference and felt he should offer some support for the master.

'They are large sums of money but, along with Mr Grady and Mr Hancock, he reports to the vestry on income and expenditure each month. Your figures might well be generous, Henry, as the workhouse inmates may not be hired every day. Indeed, there are days when all of them stay inside the guildhall.'

'That may be so, John, but a more conservative estimate would certainly be more than £300 per annum,' Henry replied, his numbers being met with agreeing nods from Mark, Tom and James, the last of these having been quiet, listening to the conversation.

'The temptation to stick his nose in the trough must be great for any man without strong morals and ethics. I do hope the vestry is able to audit the reported figures.' Having listened, James Ferguson said it plainly.

John Brownwigg felt somewhat under siege as he was one of six members of the vestry, who were responsible for the collection of rates and their distribution for the relief of the poor. He was sensitive to the sentiments of ratepayers like these four men before him, who paid rates as homeowners of properties of value, as well as owners of farmland and businesses. Moreover, he was one of them himself, paying more than his fair share.

'You are quite correct to raise these points gentlemen, and I can assure you the vestry takes prudent accounting very seriously,' John said reassuringly.

'Thank you, John, I am sure you do everything you can on behalf of Hadleigh ratepayers to ensure the accounts are correct,' Henry said, and the mood of the meeting became more convivial as they finished the carafe of port.

Walking home to his house at the top of Angel Street,

John Brownwigg thought about the conversation upstairs at the George. Comments alluding to Daniel Ward's ethics and integrity regarding revenue for casual workhouse labour had planted a seed in his mind. They all appreciated the affordable labour costs but was there something he was missing? 'Perhaps I should keep a closer eye on the figures for inmates' labour as reported by Daniel Ward,' he thought. 'Ten pence I paid for Benjamin Squirrell's labour for the day, and ten pence should have been passed on to the vestry.'

9 Toppesfield Mill

'Squirrell!' the master called, as Ben was eating his porridge. 'Get that down your throat, you're required at Toppesfield Mill, and the working day starts at seven o'clock.'

Ben looked up, initially startled, but then pleased with the instruction. He had enjoyed the day of labour the previous week at the mill with Mr Crabb, Peter and Will. The miller's kind words about appreciating Ben's efforts and contribution, along with the gift of a thick piece of cheese, had remained in his memory, providing some cause for optimism. He did not dare to expect them to offer him a permanent position, but such an ambition was not an impossibility for the future.

'Yes, Mr Ward,' he replied, and with four rapid scoops of his spoon he transferred the remaining porridge from the bowl into his mouth.

Ten minutes later Ben was walking alone across Toppesfield Bridge towards the mill, just as he had the previous week. The pair of swans and their three cygnets were not immediately in view, but as he was almost across the bridge and about to turn left for the last 100 yards along Tinkers Lane, he heard squawking upstream from the other direction. Ben paused and crossed to the other side to see the cause of the noise, where the family of swans came into view. The two adults looked much larger than the previous week as their wings were unfolded and flapping as they hissed at seven geese that had the temerity of getting too close to the three cygnets. It was the geese that made the noise, squawking as they hastily made their exit from the space occupied by the swans. Taking a few moments to observe the scene, Ben smiled at the geese in their state of fright whilst admiring the majestic adult swans caring for their young, as parents should. Once the geese were safely distanced, calm returned to that little stretch of the Brett and the family of swans proceeded upstream. He watched them disappear around a gentle bend in the river, then he crossed back to the other side of the bridge, onto Tinkers Lane and made his way to the mill.

'Good morning, Benjamin Squirrell,' Steven Crabb called with a smile as Ben approached. 'We are in need of your assistance again. Come in, I hope you're ready to work.'

'Thank you, sir,' he replied with a smile, 'I am.'

'Very good, but don't forget, once in here, I'm Steven,' the miller said stepping aside to allow Ben through the door, giving him a friendly pat on the back. Ben immediately felt at ease and to reinforce his welcome, Betsy appeared from a shadow and trotted over, tail wagging.

'Betsy, hello girl,' Ben said, leaning forward to stroke the little terrier.

'She will make a fuss and stay with you for the day, but she will get in our way fussing about us. So, come Betsy, out you go,' Steven said opening the door and gesturing with a click of his fingers. The obedient dog knew her work in the mill ended when the sun rose that morning, and she trotted out into the sunlight to find a sheltered place to rest and sleep.

Peter and Will came down from the top floor, where they had been readying the sacks of grain to be poured through the chute to the grinding stones on the middle floor.

'Good morning to you, Ben,' Peter called from the bottom of the stairs, his voice raised so it could be heard above the noise of the water wheel that powered the production process inside the mill.

'Good to see you, Ben!' Will called out, echoing his colleague. As Will spoke they could just hear above the sound of the gushing water St Mary's bell striking seven times, signifying Ben had arrived in good time and the day's work was to begin. Steven set the three young men to work, with each of them on one of the three floors of the mill, just as they had worked the previous week. After an hour of watching and ensuring Ben had remembered what was required, Steven moved each of them to a different floor, and repeated the change after the second hour. The result was that by ten o'clock each lad had worked each of the three stages of the flour making process on the top, middle and ground floors of the mill. As St Mary's bell was struck ten times, Steven called them all down to the ground floor, where they tidied the flour into the waiting 10lb sacks and they went outside for a mid-morning break. He liked to rotate the tasks as experience taught him that varying the work kept them alert, which resulted in fewer mistakes, less waste of grain and flour, as well as less likelihood of injury. They sat outside on the bench, where Steven produced a quart pot of weak ale and half a loaf of bread.

'You've retained the skills of a miller that you learnt last week, Ben,' Steven said as he broke the bread into four and passed three parts to the boys.

'Thank you, sir, I mean, Steven,' Ben replied.

Steven took a deep draught of the ale, wiped the excess from his mouth with his forearm, and passed the quart pot to Peter, who repeated the procedure. There was no conversation for a few minutes as the bread was eaten and the pot of ale was passed between them several times. With the bench facing directly south, they were all content to close their eyes for a minute, enjoying the warm sunlight as the bread and ale settled in their stomachs.

'There's probably still a pint or so left in the pot, lads, if you would like to finish it,' Steven said shaking the pot, producing a soft sound as the ale swirled inside the clay container. But no one was in need of more, so he placed it in the shade. 'Very good, we can finish it later. Let us get back to work then. I am going to ride down to Layham Mill to meet Mr Brownwigg, who wants me to have a look at how they are getting along. Then I will call in to town to collect a few things, before returning to see how you have progressed.'

'How long will you be?' Peter asked.

'Well, it is about a mile and a half to Layham Mill. The same distance back to town. So, with Jessie in good health, and allowing some time for discussion at my two stops, I should not be more than an hour. Stay working on the same floor until I return, then we can change over. No slacking, I've counted twenty sacks of flour, and expect to see them greater in number when I return!' Steven said the last sentence with a stern look, but then could not suppress a smile, adding, 'Don't let me down, boys.'

'We won't,' Will replied.

Steven's mare, Jessie, spent most of the day in a meadow by the river fifty yards downstream of the mill, where the grass was rich and there was plenty of water. Within ten minutes Steven had set the three young men to work, saddled Jessie, and was riding at a gentle trot along the path that followed the river to Layham.

Ben was assigned to the top floor and the task of pouring the grain carefully down through the chute to the grinding stones, where Will worked, whilst Peter was responsible for bagging the flour on the ground floor. As he got on with his task, Ben looked out of the large windows through which the sacks of grain were hauled from the ground outside with the assistance of a pulley. Seeing Steven riding eastward alongside the river, Ben felt a sense of admiration and gratitude to the miller, who had shown him nothing but respect and kindness. It struck him as odd that some employers of inmates could be generous and kind, like Steven and James Pike, whereas others, like John Humphries at Benton End Farm, were the opposite in both words and actions. He pondered these vicissitudes of human character and resolved to work hard for Mr Crabb, so that the miller would not regret the trust he placed in a workhouse inmate.

St Mary's bell struck eleven and a short while later Steven arrived back at the mill, having returned from the town via Toppesfield Bridge. Jessie was led to her meadow for a well-deserved rest, and within minutes the miller was back inside the mill. The lads were working and he saw no reason to change the three job roles for the last forty minutes until mid-day, so he simply visited each floor to let them know he had returned.

Steven welcomed the opportunity to sit outside on the bench in the sunshine for a short while, allowing him some solitude and time to think. Betsy had heard him return but did not stir from where she lay on some old grain sacks until he sat on the bench, at which point she emerged from the shadows to greet her master.

'Good girl, Betsy,' he said as she trotted towards him.

She stood on her hind legs, her front paws placed on the bench, so Steven did not need to lean forward to stroke her head. 'What do you think of young Benjamin?' he asked the terrier, whose response was positive, her tail wagging and tongue hanging from her mouth. 'I think you approve of him as well,' Steven said as he tickled her neck. Encouraged by the attention, Betsy hopped up onto the bench and curled up close to Steven, enjoying the intimacy. Her head rested on the seat, protective and watchful for any danger that might approach.

'John Brownwigg seemed to appreciate the contribution to productivity of an extra pair of hands last week,' Steven thought, 'as the increase in sacks or flour was certainly greater than the ten pence he paid for Ben's labour. Indeed, it was greater than the sixteen to eighteen pence we pay each of the lads here and at Layham Mill. I would estimate there must have been four to five shillings worth of extra flour.' He was looking across the river, thinking about the meeting with Brownwigg and Jacob Wright, the miller at Layham, less than two hours earlier. Stroking Betsy's stomach, encouraging her to uncurl and stretch, she lay on her back, inviting him to continue. Gently scratching her stomach, Steven told her his thoughts, 'Jacob is in the same position as us, Betsy, operating the mill with just two lads. You should have seen his face when I mentioned Ben's contribution last week, so I suspect he may have enquired further with Mr Brownwigg when I departed for town. I think the boy could be employed most gainfully by Mr Brownwigg six days a week, working here, at Layham, or at either mill as required.' Betsy listened, enjoying the attention to her stomach and the kind tone of his voice. 'Surely he must be amenable to employing another lad. Eighteen pence a day is nine shillings a week, for an increase in output of more than two pounds worth of flour,' Steven added. But he knew John Brownwigg's reasoning. 'Why pay eighteen pence to employ the boy at the usual rate, when he can get him for ten pence through Daniel Ward?' he thought. 'Somehow we need Ben's labour to become more important to the mills, so Brownwigg has to employ him to guarantee his labour rather than lose revenue, Betsy,' he said, transferring from thought to speech. 'Perhaps if we lost business because Ben was working somewhere else, when he was needed here, Mr Brownwigg might be persuaded?' The dog looked up at him sympathetically. 'I must invite Jacob to join me for a pint or two of ale, Betsy. But now it is time for some lunch!' With that the miller left the dog on the bench and went into the mill to stop the boys from their toil.

In town Steven had collected another quart of ale, a small loaf of bread, and a meat pie, which the four of them settled down to enjoy beside the river. It was a repeat of the previous week, and Betsy was even more friendly as a result of the smell of a mixture of beef and lamb emanating from the pie.

'Get down, Betsy,' Steven said sternly to the dog when she attempted to cross the line of acceptable behaviour by getting too close to the pie. 'You can wait!' Having put the terrier in her place, Steven's tone changed as he spoke to the boys.

'It looks as though you worked well this morning, lads. Did you encounter any difficulties whilst I was absent?'

'No, Steven, we seem to have managed,' Will said as he broke off a handful of bread.

'Aye, we worked well together,' Peter added.

'What about you, Ben?' Steven asked.

Ben was holding a piece of the meat pie in one hand, a handful of bread in the other, considering which to try first. He looked up at Steven.

'Thank you, sir, I mean Steven, this pie looks delicious. Sorry, I mean, I think there were no problems this morning…'

Steven laughed, seeing Ben would rather eat than talk at that precise moment.

'Forgive me, boys, I am forgetting you have toiled, so let's eat and speak after,' and without reply the three young men tucked into the lunch generously provided by the miller.

Ten minutes later, the four of them were sated, the bread and pie were gone, except for three morsels of meat to reward Betsy for her good manners, and the quart pot was passed between them to quench their thirst. Steven waited a minute or two more, enjoying the sight of the three content young men, relaxing as they digested their lunch. The quiet was punctured by Will leaning back on his elbows on the grass by the river, staring up at the sky, and emitting a loud belch, which was met with laughter from the other two lads.

'Ooh, excuse me, gentlemen,' the offender said with a smile.

'Ah, well it is a sign of an enjoyable meal, so it is, Will,' Steven said, 'and I'll wager so-called gentlemen do the same in certain company.'

'What company would that be, Steven?' Peter asked, and Ben listened carefully for any illumination that might be offered about polite company.

'I think they might be partial to sounds from both mouth and arse when they are together, sipping wine or port, Peter,' Steven replied, drawing more laughter from the young men in his charge. 'But mind you refrain from such noises and smells when in the company of a young lady, boys. That would not do, as they should be shown more respect from a man, especially if he be of a mind to courting that young lady.'

The laughter ceased as they listened to their elder, the worldly-wise miller, who they trusted in his guidance about such matters. Peter and Will had never heard him speak coarsely of women, which was not the case with other older men they knew or overheard in ale houses. Ben was also impressed to hear the miller speak respectfully of women, appreciating this little piece of advice, and for a moment he thought of Sarah, making a mental note of what he must never do in her company.

Steven looked at Ben and thought it was time to broach the subject he intended to get to earlier.

'The three of you work so well, I fear I may become redundant as the miller of Toppesfield Mill,' which was met with smiles, the biggest on Ben's face as he could not hope for a finer compliment. 'Do you enjoy the work here, Ben?' he asked getting closer to what he had in mind.

There was a pause as Ben considered the question to ensure he had not misheard.

'Yes, sir. I do enjoy working in the mill with your good selves, sir.'

'Steven,' the miller said.

'Sorry, sir, I mean, Steven,' Ben replied nervously, stumbling over the words, hoping they sounded correct.

Peter and Will both smiled, seeing Ben's response, guessing how he might be feeling. They had both come to like the boy from the workhouse, as well as feeling sympathy for his condition. Just the previous Saturday they had discussed his position over a pint in the Ram, both recognising his contribution towards the increased production of flour a few days earlier. The irony was not lost on them, that he was as good as them, but as they supped ale that Saturday night, he was just thirty yards away locked up inside the guildhall.

'Well, how about if Mr Brownwigg could be persuaded that between here and Layham Mill an extra pair of hands would be beneficial to his enterprise?' Steven asked.

Ben could not believe what he was hearing, it sounded too good to be true.

'I would like that very much, sir, I mean, Steven. Thank you.'

Peter and Will were also pleased to hear the possible proposition, and Will gave Ben a firm slap on the back.

'Understand this is not an offer I can make or promise, Ben, rather recognition of your hard work, and the idea of the potential to increase productivity here and at Layham.' Steven realised he should not encourage the boys to assume it would definitely happen. 'At this stage, it is something I believe is possible and would improve both mills. However, the decision would be Mr Brownwigg's.'

'Yes, Steven,' Ben said, 'thank you.'

'Following discussions with Mr Brownwigg and Jacob Wright, I believe it is something we can aim for, so I would say to you, keep working hard and your conscientious labour will hopefully be rewarded. That is all.'

Their break for lunch came to an end and they returned to work, continuing to rotate the tasks each hour on the miller's instruction, until five o'clock when Will was told to stop pouring the grain into the chute from the top floor. Will then joined Ben at the bottom, helping with the bagging of the flour that poured down from the grinding stones on the first floor where Peter worked. Eventually all of the grain had been processed into flour and bagged, leaving the three boys to tidy and clean. Through those afternoon hours Ben worked diligently but was unaware of fatigue as the conversation from lunchtime left him in an elated state of optimism. Finally, it was time to cease work for the day and, like the previous week, Steven handed Ben a small linen package containing a large slice of cheese.

'I considered a meat pie, Ben, but thought it might be difficult to eat surreptitiously,' the miller said with a smile.

'Surrep-what, sir? I mean, Steven?' Ben could not pronounce the unfamiliar word.

'I should say secretively, without others seeing you, Ben.'

'Ah, yes, you're right. This is most kind. Thank you,' Ben replied with a smile as he accepted the gift.

Within minutes they all bid each other a good evening and Ben was walking down Tinkers Lane, across Toppesfield Bridge, along the path past the Ram, and then left to the back door of the guildhall. Dinner and the rest of the evening passed in a daze and when he climbed into bed, he was able to reflect on the day. He was not hungry, so the linen parcel was placed under his bed, where it would stay cool and could be kept safe until the morning when it could be hidden beneath his pillow for the day. 'I can share it with Arthur tomorrow,' he thought, and returned to thinking about his new ambition, 'Benjamin Squirrell, a miller of flour. I like the sound of that.' Then he closed his eyes to sleep, most satisfied with the day.

10 Daisy Tappin

'Thank you, landlord,' Daniel Ward called to the end of the bar, as he placed his empty pewter tankard at the other end and turned to leave the Ram Inn.

'You are most welcome, Mr Ward,' Arthur Small called back raising his hand, a farewell gesture, knowing the regular customer would return soon enough. After several pints of ale, Ward felt relaxed and strolled the thirty or so yards back to the workhouse, where after showing his face and making sure all was well, he could lie down for an hour before supper. But as soon as he entered through the back door the look on Tess Yates' face suggested his repose might have to wait.

'I have received word from Polstead. My mother is unwell, so I need to go to my family.'

In his alcohol sedated mind, it took a few moments for him to understand how this would affect his evening, before nodding, 'Yes, of course, you must go,' adding, 'I am sure I can cope.'

'I have told the older women what is for supper, and five of them are preparing it now,' Tess said.

'Very well,' he replied, although after the ale he would have preferred to not have any responsibility, allowing him to take a nap.

'Do you expect to return tonight?' he asked, having the presence of mind, despite the ale, to consider whether to lock the doors before her return. Tess thought for a moment.

'So that it is safe for you to lock up, I shall stay at the farm and return in the morning at first light,' she replied, and within ten minutes Tess was walking towards Toppesfield Bridge. It was no more than three miles along footpaths and farm tracks to her parents' farm at Polstead, which, despite a steep uphill walk, could be reached in about an hour.

The unexpected responsibility of overseeing supper immediately affected Ward's mood, so when he walked into the kitchen where Daisy and Evy were leading preparations of the evening meal, assisted by three other women, his manner was curt.

'Supper should be on the table in an hour!' he said with a snarl.

All five women looked up from their work, startled, but not surprised when they saw him standing in the doorway.

'Yes, Mr Ward,' Evy replied on their behalf, knowing Daisy would rather not speak, as her contempt for him had deepened in recent weeks.

'Make sure it is,' he replied, leaving them to get on with their task. 'Perhaps I might steal a ten-minute nap,' he thought returning to his office, where he lay down on his bed. 'I can check on the other inmates shortly,' he muttered to himself as he closed his eyes and the ale relaxed his senses.

Minutes passed and as Ward woke from his repose it dawned on him that the overnight absence of Tess presented an unexpected opportunity, and his thoughts turned to the girl, Sarah. 'Perhaps I might enjoy her company for a short while tonight,' he thought as he got up to check on the preparation of supper.

Ward had only to stand holding his stick at the front of the eating room by the kitchen servery, through which food was dispensed, for there to be quiet amongst almost seventy inmates queuing for their supper. He enjoyed the feeling of power he wielded standing there, the vestry-appointed master of the poor, able to instil fear with no more than a cold glare. None of the inmates chose to meet his stare, not even the stronger adult men like Martin Lyndon. Why would they? They had nothing to gain by incurring his ire, only problems making their daily existence less comfortable. So, Martin kept his head looking straight ahead avoiding Ward's gaze, as did the others queuing to eat. The submissive stance of the inmates allowed Ward to survey the two lines of men and women without being seen, looking for one in particular.

Sarah was halfway along the queue on the left, stood behind two younger girls, and behind her was Amy, making it easier for Ward to spot her amongst the shorter girls. His eyes were fixed on the tallest girl and he waited as the line of women and girls shuffled forward to collect their plate and be seated. When Sarah was no more than five persons from reaching the servery, he stepped forward to where she stood, lowering his stick between her and the girl in front, causing her to stop. Her head remained lowered, knowing who it was who had halted the queue, so he gently used his stick to raise her head, pressing it upwards against her chin. No words were spoken, but as Sarah's eyes unavoidably met his, he grinned. Sarah felt a cold chill and wished she could escape, however she had no choice but to wait until he had satisfied himself at her expense. Finally, after some moments that seemed like minutes to Sarah, Ward lowered his stick down to his side allowing the queue to move forward. Despite the interruption to the smooth progress of serving supper only a few others noticed; one being Amy immediately behind Sarah, who felt uncomfortable seeing Ward's use of his stick to control and the look on his face as he leered at her friend; another observer being Daisy from the other side of the servery, who found her grip on the wooden ladle tighten as she witnessed Sarah's brief ordeal. Following the incident in the rope picking room, this was further evidence supporting her suspicions.

After providing supper for about sixty-five souls, the five older women could take their own portions and join their housemates. The amounts of ingredients were calculated carefully for each meal to avoid waste, but there was invariably a little left in the pots, which Daisy, Evy and the others could enjoy. However, at their age appetites began to wane, so they could take their heaped plate to the table and give some to an inmate who might welcome a little more. Daisy saw the bench where Sarah sat with Amy had space and joined them.

'May I join you two girls?' she asked.

Amy looked up and smiled but Sarah just glanced at the old woman who had become a friend, clearly unhappy, and Daisy feared she knew why. Both girls moved slightly to create a space for Daisy to sit between them.

'Here, Amy, have some more of the mutton, which is very tasty,' Daisy said and pushed some of the stew from her full plate onto Amy's almost empty one.

'Thank you, Daisy,' the little girl said gratefully, and

immediately set about satisfying her hunger. However, Sarah's plate had less space for extra mutton stew as only a small amount of her original portion had been eaten.

'You have not eaten your supper, Sarah. Are you ailing?' she asked, a loss of appetite by workhouse inmates usually being a symptom of an ague.

'I am not unwell, thank you, Daisy. I just seem to have lost my appetite,' Sarah replied, trying to be polite and not cause the kind old lady concern, but she was unconvincing. Daisy knew it was more than a simple loss of appetite, so paused for a few moments before asking, lest she made the girl feel she was being interrogated. Turning her head so she was closer, and no one could hear, she almost whispered.

'Sarah, I can see something troubles you.' She moved her right hand, so it rested gently on Sarah's left. 'You can tell me anything in confidence, young lady, I would never betray you, and a problem shared is a problem halved.' Her kind voice cut through Sarah's visage, behind which she was in emotional turmoil, and tears began to slip down her cheeks.

'I cannot speak of what troubles me, Daisy,' she said wiping the tears with her cuff. 'It is the condition of my life, over which I have no control.'

'Perhaps others can help, Sarah. If not persons in here, perhaps the likes of Reverend Watson, or Dr Parsons?' Daisy was convinced it concerned Ward and those two men outside these walls might be able to help.

'I have a heavy weight hanging over me, and if I do not do as demanded of me, others more innocent may suffer,' Sarah said, looking down sadly at her plate.

As they sat speaking quietly, they were unaware of the master walking between the tables and benches, exerting his control over the inmates simply with his presence.

'That food has cost Hadleigh ratepayers good money, so eat it girl, as you need your strength and sickly inmates are not productive,' Ward said, as he stood behind Sarah and Daisy. Sarah felt a chill down her spine, realising he was leaning over her shoulder, but did not want to see his face, or for him to see her upset, lest he blamed Daisy, treating her cruelly as he had in the rope picking room.

'Yes, sir,' she replied, and continued eating.

Ward moved forward and felt aroused by being so close to the girl that they were almost touching. Daisy could feel his presence and her suspicions grew more certain. 'Damn you, Ward,' she thought, and without hesitating she started to cough repeatedly, causing him to step back. The master looked at her with disgust, but her coughing fit had the desired effect.

'Keep your malady to yourself, you old harridan. You would have us all infirm,' and he walked away to escape any threat of infection. Sarah looked at Daisy, feeling relief that he was no longer leaning over her.

'Thank you,' she whispered.

Shortly after Ward's departure, supper ended and Daisy was required to supervise the clearing up and cleaning after seventy or so inmates had eaten, assisted by the four older women who had helped to prepare the meal, as well as four of the girls. These four included Sarah and Amy, who collected plates and wiped the long tables, before joining the five older women to clean up in the kitchen. Everyone knew what was required as it was a choreography played out each evening. Ward stood at the end of the room furthest from the kitchen, his presence ensuring order and application, as well as allowing him distance from the old woman and her coughing. It also gave him the opportunity to observe the girl who since Tess's departure filled his mind with lustful thoughts. Sarah was aware of his presence and when she looked up could feel his stare, so tried to stay at the kitchen end of the room collecting plates and cleaning tables furthest from where he stood. But she was not to be free from his attention.

'Girl! Sarah, come here, there are plates and mess to be cleared,' he called with authority, causing her to feel discomfort and dread.

'I can do it, sir,' Amy said, seeing the fear on Sarah's face, and it was a reasonable statement as she was closer to where Ward stood. But the master would not have a small girl interfering in his evening endeavour.

'Be quiet, girl, and carry on taking those plates to the

kitchen.'

Amy, despite her young age and having experienced Ward's wrath in the rope picking room, knew better than to defy him, so continued with the table clearing to the side. 'Yes, sir,' she replied and carried a pile of seven plates to the kitchen.

With her head lowered, fearful of looking into his eyes, Sarah walked to the end of the room where Ward waited. As she gathered plates and spoons from the table, Ward continued to stare, then finally as she had an armful of the wooden eating utensils he spoke.

'That's good. Come here, girl.'

Sarah was isolated. She felt alone with no one to help or witness what he might say or do. She felt weak as if any strength had been sucked from her body, and she wanted to cry, but she found herself unable to do or say anything and stood frozen.

'What is wrong, are you unable to follow simple instructions, girl.' Ward walked the five steps to where she stood holding the plates and spoons. 'Do I need to remind you of the agreement we made with your mother so that your family can remain in that cottage?' he said in a lowered voice so others in and around the kitchen could not overhear. But Sarah, trembling with fear, was unable to reply. 'I said, do you remember the agreement we made, well?' he repeated, his patience wearing thin, and Sarah knew what her answer had to be.

'Yes, sir. I do remember, sir.'

'Good, well get yourself along to my office later shortly after lights out.' She did not reply. 'Do you understand me, girl?'

'Yes, sir.' Sarah could not bring herself to look at him, and a single tear fell from her eye, sliding down her cheek and falling onto the top plate held in her arms.

'Good. Now get on with your cleaning.'

Sarah turned and did as instructed, carrying the armful of plates and spoons into the kitchen, where they would be washed. Her ashen face was noticed by Daisy, who had observed the conversation with Ward. Daisy could not intervene in a conversation between master and inmate and could not hear what was said by him to Sarah, whose head remained lowered throughout. She watched carefully to see if he laid hands on the young girl, not knowing what she would do if he did, and not for the first time she found herself cursing Daniel Ward under her breath.

Nine of them in the kitchen washing, drying, putting the wooden spoons and plates away ready for the next day created a busy environment, which was not conducive to quiet, discreet conversation, so Daisy was unable to speak to Sarah about her exchange with Ward. However, it was plain to see she was affected as her cheeks lost their pallor, her head was lowered as if in shame, and she did not speak to any of the other women and girls. Daisy also noticed Sarah was the first to leave as their duties were completed, without word, which was unusual as the women and girls enjoyed the opportunity to speak informally without the presence of the master or mistress. She had a strong suspicion that Ward was going to do something and feared for the girl, but unless Sarah would share what troubled her, it was hard to think of what more she could do. Then she heard a young voice and she had an idea.

'Daisy, I think we have finished. Shall I go now?' Amy asked.

Daisy looked down at the eight-year-old and smiled.

'Yes, of course, beautiful girl. You've worked hard and deserve a rest.' But as Amy was about to turn and leave the kitchen, Daisy added, 'Amy, I wonder if you can help me?' and she sat down on a stool, wiping her hands with a linen cloth. A smile appeared on Amy's face, as she was delighted to spend time with the kind old woman.

'Yes, Daisy, I would like to help you.'

'Well, sit here my darling and let's see if you can help me and someone I think we both care about,' and Daisy pulled another stool towards her, so they could sit closely together for a few minutes as the other six left the kitchen.

Evy was the last to leave, giving Daisy a knowing look and Amy a gentle stroke of her hair. She was aware of what concerned Daisy having also noticed Sarah's forlorn demeanour, and guessed Daisy was up to something concerning the girl's well-being.

Once they were alone, Daisy could ask the little girl for her help. She looked round to see if anyone could overhear, then explained to Amy how she might be able to assist with her plan.

'Sarah is such a nice girl. I have seen how she has become a "big sister" to you,' Daisy said with a kind smile, which was returned by Amy.

'Yes, she is lovely, and I like to be in her company.'

'I like her very much too,' Daisy said and paused. 'But sometimes I am concerned for her and I was wondering if you have noticed that she can be melancholy?'

'Melancholy?' Amy asked.

'Sorry, my darling, melancholy means sad. Although I know we can all feel that way living in this place.'

Amy was quiet for a moment, thinking about Sarah and Daisy's question.

'Yes, she can be sad sometimes, like this evening,' and the smile disappeared from her little face.

'I saw that too, Amy. Do you think there is a cause for her sadness?' Daisy was probing to see if the eight-year-old was aware of Ward's effect on their friend.

'I think Mr Ward scares Sarah,' the little girl said.

'Why do you think she is afraid of him?' Daisy asked.

'I do not know, Daisy. I think he is mean and cruel, and he scares everyone,' the little girl said innocently.

Daisy felt some relief that Amy was not yet aware of the ways of the world, and particularly how the carnal desires of men can lead to the mistreatment of girls and women. She hoped the little girl's innocence would remain for some years to come.

'Perhaps we can look out for Sarah,' Daisy said, 'and if we think Mr Ward is going to hurt her, we can tell each other, so we might interrupt him.'

A smile returned to Amy's face, as she liked the idea of looking after her "big sister" and having Daisy's help was more likely to make that achievable. But how could they, a little girl and an old woman stop the master?

'What shall we do, Daisy?'

'Well, if we witnessed him trying to hurt her, we can call for help, or tell someone with greater authority, like the doctor or the reverend. What do you think, Amy?'

Daisy's question was met with a nodding head, followed by, 'Yes, I think this is a good idea.'

'But we must take great care, Amy, lest Mr Ward realises what we have agreed to do as then he might turn on us, as he did in the rope picking room.'

'I remember, but I am not afraid of him, Daisy,' Amy replied, and her smile disappeared again to be replaced by a stern resolve that belied her age.

'God bless you, Amy, you are very brave,' and Daisy moved close to give a warm hug that was much appreciated by the little girl. 'We should still take care, Amy. Let us make this our secret that we will keep and help each other in looking out for our friend.'

'Yes, I understand,' Amy replied. 'Shall I come to you if I think he might hurt her?'

'Yes, darling, particularly if it is after lights out, when no one else is likely to notice.'

Amy nodded. 'My bed is next to Sarah's.'

'You cannot stay awake all night, sweet girl, as you need to sleep, but if something happens that causes you concern, you can come and tell me.'

'Yes, I will,' Amy said, and she decided she would try to stay awake each night until Sarah was asleep, to keep her "big sister" safe.

Daisy smiled and held Amy's tiny left hand gently in both of her gnarled and wrinkled hands, deformed by years of rope picking and other hard labour. They agreed they would both keep an eye on Sarah and tell the other if she seemed threatened, particularly if the threat came from the master. Thanking her again, Daisy told Amy they should both return to be with the others, lest it drew suspicion, and minutes later Daisy was able to close the kitchen door for another day.

As preparations were made for bedtime, Amy found herself looking at her friend, whose demeanour had not improved since supper. Sarah seemed to become more morose as the time crept towards lights out, and Amy noticed how when they changed from their uniforms into their linen nightshirts, her friend moved slowly, as if going to bed was something that filled her with dread. Despite her innocence, the little girl sensed impending danger and resolved to stay awake to keep watch over her friend, as she had promised Daisy.

Oil lamps placed at strategic points around the four bedrooms produced a soot that stained the walls and ceilings in their immediate area, along with an accompanying foul odour. They laid in their beds waiting for lights out, a task usually carried out by Tess Yates in the girls' and women's bedrooms, whereas in the boys' and men's the duty was performed by the master. With Tess Yates' absence this responsibility would fall to one of the older women. Amy lay on her side looking at Sarah, wanting to speak but reluctant to intrude into the space in which she seemed to have retreated, as she stared up at a nearby light and the thin thread of smoke drifting up towards the darkened ceiling. The light coming through the small, barred windows ten feet above the floor began to disappear as night replaced day, leaving the oil lamps as the only source of light, and Amy could wait no longer to speak.

'Sarah, are you unwell?' But there was no reply. 'Sarah? I am concerned for you.' These last words pierced her shell and Sarah was drawn from her solitude to reassure her little friend in the next bed.

'Do not worry, Amy, I am just feeling melancholy and will be well tomorrow,' she said turning her head, so she faced the eight-year-old rather than the ceiling. Sarah attempted to smile but was unsuccessful, which Amy noticed and responded by reaching across the short space between their beds, offering her hand.

'I am sorry you feel sad, Sarah,' Amy said, remembering Daisy's explanation of the word she had now heard twice that day. 'But I am glad you will feel better in the morning,' she added clutching Sarah's left hand in her right.

'Good night, little angel,' Sarah said.

'Good night, Sarah.' Amy released her grip on her friend's hand so they could both get comfortable in their beds, and she turned over, so she faced away from Sarah, and pretended to sleep.

Within a few minutes, the girls' bedroom door opened, and Daisy entered quietly, moving around the room, extinguishing the oil lamps. As she passed by their beds, she looked down at Amy and smiled. Without any sound, Amy returned the smile and closed one eye to signal that she would feign sleep, whilst she waited for Sarah to fall asleep. Once Daisy smothered the flame from the last oil lamp closest to the door, the bedroom was almost in darkness. Daylight had disappeared a while ago, but there was a faint light coming through the small window from a full moon and clear sky outside. This had the effect of providing just enough light for shapes to be identified in the bedroom, and Amy could see the silhouettes of the other girls in their beds. If someone were to get up to move about the room, perhaps to use the large chamber pot near the door, she would certainly see their form, even if she could not identify their face. She felt tiredness overcoming her, with a desire to close her eyes and sleep, but she was determined to stay awake a while longer and pinched herself beneath the blanket and rubbed her eyes.

Sarah had lain still after Daisy extinguished the oil lamps, keeping her eyes closed to avoid contact with the kind old woman. What she had to do was tormenting her, filling her with revulsion and fear, and she knew that if she looked into Daisy's suspecting eyes, she would break down, with possible dire consequences for her family. It was them, her mother, younger sister and brothers, that she tried to focus on, rather than Ward and what he might do to her, as she lay still waiting five or ten minutes until the other girls should all be asleep.

It was only a faint, imperceptible sound as the blanket was moved and someone got out of their bed. If it had been one of the girls fifteen, or twenty feet away, Amy may not have heard anything, but Sarah was just four feet from her. She waited for Sarah to get closer to the door, then turned to see the empty bed and the silhouette of the tallest girl open the door and exit the bedroom. She was wide awake and waited a minute, then got up and made her way quietly but quickly to the women's bedroom.

Sarah stopped when she got to Ward's office, as she felt nauseous and faint, wondering if she could go through with the ordeal that she faced the other side of the door. For a moment she closed her eyes as tears welled up, then she wiped her face with the linen sleeve of her nightdress, gently tapped on the door and entered the room.

Daisy was in her bed, and like Amy had resolved to stay awake fearing something might happen, but her understanding of the threat Sarah faced was greater than the eight-year-old's. When the door of the women's bedroom opened, Daisy was alert and guessed why when she saw the shape of a small girl enter the room. In the dark Amy could not see which of the twenty or so beds accommodated Daisy, so she spoke quietly.

'Daisy.'

Several women were wakened, and she was met with, 'Sssh!' and, 'Go back to bed, girl!' A small girl coming into the women's room was not unheard of; perhaps the poor mite was having a nightmare and in need of a motherly hug; it was understandable, and the older women even enjoyed that warmth they missed from life outside.

'I'm here, Amy,' Daisy said sitting up, and the little girl made her way over to the bed of the woman with whom she shared a secret. Daisy put her arm around Amy's shoulders, so they were close and could whisper.

'Sarah got up and left our bedroom,' she said in a barely audible voice.

'Very well, let's get you back to bed, darling,' and Daisy led Amy by the hand, out of the women's bedroom.

'What is it, Daisy?' Evy asked seeing them walk past her bed.

'Amy is concerned about one of the girls,' Daisy replied without stopping. Behind her, Evy threw back her blankets and followed a few steps behind.

At the door to the girl's bedroom, Daisy stopped and Evy caught up.

'Perhaps you should go to bed, Amy,' Daisy said.

'But I am concerned for you and Sarah, Daisy. Perhaps you need my help,' Amy replied, causing Daisy to smile.

'Bless you, Amy, you are so brave, but do not worry as I have Evy to help me. I am sure Sarah is unharmed and will be back in bed very soon,' and she leaned down to kiss the little girl's forehead. Reluctantly, Amy returned to her bed, where she would wait for her friend to return.

In the darkness Daisy and Evy continued along the corridor to Ward's office, where upon arriving they could hear muffled voices from inside. Uncertain of what to do, they stood and listened, trying to establish if they should burst in, or knock on the door. For a moment they were inert; the consequences of their actions were apparent in their minds, as they had witnessed the brutality of Ward's temper on many occasions. Then the voices were raised.

'Come here, girl. I own you and you will do as I wish!'

'No. Please, sir, I do not want this…'

There was a knock and without waiting for reply the two old women were stood in the doorway.

'Pardon us, sir, Mr Ward. One of the girls fetched us as they said one of them was unwell,' Daisy said with a concerned look.

Sarah looked round, tears streaming down her cheeks, and Ward stepped back from his body almost touching hers. The shock of the two old women appearing was unexpected and stopped him, leaving him speechless, so for a few seconds he simply stared. Then initial shock turned to suspicion and anger, but he could not see his enterprise through that evening as word would soon spread.

'Yes,' he said through gritted teeth, 'the girl has been poorly, and it is my misfortune to deal with such matters in the absence of Mistress Yates. However, apart from some tears, she appears to be well enough. Aren't you, girl?'

'Yes, sir. Thank you,' Sarah replied and looked to Daisy.

'The poor girl. Perhaps she is suffering with her time of the month, Mr Ward. It can affect women in both physical and emotional ways, so it can, sir,' Evy said, adding, 'Shall we take her back to the girls' bedroom, sir?'

Ward had no choice. 'Yes, yes, take her away,' and he contemptuously gestured with his hand towards the door. Without need for further word, Daisy and Evy put their arms around the tearful girl and escorted her through the doorway, where Daisy paused to close the door, saying, 'Goodnight, Mr Ward.'

Inside his office, Daniel Ward was seething with rage.

'I will make the old bitch pay for this...'

11 Chimney Sweep

Daniel Ward was sitting alone at a booth in the Ram. There were few other customers, apart from some old men who managed to pass the afternoon reflecting on their lives with no more than a pint or two. He was content with his own company for a while, the Ram being barely thirty yards from the backdoor to the guildhall. Most of the inmates were out working in the fields or places of manufacture, keeping labour costs down for local farmers and men of business, and Tess Yates could supervise the twenty or so who remained.

'She can manage the place while I take a break for an hour,' he thought as he raised a pewter tankard of ale to his lips, then placing the vessel on the table and wiping his mouth along his forearm, 'God knows I do enough on behalf of parish ratepayers,' but his thoughts and solitude were interrupted.

'Daniel Ward?' asked a man dressed in clothes totally blackened in colour, as were all visible parts of his flesh. His hair, like his skin, may have been naturally fair, but it would remain a mystery as it was discoloured with dirt, or some other substance. He stood to the side of the booth, waiting for a reply and perhaps invitation to sit down, but Ward simply looked at the man who resembled a scarecrow that had been blown over and left in a muddy field all winter. After a few moments, Ward recognised the trade of the man who stood before him holding a pint of ale.

'Master Sweep, what can I do for you?'

'Good afternoon, Mr Ward, I seek to discuss a matter of business with your good self.'

'Then you had better sit down.'

'Thank you, Mr Ward. That is most hospitable of you.'

The man referred to as 'Master Sweep' was used to folk being reluctant to get too close or sociable on account of his appearance. Master Sweep was not the name with which he was baptised, it being a generic name for all men of his profession across England. His real name was John Smogg, but like all chimney sweeps he was commonly addressed with the title used by Ward.

John Smogg, like other master sweeps, had developed a thick skin to protect himself from the hurt of being shunned at almost all levels of society. They were usually the sons of master sweeps and if they had the good fortune to wed, it would usually be to the daughter of a master sweep. Their lives were spent covered in grime, their hands permanently discoloured, so John Smogg could understand the reluctance of virtually everyone to shake his hand. The irony was that whilst he was a man no one wished to be near, he was a man everyone needed, as much as they might need a doctor, lawyer, or some other more respectable profession once every year or two. Since the Great Fire in London almost 130 years earlier, chimney sweeps had become recognised as an essential profession, lest a rich man, or poor man, should find him and his family perishing in the burning to the ground of their homes. However, being invited to sit down at a booth in a tavern was likely to be the extent of social interaction outside the small circle of his profession for a man like John Smogg.

'What business would you speak of, John Smogg,' Ward asked, showing the courtesy of using his real name, partly because he guessed what that business might be.

'Thank you for asking, Mr Ward. I will be direct, sir, and would ask if you might have a boy who would be suitable for my trade,' Smogg replied, confirming Ward's suspicion.

'Do you require a boy to assist you for a day or two, or are you in need of an apprentice, Mr Smogg?' Ward asked, showing even more courtesy as he realised a lucrative transaction might result in their mutual benefit.

'Yes, well let's say both, Mr Ward. Perhaps a day or two to begin with, paid at a daily rate, and if the boy is suitable, then a purchase of the boy as an indentured apprentice.'

Ward was immediately more interested. Ten pence or so a day was steady revenue, but the sale of a boy offered far greater reward. A master sweep such as John Smogg supervised the clearance of soot and other blockages from chimneys, but they were unable to climb up into chimneys, which by design narrowed from a wide hearth as they rose to the aperture in the roof. It was work that could only be performed by a very small person, making it the trade of young boys across England. There were even rumours of small girls employed for the same purpose in the growing cities. The problem was it was an infamously dangerous occupation for small children, with fatalities commonplace, or debilitating illness if they survived to adulthood. This made Ward's position more difficult in some ways, as the likes of Reverend Watson and Dr Parsons would not be supportive of such a transaction, but it also made Ward's position in negotiating a price stronger. Smogg would not find it easy to procure a boy from many other sources, although some families were known to sell their children, reducing the number of mouths to be filled with food.

'Let us address each other with the Christian names with which we were baptised, John,' Ward said warming to the idea.

'Aye, thank you, Daniel,' the master sweep replied. Clearly, they knew each other.

'There are boys of a suitable age and dimension in the guildhall, John, but the problem we face is interference in the practice of commerce by bothering do-gooders. I have to operate the workhouse cost effectively to the benefit of ratepayers, but there are constantly men like the church minister and town surgeon looking over my shoulder.'

'I understand, Daniel, but mine is an unusual trade that cannot operate for the purpose of keeping folk safe without the employ of small children. Would the vicar and the doctor prefer to go to bed at night uncertain whether they and their families are safe from fire?'

'You do not need to persuade me, John, but I mention it as I have to listen to their prating about child labour.'

'Allow me to buy you a pint, Daniel, as I know resolving such problems is thirsty work,' John Smogg said, standing to fetch a refill.

'Aye, thank you, John, that would be most welcome,' Daniel replied, seeing no reason not to mix business with pleasure.

Two hours later, Daniel Ward wandered back to his place of work and his responsibilities. The effects of four, possibly five, pints of ale included his clumsy, unsteady gait, but it was just a short distance. Once inside the workhouse, he made only a cursory appearance in the work rooms, along with an unintelligible grunt, to let everyone know he was back. Within no more than two minutes of entering through the rear door of the guildhall, he was in his office, where he relieved himself into his chamber pot and lay down on the bed behind a curtain to satisfy another effect of numerous pints of ale.

An hour or two later Daniel Ward was stirred from his afternoon slumber by the need to use his chamber pot again, after which it needed emptying, so he made a mental note. 'Perhaps the girl, Sarah, can come and attend to me, without any interruption from those old hags,' he thought, remembering the incident the other night. It had been a pleasing afternoon, with about two hours spent supping ale in the Ram, followed by a similar period asleep, and thoughts of the girl were also pleasurable, but perhaps even better was the opportunity to make some good money. 'Right, how shall I go about this?' he thought. 'There's the selection of the boy, and there's also the possible objection of the priest and the doctor. Do they need to know?' He knew he could assign a boy to work for Smogg for a day without informing Watson or Parsons, but the sale of the boy would be more difficult to conceal. 'We will see,' he said to himself as he left his office to get ready for the return of the teams of inmates from their different places of work.

Following a day of labour, the inmates sat down just after six o'clock for a supper of vegetable stew and bread prepared by Tess Yates, Daisy and Evy. The two old women enjoyed working with the mistress of the workhouse, who appreciated their efforts and never had cause to chide them. Indeed, she felt some sympathy for their predicament, reflecting on the cruel nature of fate that two old women were likely to spend their last years locked-up, as if they were criminals, because of poverty. Unlike Daniel Ward, Tess was not familiar with the niceties of the poor relief system, often wondering why the likes of Daisy and Evy could not be afforded an almshouse. Unfortunately, such decisions were made by men, not women, who sat as members of the vestry and trustees of the feoffments. If she could not effect a change in the circumstances of the two old women, she resolved to ensure they should be spared the excessively demanding work set to the younger inmates, so requested they assist her with the preparation and clearing up of meals. When she heard of Ward's treatment of Daisy a couple of weeks earlier, she was not impressed, but when she broached the subject with him, he waved her away saying, 'the old woman was insolent and part of an attempt to deceive me,' which was all he needed to say.

As the inmates ate supper, Tess, Daisy and Evy were tidying the pots that had been used to cook, before sitting down themselves, when Daniel Ward appeared at the door.

'Would you two leave us alone, I have a matter to discuss with Mistress Yates.'

'Yes, sir,' Evy said. Daisy remained silent, having no desire to speak to him, and they took their bowls and lumps of bread that sat in the servery, and went out to join the others.

'What is the age of the new boy, the orphan we admitted last week?' he asked once the two old ladies were gone.

'The new boy? You mean Jamie Bell. We believe he is six years of age. Why?' Tess replied, curious as to why Ward was asking, as he did not normally show much interest in the personal details of the inmates, whatever their age.

'We may have work suitable for a boy of his size.'

'What work would that be?' Tess asked, becoming slightly suspicious.

Ward paused, wondering whether he should tell her, 'She might as well know now, as she will find out soon enough,' he thought.

'John Smogg, the master sweep, needs a boy.'

Tess was taken aback, somewhat surprised but not shocked. She knew of the practice of procuring boys from workhouses for this trade, and Ward was a man who would not hesitate to provide such labour if the price was right. However, the boy he asked of was so young and small. The women had all expressed a fondness for the little mite, expressing sadness that he was without family. But then that was the case for virtually all the children.

'He's very young, Daniel. Is there not one who is older?'

'Aye, there are older boys, Tess, but with age comes longer arms and legs, and they are enemies of an effective climbing boy.'

'It's a cruel trade for a small boy, Daniel. Can Mr Smogg find another boy?' she asked, but Ward's patience was wearing thin.

'No, there are no other boys available, and the good folk of this parish and surrounding parishes do not want their families to die in their own homes because the chimney was not cleared.' His supposedly altruistic reasons were enough to win the argument, but he added, 'It's all very well for do-gooders in Parliament and charity trustees to talk about the sins of child labour, but we have to provide that labour to keep them safe at night.'

Tess took a deep breath and sighed, knowing she had neither the argument nor the authority to stop Ward.

'Is he going to work for Smogg at a daily rate and stay here?' she asked. 'Or is he to be indentured?' She knew the difference, and hoped it was not the latter, as she had heard stories of how such boys were treated if their master was prone to cruelty. 'At least I could keep an eye on his welfare, if he stays here,' she thought. 'If necessary, I could alert Reverend Watson, or Dr Parsons.'

'We will see,' Ward replied, causing her further concern as she knew his priority would be the money, not the boy. With nothing more to say, Ward turned and went out to keep an eye on the inmates.

Tess was quiet, trying to think of something she might do, but nothing came to mind. Ward was in charge and perfectly within his rights to indenture the boy to an apprenticeship. So, she stood at the servery looking out at the inmates, trying to find Jamie, who was not initially to be seen because of his size, but then she spotted him sat between old

Harry and the much younger Ben. What she could not see and had been unnoticed by Ward as he left the kitchen, was that there was no space for Daisy and Evy at the tables, so the two old ladies had sat on two stools either side of the servery balancing the bowls of stew on their laps, and between them heard every word of the conversation.

***

The next morning at breakfast Daniel Ward told different groups where they were required to go to for the day, and that he would be along in the course of the day to check they had not arrived late. As he read aloud the last list of seven inmates to report to farmer Humphries at Benton End Farm, he paused.

'Jamie Bell, where are you?' he asked looking up.

A small hand on the end of a short thin arm was raised by the nervous looking boy.

'Here, sir.'

'Do not be afraid, boy, you are not in trouble. I have a job for you.'

Most of the inmates heard, and whilst being intrigued as to what work the master had in mind for the small boy, they were not alarmed. It was no more than they would expect of Ward, his desire to raise revenue by putting all inmates to work being well known. However, two inmates were immediately concerned with what they heard, and Daisy looked at her friend, Evy, then over to where the boy sat. Her heart sank as she guessed the 'job' to which Ward referred, and she could see Evy was thinking the same. But there was nothing they could do, other than hope Jamie would stay safe and return later.

As the inmates gathered in their work teams on the footpath outside the guildhall, Martin Lyndon saw an anxious Daisy approach him and his group.

'As much as I would enjoy your company, Daisy, I fear the nature of our toil may not be appropriate for a lady such as yourself,' he said with a warm smile. Along with six other men, he had been assigned to Benton End to remove a tree, roots and all, which was hindering the construction of a new barn. It promised to be a day, possibly two, of hard labour.

'I am not coming with you, Martin,' Daisy whispered,

showing no mood for levity, removing the smile from his face.

'What is it, Daisy,' he asked, worried for her, it not being long since Ward's mistreatment of the kind old woman liked by everyone.

'It's the new boy, Jamie. We think Ward is taking him to work for a chimney sweep. Evy and I heard him speaking to the mistress about this matter last night.'

'I see,' Martin replied, immediately sharing their concern, but like them unable to do anything. He quickly thought about what options they had. 'We could try to speak to the reverend later after our return. For now, all we can do is pray he comes to no harm.'

Daisy knew Martin would be concerned as he had knowledge of the condition of boys who toiled by climbing for chimney sweeps, having told her a story about something he witnessed in Ipswich some years ago. However, he was right, there was nothing they could do there and then. At least his idea of approaching the reverend offered some hope.

'Thank you, Martin. Yes, that is a good idea.'

It was time to leave as the work teams were complete. Daisy returned inside the guildhall to get on with her tasks, and before Martin departed with his group, he looked over to where Ward stood with the small boy at his side. Martin whispered quietly to himself, 'You bastard, Ward.'

At Benton End Farm the removal of the tree by the seven men, who included Ben, was a great physical task. Felling the tree, cutting it into sections that could be moved, stored, reducing some to firewood size, then digging down and removing as much root as possible, was going to take at least a day. Perhaps some of them would be required to return the next day once the heavier tasks requiring all seven men were completed. For Ben it was interesting to return to Benton End Farm, where he had worked weeks earlier, when he was the eldest of the group of nine children. At seventeen years he could be assigned to work with the children, with whom he still shared a bedroom, acting as leader. Or, as now, his strong young body qualified him to work with a group of men, which he enjoyed as he had less responsibility, listening, observing, learning from the likes of Martin. He had never felled a large tree and was curious to learn, particularly when farmer Humphries produced an array of saws. It did not escape his notice that the farmer adopted a different manner with grown men, albeit workhouse inmates, than he had previously with the children. Humphries was not friendly, but nor was he threatening or bullying as he had been. There would be no waving of his stick, just simple instructions of what was required; the size of the cut wood and where it was to be stored. Then he left them to proceed with their task.

Martin led the team, explaining how they would bring the tree down so it fell where it would cause no damage, which involved two axes, a large crosscut saw and rope. They took turns to wield the two axes to hack a deep wound into the base of the trunk about four feet above the ground. Each pair swung their axes for a minute or two, alternating the blows, before handing to the next two men, who did the same before handing the axes to the next two men, repeating this for what seemed a long period of time as their arms and backs began to tire. Once a deep fissure had been cut into the trunk, the axes were placed to the side, rope was thrown up around the trunk and thick lower branches. Then the large crosscut saw with a perpendicular wooden handle at each end was used to saw deeper into the trunk, again with two men sawing and passing the task on to two others after some minutes. A strong sweat was developed by each man from the effort required to power the axes and saw. Eventually it was clear the tree was close to coming down and the men who were not sawing took up the rope and began to pull, directing the trunk towards where they wanted it to lay. Finally, it was toppled, slowly at first, allowing the men to move clear of its destination, but then falling quickly, completing the last part of its journey with a loud crash to the ground.

Six of them let out a cheer as the tree lay still and dust that had been thrown up settled, but one of them was unusually quiet. Working through the morning, it was clear to Ben that Martin, their leader, was not in his normal spirits when away from the workhouse toiling outside in the fresh air. He would usually be ready to joke and laugh, looking to make others smile, which along with his knowledge and experience made him good company for younger inmates like Ben as they all tried to get through the day.

This first stage of their task had taken them to almost midday, apparent from the sun moving halfway across the sky from east to west. Farmer Humphries had watched from a safe distance and satisfied with their progress suggested they stop to rest and eat before continuing.

'Aye, this is a good time to pause,' Martin said, and they walked the 100 yards down to the riverbank to sit on the foundation stones where the old mill had been located, just as Ben and the other eight children had weeks earlier. 'Let's get away from farmers, employers and masters for a short while,' Martin said after Humphries had gone back into his farmhouse, which also struck Ben as odd, as he did not usually bother to make such remarks, knowing the relationship between master and inmate was the nature of their condition. Once they were sat down, eating bread and cheese, and passing amongst them two quart pots of ale, Ben felt he could ask what was wrong.

'Martin, are you unwell today?'

'No, thank you, Ben, I am not unwell,' the muscular man replied looking at the river.

'You look troubled, Martin, is there something wrong?' Ben asked with a kind voice. In another time and place, like a tavern before he was a workhouse inmate, Martin might have answered differently, even with his fists, but he liked the young man sat alongside him, who he knew was sincere in his concern. He looked round and decided to share what had filled his mind all morning.

'What is it, Martin?'

'It's Ward. He's taken that small boy to a chimney sweep.'

Ben was unsure what Martin meant.

'Which boy and which chimney sweep, Martin?' Ben asked, but as soon as the words left his mouth, he remembered Ward calling out the name of Jamie four or five hours earlier, at which time he thought there was nothing sinister, just the master wanting to set the boy to some work. Ben's mood changed and Martin explained his concern.

'It is a most cruel trade to which a boy can be committed, Ben.'

'I have heard that, Martin. Clearing chimneys of soot and other obstructions must be difficult,' Ben replied, and it was true, he had heard stories of the dirty nature of such work.

'It's worse than just being dirty work, Ben. The life of a climbing boy is usually brief, most not living long beyond your age.'

'Because of the danger of fire?' Ben asked.

'Aye, fires are not always fully extinguished, and sometimes can re-ignite once the flue has been cleared and air flows freely. But the hazards are more than burning alive, as awful as that is,' Martin said solemnly. The five other men joined Ben in listening attentively.

'What other dangers do they face?' Ben asked and Martin took a deep breath.

'A chimney sweep is usually a grown man, known across England as Master Sweep, who plies his trade performing an important service to rich and poor. Without their skills more families would surely perish in their homes, as fires in blocked chimneys can spread to wooden timbers and thatched roofs.'

'So, they do good work,' Ben said.

'Aye, important work, Ben, but they use small boys, like Jamie, to clear the chimneys.'

'I thought they used long poles with wide broom bristles, pushing them up the chimneys to clear blockages,' Ben said in defence of master sweeps across the country.

'Indeed, but sometimes there might be a bend in the chimney flues of large buildings, or sometimes the soot is packed hard to the sides of the chimney requiring chiselling to break it away from the brickwork,' Martin explained as all six of his colleagues paid careful attention. Everyone knew of chimney sweeps and climbing boys, but not necessarily the details of how they worked. 'A master sweep might employ a team of six to twelve small boys who climb up into chimneys, which a grown man, or even a lad of fourteen or fifteen could not attempt unless his growth was stunted. At the level of the hearth the chimney is wide enough for you or me, Ben. But as it rises to the roof of the house, it narrows to only fourteen or sixteen inches.'

'Fourteen inches?' Ben exclaimed, 'That is only this wide,' and he held his hands apart to indicate the short distance.

'Yes, and that is where most of the problems occur. Only a small boy can fit into such a space as the chimney narrows, so master sweeps will often use six to eight-year-olds as apprentices, and they often starve them to ensure they stay small.'

'How can they climb in such a tight space?' Ben asked, mystified by the thought of anyone moving inside the chimney beyond its lower section.

'They clamber up the chimney using their elbows and knees, pressing themselves against the wall with their elbows, then raising their knees to do the same,' Martin tried to explain, but Ben looked confused. 'Think of a caterpillar, Ben, the way it moves part of its body forward, then drags the back end forward so the two ends meet and repeats the movement to proceed. A climbing boy moves up the chimney the way a caterpillar moves along a twig.' Ben nodded his head as he began to understand the mechanics of a small boy climbing up a narrowing chimney.

'It must be damaging to their knees and elbows,' Ben said sympathetically, trying to imagine what it must be like in the darkness of a chimney flue.

'Aye, their knees and elbows can be burnt, and disfigured by the extreme nature of the work. But worse is that a caterpillar does not climb along a space in which it can become stuck. Whereas a climbing boy can find himself in a space where he cannot move up or down. Unable to move his knees or elbows, he becomes stuck!'

'What happens to him? How do they get him out?' Ben asked, horrified by the image of such a scene.

'He usually dies in the chimney, Ben. They cannot reach him and if the heat does not do for him, then he usually suffocates.'

'But they cannot leave him there in the chimney,' Ben made a statement, but he meant it as question that needed answering.

'You are right, Ben. If they cannot get the body down by force, they have to take the bricks of the chimney breast apart to extricate the corpse.'

'How do you know all this, Martin?'

'Because I saw it, Ben, some years ago when I worked in Ipswich. At the time I was working with a house builder as a hod carrier, and my master was called to an emergency to carefully take apart the chimney and rebuild the structure after we cleared its obstruction, a small boy's burnt and blackened body.' Martin looked down, his chiselled jaw firm, and they could all see that even after some years he was still scarred by what he had witnessed. His chilling account shared, the other six had the same thought; was the boy, Jamie, who had come to the workhouse as an orphan just a week or so ago, now being used for the same purpose?

The eldest of the group was George Maguire, an Irishman approaching his sixth decade but still as strong as a horse, who had been resident in the guildhall for several years after falling on his own hard times. George had been listening silently, like the other five, but after considering a response to Martin's story, he added his own comment.

'He's a wrong 'un, that Ward. He'd sell his own mother,' followed by him gathering a mouthful of phlegm and spitting it in the direction of the river. The others looked at George, sharing the sentiment, and like Daisy and Martin earlier in the day, they felt a helpless frustration at being unable to do anything. So, they sat quietly with their thoughts, hoping the boy would appear later back at the guildhall. Ben's mind was thinking about the plight of climbing boys, and a question occurred to him.

'Martin, may I ask, what happens to them? The climbing boys, do they grow up to become master sweeps themselves?' It was a reasonable question. Why should they not progress, like other apprentices of other trades? But Martin's answer did not offer hope or optimism for those who did not perish inside chimney flues.

'In truth, I do not know for certain, Ben, but I do not think chimney sweeps were once climbing boys. More likely they were sons of preceding master sweeps who owned apprentice climbing boys. Just think, we live in the workhouse but we're unlikely to become masters. It's hard to imagine Ward was ever an inmate judging by his treatment of some of us.' Martin paused as his rationale was met with nodding heads. 'I have heard stories that the small boys who climb chimneys become afflicted with terrible diseases folk like us do not know, and they rarely live to be called a man.'

Martin concluded his account of what he knew about the life of apprentice climbing boys, and looking across the River Brett towards Lower Layham, they all reflected on how their own conditions in life were far from ideal, and yet there were small children whose lives were worse. After a short period of resting and thinking, the seven men returned to their task of sawing the fallen tree into smaller pieces of wood. The physical nature of the task helped them focus their minds on something different to the condition of apprentice climbing boys and Jamie Bell, but the subject was never far from their thoughts as they worked through the warm afternoon.

12 Sir Percival Pott

Sitting at his desk in the study of Church House, John Parsons looked out through a large window across the shaded graveyard on the western side of St Mary's. He had no appointments that evening, so was content to tidy his papers before dinner whilst enjoying a glass of claret. The appearance of a man opening the iron gate and approaching the front door did not escape his notice, although it was just in the corner of his eye, so he was unable to identify him before he heard the knock on the door. There was no cause for alarm, as he was used to people coming to the house, particularly if there was an emergency, like a premature birth and a midwife requiring his support. He knew that if it was about a medical matter Caroline, his wife, would alert him.

'John, there is a man at the door who wishes to speak to you.'

'Is it an emergency, my love?' John asked, knowing that was always her first response to any unexpected caller.

'He said it was not an emergency, John.'

'Is he ailing?'

No, he looks in good health.'

'Oh, then what is it he requires, I wonder?'

'John.'

'Yes, my love.'

'He wears a workhouse uniform, and he looks troubled.'

'I see, then I will speak to him. Please ask him to come into the study.'

It was uncommon for him to see any patients in his study, but it sounded as though the man wanted to simply discuss some matter, and John Parsons suspected it might be serious as such visits from the workhouse were rare.

Martin Lyndon stood holding his cap with both hands. His linen shirt was slightly discoloured by the day's sweat drying, leaving patches of stains. He had taken care to wipe off as much soil and dirt as possible from his boots at the front door, but some stubborn pieces had remained until falling off onto the polished floorboards, causing him some embarrassment.

'Apologies for the dirt, Doctor Parsons.'

'It is of no consequence, where have you been working?' John asked, seeing the man was nervous.

'Benton End Farm, sir.'

'Ah, I heard farmer Humphries needed men to remove a tree.'

'Yes, sir.'

'Challenging work for strong men…what is your name? And are you all well on your return?'

'Sorry, doctor, I am Martin Lyndon, and we are all returned safe, sir.' Martin's reply was followed by a short silence.

'What is it you would speak of, Martin? Please call me doctor.' John Parsons was curious of the reason for the unusual visitor.

'Well, sir, I mean doctor, it is a sensitive matter, and some of us in the workhouse are most concerned for the welfare of one of the boys.'

John became more curious.

'Which boy, Martin, and what is the nature of your concern?'

There was another pause as Martin considered his words.

'A small boy, an orphan not long an inmate of the workhouse, is being sent to work for a chimney sweep, doctor.'

John became more interested. He had knowledge of the iniquitous use of young boys by chimney sweeps from his time training as a doctor in London, where he had experience of its effects. However, as a member of the vestry, he had to be circumspect in what he might share of this knowledge and experience, particularly with an inmate of the guildhall. The use of climbing boys was not illegal and assigning boys from workhouses to such apprenticeships was commonplace across England. He could not let his personal view on the matter interfere with the day to day running of the workhouse by the master.

'It is a hard life, but it is one that keeps folk safe.
Which boy is it and how old is he, Martin?' the doctor asked,
curious to know a bit more detail.

'The boy is called Jamie. Forgive me, doctor, I do not
know his family name, and he is just six years in age.'

Dr Parsons felt a sharp stab in his mind, his conscience
assaulted by Martin's last four words, but he maintained his
composure despite a sense of alarm.

'I see, that is young, and I can understand your
concern, Martin.' Now it was John's turn to pause. 'Let me
make some enquiries and I will not mention to Mr Ward
anything about our conversation. Nor will I share your identity
with anyone else.'

'Thank you, doctor. I appreciate your discretion.'
Martin was as strong as any man in Hadleigh, afraid of no one,
but there was no reason to seek enmity with the master who
had so much control over his life as an inmate. He was grateful
to the doctor for keeping their brief conversation private.

'Leave it with me and I will speak of this to Reverend
Watson before looking into the welfare of this boy.'

'Thank you, doctor.'

Martin was escorted to the front door, from where
he made his way the short distance to the back door of the
guildhall. Dr Parsons went straight to his wife.

'Caroline, I must go to see George Watson to discuss a
matter that has arisen.'

'Of course, John, dinner will not be ready for an hour.'

'Very good, my love. I will return shortly.'

Within five minutes Dr Parsons was inside the deanery.

'You say it is a sensitive matter,' George Watson said,
'Let us go to the library in the tower.'

'Thank you, George.'

Sitting down in two high backed leather chairs, the
reverend poured two glasses of port from the crystal decanter
into two matching crystal glasses.

'What is it, John?'

From the comfort of their chairs in the Pykenham

Tower library, John Parsons could see across the circular room through the old windows down to the guildhall, to where he hoped a small boy had safely returned.

'It has been brought to my attention that a small boy, named Jamie, has been sent out from the workhouse to work for a chimney sweep.'

George Watson was immediately concerned, as he knew of only one boy with that name, the orphan who was brought to the workhouse just a couple weeks ago. He was there when the boy arrived and was struck how sad his predicament was at so young an age.

'I know of only one boy by that name and we believe he is only six years of age. Which is surely too young, John?'

'Was he admitted to the workhouse recently?' John asked.

'Yes, barely two weeks ago.'

'It must be the same boy.'

'Too young for any labour, I would say, particularly a trade so harsh,' George said. 'He should be spending his time learning his words and numbers, with no more than light work, an hour or two each day.'

'We have been saying this to Ward for some time, George, but I fear the master ignores our requests for education alongside work,' John said with a sigh and seemed visibly upset.

'Ward goes too far, John. I am sorry this seems to have affected you.'

'You are right, he has gone too far, George. If the boy is only six years of age, Ward has broken the law. Parliament passed the Chimney Sweepers Act five years ago, which decreed a chimney sweep could have no more than six apprentices, and that they should be no younger than eight years of age.'

'Then we must challenge Mr Ward, and bring the law into it, if necessary,' George said.

'Yes, but sadly convictions of chimney sweeps are rare as ages of young boys are not easily proven, and employers can claim they were assured the boy was eight, proof otherwise being difficult. Also, magistrates are often unsympathetic as they care more about their homes than the welfare of a pauper being put to work.'

'This is most heinous, John. Thankfully, you appear to have a good understanding of these matters,' George said, curious to hear more.

'Sadly, I saw the effects of this trade on small boys when I trained for medicine at St Bartholomew's Hospital in London fifteen years ago.'

'There must be many more chimney boys in London, John?'

'Yes, thousands, but few lived to adulthood, George, and if they did, they suffered wretched health making life not worth living.'

'Did they all perish in the chimneys?' George asked, having heard stories like the one told by Martin to his workmates.

'No, George. Many would get stuck in the chimney flues and suffocate, but those who survive the daily ordeal are usually killed by a most cruel disease,' John explained, paused for a moment, then continued. 'Few climbing boys, as they are known, live to be men, dying of a terrible cancer caused by the poisons they are exposed to inside chimney flues.'

'A cancer caused by the soot? Is this a new idea about the cause of such diseases?'

'Aye, George. When I was training at St Bartholomew's, I had the honour and privilege to be taught by Sir Percival Pott, a truly great surgeon and physician. After witnessing the death of so many climbing boys from this specific cancer, he made the link between their malady and the environment they inhabit, something no doctor had ever done before.'

'What is the cancer that is so specific to chimney boys?'

'It is a cancer that appears on the scrotum of their testicles, George. A dark tumorous growth, which the boys call a soot wart, then over time the disease spreads throughout their bodies and kills them. It is so specific to these poor boys that it is called chimney sweeps' carcinoma, a most horrible condition and death for a boy unlikely to live past adolescence.'

'Dear God! This is an execrable condition and this doctor is a great man, John.'

'Yes, without doubt, Sir Percival most certainly was, having sadly died a few years ago. He saw so many that the evidence was incontrovertible, and his findings and lobbying of MPs was an important argument for passing the 1788 Act I mentioned earlier. Sadly, he and others were unable to outlaw the practice but have at least made a start.'

'Thank you, John, I understand more now, and the reason for your concern for this boy. Let us go to the guildhall now, challenge Ward and put an end to this matter.'

Tess Yates was busy getting supper prepared for more than seventy inmates, but her face was not just one of concentration, there was a worried, distracted look about her. Daisy and Evy were both assisting, and they too looked concerned about something other than preparing the evening meal. Moreover, there was no conversation, all three working in silence.

Reverend Watson and Dr Parsons entered the guildhall from the front door, just fifty yards from the deanery, as they were in no mood for delay, so they passed through the entrance hall and second door to the area given over for the purpose of providing habitation for the poor. George Watson could not see the master, so he went straight to Tess.

'Good evening, Mistress Yates, we need to ask about one of the inmates,' he said, conscious of the two older women overhearing his enquiry.

Tess looked up from the large pot of vegetable stew she was stirring, she glanced at Daisy and Evy, then at the reverend.

'Yes, sir.'

George sensed there was something wrong by seeing the same look on the faces of the three women.

'Is it about the boy, sir?' Tess asked, and George realised the three women knew something and that it was not good.

'Yes, the orphan, Jamie, who has been here but two weeks. Is he safe?' John Parsons asked.

'Sir, we are worried as he has not returned since leaving this morning,' Tess replied, and it was clear the two old women were aware of the situation. Tess had shared with them her concern earlier when the boy failed to return, unaware that they both knew of where he had been taken by Ward. Like her they both feared for the boy.

'Where is Mr Ward?' George asked, his and John's concern intensifying.

'He has not returned either, sir,' Tess said.

'Perhaps they have been delayed because the chimney sweep was working at a house a distance from Hadleigh. Bildeston, or even East Bergholt?' George said, looking at the doctor doubtfully.

'That is possible, but why would Ward not be here, attending to his duties?' John said, suspecting the worse and not of a mind to give the master benefit of the doubt.

There was a pause and quiet for a moment as the five of them considered possible reasons for a delay to the return of the master and the boy.

'I hope they return soon, sir, as I fear for the boy.' Daisy spoke and the reverend and doctor could see a small tear in the corner of her eye.

'I think we all do, Daisy,' George said, familiar with the name of the old woman who had been resident in the guildhall for as long as he could remember.

'We should let you continue with the important task of feeding everyone, Mistress Yates, and we will return to our homes to have our dinner. But please send for us as soon as the boy and Mr Ward appear.'

'Yes, sir,' Tess replied.

Neither George or John had an appetite, nor were they much good for conversation over dinner with their respective families, their minds elsewhere.

'Are you unwell, John? Or is something troubling you?' Caroline Parsons asked.

'I am in good health, my love. I apologise for being

distant this evening. There is a problem in the guildhall, which will hopefully be resolved this evening.'

Caroline knew he meant the workhouse, and it could be a subject he would not wish to discuss in the presence of their young children, so she refrained from asking for further detail, but noticed John was not eating his dinner with his usual enthusiasm.

An hour later, supper inside the guildhall had been served, eaten and cleared away, and the inmates were in the four bedrooms, relaxing as they waited for lights out. Whispers spread quickly during supper, made easier by Ward's absence, so by the time they were in their bedrooms, everyone was aware of the boy not returning from working for a chimney sweep. Ben looked across the boys' bedroom at the empty bed and thought about everything Martin had said at Benton End Farm. In the men's bedroom, Martin was seething, fearing the worse.

'Damn that bastard, Ward,' he said to George Maguire, 'I could do him, and hang for it.'

'Aye, Martin, you and me both,' George concurred, not caring who might hear.

They did not hear the back door open, otherwise they may have been spurred to violence. Daniel Ward finally returned as lights out approached and he walked slowly along the corridor to his office, where he could lay down for the night. But Tess had left her door ajar so she might hear his return, so as he reached his office, she walked out to confront him.

'Where's the boy?'

Ward looked up slowly and Tess immediately knew he had been drinking, smelling ale on his breath as she got closer so others would not hear.

'The boy? The boy is well, do not fret over him,' Ward replied. He walked into his room, followed by Tess, who wanted further explanation.

'Where have you been?' she asked, not really needing to be told, 'and where is Jamie?'

Ward looked round, his demeanour changing to

indignation that he should be questioned in this manner.

'I have been enjoying a pint or two of ale, having achieved some success for the parish, mistress. The boy, or Jamie as you call him, is now an indentured apprentice climbing boy with a respectable employer. We were paid six pence for his work today, and Mr Smogg was so impressed he took him on at a price of three pounds five shillings six pence.

'You've sold him for three pounds,' Tess said, exasperated.

'And five shillings and six pence,' Ward said grinning, pleased with himself.

'He's only six years of age, Ward,' Tess said, exasperation turning to anger.

'Ward? Do you forget yourself, mistress, I am the master of this workhouse and it is my job to place children in apprenticeships to their benefit and the benefit of the parish. Besides, we do not know he is six years.'

'The boy is so small, Daniel,' she replied, hoping use of his Christian name might help her cause.

'His small stature makes him perfect for that profession. He can work and pay his way, no longer a liability for Hadleigh's ratepayers. Anyway, it is too late to change, and he now belongs to Mr Smogg.'

Tess had nothing more to say. She felt her heart sink and was filled with contempt for the man stood before her.

'And now I would like to sleep. Be so good as to lock up for the night, mistress, I have had a long, tiring, but productive day.'

There was nothing more to add, so Tess left Ward in his office, taking with her the keys. Before locking the doors of the workhouse for the night, she got a shawl from her room and went out for ten minutes to inform the reverend of Ward's return.

13 Apprenticeship

'Squirrell!' the master called, as the inmates were eating their porridge. 'You're working at the mill again today, so finish your breakfast and come with me.'

Ben looked up. His contempt for Ward had deepened, following word of what had happened to the boy, Jamie. But hearing that he would spend the day at Toppesfield Mill with Steven, Peter and Will, was welcome news. Since the last time he worked there, his private thoughts seemed to alternate between the possibility of a life outside the workhouse and his feelings for Sarah. His hopes pertaining to both were connected; the ambition that one day he and she could live together would depend on him being able to support them both through a trade or profession. He scooped the remaining porridge into his mouth and followed Ward towards the back door.

'I will return shortly, Mistress Yates, to organise the work teams for the day,' Ward called as he left the eating room.

It struck Ben as slightly suspicious that Ward was accompanying him the short walk of five to ten minutes past the Ram, over Toppesfield Bridge, and along Tinkers Lane, as previously he was just sent on his way with a warning to not be late. 'Perhaps he wants to discuss the daily rate of pay?' he thought. 'If he knows Mr Brownwigg and Steven are pleased with my labour, he will probably ask for more,' and following Ward along the path and past the Ram, looking at the back of his head he felt his dislike increase as he considered the man's seemingly boundless capacity for greed and cruelty.

'Good day, Mr Ward,' Steven called as he saw them approach along Tinkers Lane, 'and to you too, young Benjamin.'

'Good day, Master Miller,' Ward replied, 'Is Mr Brownwigg joining us?'

'Aye, he should be along shortly. Come in.' Steven led them into the mill, where Peter and Will were moving bags of flour from the previous day, which were due for collection by a merchant who would sell them in surrounding villages and hamlets. 'Ben, whilst Mr Ward and I await the arrival of Mr Brownwigg, perhaps you can assist Peter and Will.'

'Yes, sir,' Ben replied willingly, refraining from referring to the miller by his first name in front of the master, and joined his two young work mates with a broad smile.

'What brings you to the mill, Mr Ward? I trust there is not a problem?'

'There is not a problem, Master Miller.' Ward continued to refer to Steven with the generic name applied to all men of his profession despite knowing his name, suggesting to Steven his presence was for a serious matter, which he guessed was financial. 'I need to discuss with Mr Brownwigg and yourself the terms of the boy's employment,' Ward added glancing over towards the three young men.

'Indeed,' Steven replied, his curiosity piqued, but before he could enquire further John Brownwigg appeared in the doorway.

'Good morning, Mr Ward,' the mill owner said, 'I am glad you have been able to find time from your duties at the guildhall to come here.' His thanks were made knowing Ward was sure to attend the meeting as it concerned money.

'Good day, Mr Brownwigg, I am pleased to help in any way I can, you being a local businessman who employs Hadleigh folk, and a ratepayer. The latter are the people I am duty bound to serve.' Ward's altruism expressed with a false sincerity was transparent, but John Brownwigg could not be bothered to question it at this time as he had pressing matters.

'I am glad to hear this, Mr Ward, as I have a proposition, which I hope will be of benefit to all concerned, whether they be employer, ratepayer, master or worker.' Both Ward and Steven leaned forward, lest they missed something of importance spoken by John Brownwigg.

'Go on, sir,' the master said, realising he had to concentrate on a matter of business and finance whilst trying to clear his mind of the fog left by the previous evening's ale.

'Very well, let us get directly to the matter, gentlemen. Perhaps we should speak outside, where we can do so openly, with no one near and the boys in here will not be tempted to eavesdrop.' Brownwigg nodded towards the door, which was understood by Ward and Steven who followed him out of the mill into the sunshine. Once they were twenty yards from the mill, where they sheltered under a willow tree downstream from the mill wheel, they were safely isolated, the noise of the gushing water providing extra privacy. 'Steven has informed me that the boy, Benjamin Squirrell, has made pleasing progress here and has the makings of a miller. It could be in my interest, if the price is right, to have him employed here and at Layham Mill on a permanent basis, Mr Ward.'

'Ah, I see,' Ward replied.

'Now, whether that be as a workhouse inmate reporting for work each day at an agreed daily rate, or as an employee no longer living as an inmate, we have to discuss and agree, Mr Ward.'

'Yes, I understand, Mr Bownwigg,' Ward said, quickly trying to think what the two options would mean for himself. The loss of a valuable worker was not to be underestimated and he immediately thought of the two pence he kept of the ten pence received daily when Ben worked at the mill. Against that was the prospect of a fee paid for an apprentice, as profited the previous day with the sale of the boy, Jamie, to John Smogg. Two such sales in a week was enticing... 'As you well know, Mr Brownwigg, I have a duty to the vestry and the ratepayers of Hadleigh to maximise income for the labour of the inmates.'

'Precisely, Mr Ward, I appreciate how seriously you take your responsibilities on behalf of the town. Therefore, we must decide which is the best option for all concerned,' Brownwigg replied, realising he might use Ward's thinly veiled altruism as leverage to further his own gain. 'We can continue employing the boy at a daily rate, although it is normal practice for that rate to be reduced if it is on a regular six days a week basis, perhaps to seven or eight pence a day, and of course against that we must offset the cost to the workhouse of housing, feeding and clothing the boy.'

'Indeed, Mr Brownwigg,' Ward concurred, trying to compute the different rates.

'Added to that, we must consider the advantage of a price for the boy, to be agreed, as well as a spare bed that might be filled by a replacement able-bodied male who could take the place of the said boy as a worker producing an income.' Brownwigg had come ready with his reasoned arguments for finding a mutually beneficial resolution, and Ward felt himself losing ground.

'Perhaps he is right,' the master thought, 'I can accept a price to apprentice the boy, and whilst Squirrell is a good worker, there are plenty of his like seeking shelter.' He nodded, then spoke, 'Yes, I think you are correct in your overall appraisal, Mr Brownwigg, we just need to agree a fair price.' Negotiations with one of the town's leading businessmen were proving more challenging than with the likes of John Smogg, but he was not about to let a strong young man go for a pittance. 'Will the boy earn enough to pay for his lodgings?' he asked, a gesture to give the impression that he cared about Ben's welfare, not just his price.

'You have no need to worry yourself over those details of his apprenticeship, Mr Ward. He will be paid a wage that should secure his accommodation. We have several homes willing to take in a lodger, have we not, Mr Crabb?' Brownwigg said looking at Steven.

'Yes, Mr Brownwigg, we have families who will be happy to give the young man a room, or at least his own bed in a shared room,' Steven replied, knowing that Ben would be welcome in his own house, or sharing a room with Peter or Will in their family homes.

'Very good, then we can consider a price for the boy,' Ward said, seeing no reason to waste further time on niceties. 'He is a strong young man, one of our most valuable workers, who whilst being replaceable, would be sorely missed.' Ward was putting forward the case for a high price. 'I think eight pounds would be a reasonable price.' He did not know where he got that figure from, just that it was over twice the amount he accepted for a climbing boy the previous day. But John Brownwigg was not going to agree to the first figure Ward thought of.

'By my word. That is a high starting price, Mr Ward. Am I correct in understanding that you sold a boy to a chimney sweep just yesterday? May I enquire how much was paid?' Brownwigg asked.

'You are correct, Mr Brownwigg. A boy was sold as an apprentice for three pounds...' Ward was about to say three pounds ten shillings, but stopped himself, realising it would not take too much enquiring by Brownwigg to discover the vestry received three pounds five shillings and sixpence for the boy. 'Three pounds five shillings and sixpence was charged for the boy, but he was much younger and weaker than Squirrell, and sadly due to the hazardous nature of the work, upon which we all depend to stay safe in our beds, climbing boys are not guaranteed to last long. Therefore, his price was lower than we might settle on for a strong, healthy apprentice miller.' Ward had recovered his composure as a negotiator.

'That may be so, Mr Ward, but eight pounds is a large sum and leaves me to wonder if I might be better served by looking elsewhere for an apprentice. There are other young men in Hadleigh and surrounding villages who might welcome the opportunity, at no cost to myself. Until I secure a willing apprentice from a good family, we can continue as we have so far, with the boy coming to work on a daily basis as required,' Brownwigg said. He wanted Ben on account of the praise paid by Steven Crabb and was well aware that apprentices did not always work out well. Some were poor appointments who had to be discarded after valuable time training them was wasted, since their work still required constant supervision, an irksome and costly matter. Steven gave him regular reports on the progress of the apprentices, reassuring him his investment was money well spent. However, he would not pay over the odds as a matter of principle, particularly to Daniel Ward, about whom he harboured suspicions.

'Well, sir, then we must find the right price somewhere between three pounds five shillings and eight pounds. But please be mindful that I must negotiate a price on behalf of the vestry and in the interests of Hadleigh ratepayers.' There was Ward again, reiterating the supposedly noble motives of his actions, which irritated Brownwigg.

'I am sure you are, Daniel Ward, and not for your own interest,' John Brownwigg thought, before he replied, 'Well said, Mr Ward, and as a ratepayer, let me speak on behalf of them all in thanking you for your diligence on these matters. For the sake of expediency, as we are both busy men, allow me to suggest a figure halfway between the two.'

'Thank you, sir,' Ward replied in response to the thanks, but was uncertain as to the arithmetic to compute halfway between three pounds five shillings and eight pounds. 'How much would that be, sir?'

'The difference between three pounds five shillings and eight pounds, is four pounds fifteen shillings. Half of that amount is two pounds seven shillings six pence, so adding that to three pounds five shillings gives us a halfway figure of five pounds twelve shillings six pence,' Brownwigg explained and waited for a reply.

'But that is less than twice the price of the chimney sweep climbing boy!' Ward exclaimed. 'I was thinking of between twice and three times the price of the boy I sold yesterday! If eight pounds is too much, then would you not consider seven pounds?'

'I am still minded that it might be easier and less costly to find an apprentice from an alternative source, Mr Ward. Seven pounds is too high. I am prepared to offer six pounds.'

'Sir, this is not a good return for the vestry and the ratepayers.' Ward repeated the same argument, further irritating his opponent. 'What say we agree on six pounds ten shillings, which is only double the price of the climbing boy for a strong young man?'

Brownwigg did not reply immediately, preferring to stare at the man stood before him, smelling weakness and possible desperation. 'You want the money, Ward. I wonder why?' he thought.

'Mr Ward, my final offer is six pounds five shillings, which you can take or leave. We are businessmen and gentlemen, so if it is unacceptable, we can both walk away.'

Another moment of silence followed as Ward

ruminated over the offer, slightly aggrieved, as he had thought he would achieve a higher price for Squirrell. Steven Crabb stood observing the negotiations without saying a word, admiring the skill of his employer, wondering if there would be a satisfactory agreement. But he was not so sure and feared a deal would not be struck that would see the likeable young man established as an apprentice under his charge. Ward let out a sigh with a loud breath.

'Six pounds five shillings it is.'

'Very good. Six pounds five shillings for the boy, Squirrell, to be delivered from the workhouse to commence work as an apprentice miller. Shall we say in three days from now?'

'Yes, sir, in three days from today,' Ward said in a resigned tone.

'Let us shake hands on it then,' Brownwigg said with a smile, and held out his hand, which the master shook half-heartedly.

Ward was the first to leave, less happy than he had anticipated due to the outcome of the negotiations. 'Six pounds five shillings is not the return I was hoping for, so perhaps I will keep five shillings for my trouble?' he thought, as he made his way along Tinkers Lane beside the River Brett. 'Or perhaps only two shillings six pence, as there is no need to be greedy. Added to the five shillings from the deal with the Master Sweep yesterday, it makes the week a profitable one. A most profitable week indeed, Daniel Ward.' With that thought his mood lifted and he looked to his right to see two large swans and three cygnets gliding across the water in his direction. Were they curious at the sight of a man, or were they wondering if he might throw a morsel of food? However, Ward was not interested in their curiosity, rather he would prefer them to stay away, so gathered a mouthful of phlegm and rolled it in his mouth before spitting it at the leading bird. The missile fell just short of its target but had the desired effect as the beautiful creature sensed a potential threat, so she effortlessly turned to her left guiding her family in the opposite direction away from danger.

John Brownwigg and Steven Crabb returned to the mill, where the latter was delighted to call Ben over from his toil moving the sacks of flour for collection.

'Ben, Mr Brownwigg has a proposition he would like to put to you…'

'Yes, sir?' Ben replied, again uncertain whether it was appropriate to use the miller's Christian name. He felt a nervous excitement, as he hoped it would be pertaining to his ambitions.

'Benjamin Squirrell, how would you feel about entering an apprenticeship under the tutelage of Mr Crabb, working here and at Layham Mill?'

There was a pause as Ben considered Mr Brownwigg's words. He wanted to request the mill owner to repeat them, lest he was mistaken, but thought that might suggest a poor student.

'Sir? He uttered, then, 'Yes! Thank you, sir.' It was all he could do to suppress tears welling up. 'I would welcome such an opportunity very much, sir.' His eyes widened and a smile appeared.

'Excellent. Mr Crabb thinks you have the makings of a good miller, so I do hope you do not disappoint us. All being well, you will be released from the workhouse in three days, when you should report here for work at seven o clock in the morning. Come with any possessions and at the end of that day Mr Crabb will take you to temporary lodgings that we will arrange. Does that sound to your liking?'

'Yes, sir,' Ben replied, his head spinning.

'Well, this is proving straightforward, but I think you have not considered everything, Benjamin,' John Brownwigg said.

'Sir? It sounds perfect to me…'

'Benjamin, you have not asked about your remuneration.' The mill owner chuckled as he spoke. 'Careful young man, you could be entering a form of servitude worse than your current circumstances.'

'I am sure it could not be, sir, as I have never been paid any money.'

'But for your labour the workhouse has provided you with accommodation, food and clothing.' Brownwigg's reply was a point of view he had been reminded of numerous times by the master, and Ben gave it some consideration.

'I have heard of some indentured apprentices being treated harshly, sir. However, I trust and have confidence in Mr Crabb.' Ben was speaking in an articulate manner that surprised Brownwigg.

'Have you? Well, I think your trust is well placed. In case you are curious, I can inform you that your pay will be nine shillings each week, from which you will have to pay for your board and lodgings. Does that sound acceptable, Benjamin Squirrell?'

'Thank you, sir, that sounds most acceptable.'

'Let us shake on it then,' Brownwigg concluded and offered his hand.

It struck Ben that it was the first time he had shaken another person's hand, adding formality to their agreement.

'I will leave you to get on with your labour for the day, Benjamin Squirrell. Mr Crabb will keep me informed of your progress.' He turned to the miller. 'Does all of that sound agreeable to you, Mr Crabb?'

The miller was delighted to be giving the likeable boy an opportunity to be free from the workhouse but suppressed a smile in keeping with the formality of the meeting.

'Indeed it does, Mr Brownwigg,' Steven replied.

'Excellent! Good day to you both.' Without further word, the mill owner turned and left to see to other business matters in town.

Ben stood open mouthed, absorbing what had happened in the preceding five minutes. He wanted to embrace Steven, or someone, his joy filling his head with thoughts about what this meant for the future. 'I can be a miller, a respectable trade, and perhaps eventually I could offer Sarah security and a home,' he thought, before his planning for the future was interrupted by Steven.

'Well, young Benjamin, perhaps we should celebrate with a pint of ale in the Ram? However, it might be wise to wait until you are out of that place in the guildhall. So, before we do, you have a job of work to do today, then you can return in a few days to become an apprentice miller. What say you to that?'

'Yes, sir.'

'Steven!'

'Yes, Steven. Thank you so much, I will not let you down, sir. I mean, Steven,' and Ben smiled with a look that told Steven all he needed to know that the boy was sincere.

Peter and William were informed by Steven of what had just been agreed and they were able to be more open in their pleasure that Ben would be joining them on a permanent basis. There was plenty of work and he was a reliable worker, who in just a few days working at the mill increased its productivity and shared the burden of their labour. They set to their work, each young man responsible for the flour-making process on the three floors of the mill, with Ben feeling as though he could perform his duty all day and through the night if required. However, as St Mary's bell was struck twelve times, they were called to cease working and joined Steven outside for lunch on the wooden benches. It was there while he was still in a state of elation that Ben could share his delight, even telling them of his ambitions regarding a young woman called Sarah. They all shared Ben's happiness and returned to work in the afternoon with an enthusiasm created by their collective good spirits.

***

Reverend Watson and Dr Parsons marched with purpose into the guildhall through the main door that faced across the graveyard towards St Mary's.

'Mistress Yates, is Mr Ward present? We have a matter we wish to discuss with him!'

Tess had never seen the Reverend as stern as he looked at that moment. She could guess it probably concerned Jamie Bell and she feared the worst. 'Surely he has not had an accident already,' she thought. But she did not have the confidence to ask directly, so she made a general enquiry.

'Is there something amiss, Reverend?'

'Yes, Tess,' he replied, using her first name as a sign of his appreciation for her informing him of Ward's return the previous night and them sharing a mutual concern for the welfare of the young boy. 'We have decided every effort must be made to return Jamie Bell to the workhouse, so we urgently need to speak to Mr Ward, to establish his whereabouts.'

'I believe he is in his room. Shall I fetch him to you?' Tess asked knowing he would have taken a nap after his morning work and a visit to the Ram. Following recent events, she was feeling less loyalty to Ward than she had for the last three years during which they had worked together running the workhouse. He had few likeable traits, if any, but an amicable work relationship ensured the days passed smoothly. However, incidents revealing his true character were becoming more frequent, increasingly exposed by his increased drinking. It seemed he left her to supervise the inmates every day to pay a visit to the Ram, or the George, and when he returned, he was of little use in the afternoon. In just the last few weeks there was his excessive punishment of Lucy, then Daisy, and now the apprenticing of little Jamie. All of this built up, layer upon layer, causing her resentment to grow. 'Perhaps the reverend and doctor should see him as he was, probably in an alcohol induced stupor,' she thought. She was not to be disappointed.

'No need, Tess, it would be best for all concerned if we talk to him in the privacy of his room,' George Watson said and led the three of them to Ward's door.

Two polite taps on the door were met with no response, suggesting there was no one on the other side. George looked at Tess and John.

'I am sure he is in there,' Tess said. She knew he was not anywhere else in the workhouse and it was their normal protocol to inform each other if they had to leave the building.

John Parsons leaned forward, placing his ear against the door and could hear a dull sound from inside. 'I believe he may be asleep,' the doctor reported. Reverend Watson's face showed his dismay and Tess realised Ward's daily routine was about to be exposed.

Two more firm knocks and a loud, 'Mr Ward!' by the

reverend still failed to produce a reply, so he opened the door. Inside they were met with the sight and sound of the fully dressed master, wearing his boots, asleep and snoring on his bed, the curtain employed to provide privacy having been left open. The three intruders approached the prostrate master, although Tess stayed back a step, leaving the reverend or doctor to wake him.

'Mr Ward! Wake up!' George Watson's patience was wearing thin, the only excuse for his repose being illness, but he could smell alcohol. His louder voice had the desired effect and a startled Daniel Ward sat up.

'What is it?' he asked through bleary eyes, shocked by the presence of the reverend and doctor, less so by Tess, who he might expect to wake him if there was a problem.

'We need to speak to you about the boy, Jamie Bell, who you apprenticed to a chimney sweep,' John Parsons said.

For a moment Ward did not reply, absorbing what the doctor said, then feeling a deep irritation as he could guess what was coming. With a sigh he stood up from the bed, bracing himself to face their prating.

'Is this good reason for disturbing me?'

'You were asleep, Mr Ward, so we haven't interrupted your work,' George said, his ire increasing.

'Aye, Reverend, I was taking a nap. I have worked this morning and felt some rest was necessary as I have been feeling under the weather. Perhaps I should have come to seek your advice, Doctor, but know you are a busy man.' Ward thought he might deflect any insinuation of guilt over his repose, but his excuse drew no sympathy as the smell of alcohol pervaded the room.

'Do come to see me if you are poorly, Mr Ward, as we cannot have you unable to perform your work,' John Parsons said, who like the reverend was losing patience.

'What is it about the boy?' Ward asked having gathered himself and beginning to feel indignant that three of them should be stood in his room.

'He is too young to be apprenticed as a climbing boy,' the doctor said.

'How do you know?'

'Because the law states that climbing boys are not to be apprenticed until they are eight years of age, and Jamie Bell is only six,' George Watson said.

'You may be correct regarding the law, Reverend, but you cannot be certain regarding his age.'

'Mr Ward, look at the size of him. How can he be eight?' John Parsons asked, incredulous.

'Doctor, I have seen many a boy small in stature for their age, usually the result of poverty. Hence their presence in this place.' Ward was finding this easier than he thought.

'Are you telling us you believed the boy is eight, Mr Ward?' George Parsons asked.

'I was not aware the boy was so young, Reverend. Are you suggesting I would consciously break the law?' The master's veracity was being questioned and he was offended.

'I hope you would not, Mr Ward, but at the very least, a terrible mistake has been made and we must get him back,' George replied.

Tess watched and listened in silence. She tried to remember the precise words of their conversation the previous day, and whilst the exact words they spoke escaped her, she was certain she told him the boy was only six years of age. However, she was not confident of taking on Ward, even in the presence of the reverend and the doctor.

'That might be more easily said than done, Reverend.'

'Why so? There is no choice. It must be done!' George was getting irate.

'Well, there is a problem with what you say must be done, Reverend. You see, the boy was apprenticed for a price, which I negotiated and accepted on behalf of the vestry. Besides, he could be anywhere by now, Ipswich, Sudbury, Bury, Stowmarket, or any one of dozens of villages.'

'Who did you sell him to? Where does the man reside?' John asked.

'He was bought by a master sweep named John Smogg,' Ward replied, and whilst he knew the chimney sweep's home was in Bildeston just five miles to the north, he saw no reason to help undo the transaction he had successfully achieved the previous day. 'I am not sure of John Smogg's place of abode, Doctor.' Their prating was becoming tedious and he was getting impatient. 'But mind you, I think it is too late to reverse as John Smogg paid a fair price in good faith, so you might as well stop bothering yourselves.' His last words were spoken with a contemptuous sneer.

'Dear God, Ward, what have you done?' George said, but the master saw no reason for apology.

'What I have done, Reverend, is I have acted in the interests of the vestry, the ratepayers and the boy, who will have a life outside the workhouse. You and the good doctor can fuss over the rights and wrongs, but I have to make this place work, whilst being mindful of costs!' His voice had risen as he made his point to the prating do-gooders.

'The interests of the boy...Is that what you call selling a small boy into a trade where he probably won't live to become a man?' John Parsons asked.

'That is not my concern. Smogg paid a fair price for an apprentice, and that is the end of the matter.'

'Is it, Mr Ward? And how much was that fair price? And what, may I ask, have you done with the money?' George Watson asked.

Such further insinuation questioning his propriety was too much for Ward and he felt his blood boil.

'The price, Reverend, was three pounds five shillings and sixpence, and the money is here!' Ward moved over to his desk, where from a drawer, he took a small purse and threw it onto the desktop. 'Here, take it, and keep it safe for the vestry, lest you think it unsafe with Daniel Ward!'

George Watson and John Parsons looked at the master, who was clearly aggrieved, but their appeals based on reason were not getting them anywhere. Watson picked up the purse.

'If you remember anything that might help us find the boy, please let us know, Daniel Ward. In the meantime, let us hope he is safe.' Reverend Watson saw no reason to pursue the matter any further with the master of the workhouse, whose character seemed to have sunk deeper into a mire of immorality. Clutching the purse, he turned and left Ward's room, followed by the doctor and Tess Yates.

Daniel Ward stayed in his office and bedroom for a few minutes, his blood boiling. 'Bloody interfering do-gooders,' he said to himself, 'I need some ale.' It was mid-afternoon and there was time before inmates would return from their places of work, so he quietly made his way out the rear door of the guildhall to the Ram. The remainder of the day passed without further alarm after returning from the Ram, where he enjoyed several pints sitting alone in a booth in the corner of the main bar. Perhaps the ale anaesthetized his senses, but he was grateful to be away from the those who might obstruct his endeavour, who increasingly included Mistress Yates. He decided to keep his thoughts to himself that evening, avoiding conversation with Tess, if possible. With that objective in mind, at supper he positioned himself at the end of the eating room furthest from the kitchen servery, even making an effort to be more anonymous than normal, waiting for another workhouse day to end with lights out. Scanning the room and seventy or so inmates he did notice two in particular. Benjamin Squirrell was sat with a broad smile throughout the meal and spent most of it looking at the girl, Sarah, who returned his attention with her own pretty smile, which Ward found alluring.

14 Accurate Accounts

The next day John Brownwigg was meeting four like-minded trustees of the Market Feoffment in the back room of the George Inn, where half a dozen tables allowed folk to eat in more civilised surroundings away from the noise and sometimes coarse language of the main bar. Andrew Baines, the landlord, had reserved a table for five of his most esteemed customers, knowing each by name and their standing in the community.

'Here you are gentlemen, please be seated and I will return to take your orders for food and drink,' Andrew said, gesturing towards a table in a corner furthest from other possible diners.

'Thank you, Andrew,' Brownwigg said, 'let us start with a large carafe of that claret I tasted a few nights ago.'

'Yes, sir. A large carafe of claret and five glasses coming up,' the landlord replied and promptly made his way back to the bar, knowing that if they started with a large carafe, then food and more drink would in all likelihood follow, leading to a profitable lunchtime. There was plenty of claret left in the barrel he had purchased along with eight others from the Ipswich wine merchant, Alan Probets.

Joining John Brownwigg were Mark Goodwin, Henry Cuthbert, Thomas Dunningham and James Ferguson, who whilst being busy with their various business interests, welcomed an opportunity to meet men with similar interests in the convivial surroundings of the George. As soon as they were seated Andrew returned with the requested carafe and five fine crystal glasses.

'You did not need to produce your best crystal, Andrew, although I believe a French claret is more pleasing from such a fine receptacle,' Brownwigg said with a smile.

'You are most welcome, Mr Brownwigg, I think gentlemen such as yourselves deserve to drink good French wine from appropriate glasses,' and the landlord carefully poured the rich, dark fluid for each of his valued customers.

'Thank you, Andrew,' Henry Cuthbert said, 'Have you had difficulty procuring wine from France with all the turmoil afflicting that country?'

'Interesting you should ask, Mr Cuthbert, as I did wonder the same after hearing that they are now removing heads in Paris,' Andrew replied with a reference to the news of the guillotine being in an almost daily use following the beheading of King Louis in January. France's 'Reign of Terror' was just beginning and no one was to know that up to 10,000 would lose their lives in the same manner as the king. 'Fortunately for us, the revolution may have turned France upside down, with the king and aristocracy being removed from this world, but the growing of grapes and production of wine has continued, and my wine merchant, Mr Probets, has reported men and countries still need to trade.'

'Thank God for that, landlord,' James Ferguson said, raising his glass. 'Gentlemen, let us toast the vintners of France, and of all nations, as they make our lives more tolerable!'

'Indeed, James, cheers!' John Brownwigg said as four more glasses were raised.

'And more profitable for some,' James added, smiling and nodding towards Andrew.

'Thank you, sirs, your custom at the George is, as you all know, always much appreciated,' the landlord replied with a polite bow.

'Cheers, landlord,' was repeated by all five with grateful recognition of Andrew's service.

'I will return shortly, to see if you gentlemen might like some lunch.'

'Thank you, Andrew,' Brownwigg replied, and without further ceremony the landlord left them to savour the claret and commence their business.

Their mood lightened by the taste of the claret and its alcoholic content, conversation between the five men was initially about their families and businesses, which all seemed to be in good health and order. As promised, Andrew returned, and they paused in conversation to listen to what dishes he could supply to satisfy any hunger, and whilst none of them suffered from that condition, they all felt some food would be welcome. So, within a minute, Andrew was able to return to the kitchen with three orders for mutton pie and vegetables, and two orders for a simple ploughman's plate of fresh bread, Suffolk cheese and pickled onions. The five dishes were brought to the table by Andrew, assisted by a young woman employed in the kitchen, and the five men were left in private to continue their meeting and conversation.

'Is all well at the workhouse, John?' Mark Goodwin asked. He had little altruistic interest in the welfare of the inmates, although appreciated that if they were well cared for, they were more likely to work productively, his main interest in the workhouse being as a source of labour as and when required.

'I believe so, Mark. It is possible I will take on one of the young lads as an apprentice at the mill, following the request and recommendation of Mr Crabb.'

'Business must be good at the mill, John?' Thomas Dunningham said.

'Aye, trade has increased slightly,' Brownwigg replied, not wanting to lead them to think there had been a big increase. 'The miller has shown that the boy has helped us increase productivity, and he can be moved between Toppesfield and Layham mills as required.'

The other four were attentive as John explained his decision to take on an apprentice, his business acumen being widely respected in the town and beyond.

'I suspect we have lost one of the more able workers from the workhouse, gentlemen,' Thomas said with a smile.

'Haha, did you think I would take on one of the infirm or aged, Tom Dunningham?' Brownwigg replied with a light-hearted tone, which they all knew was serious, and in all truth, they would do the same if it was in their interest.

'Quite right, John. Good luck to you and the boy. I hope he and the vestry appreciate the opportunity you are giving him,' Thomas replied, and was joined by the other three nodding in agreement.

'I assume you negotiated the apprenticing of the boy with Mr Ward, John? James asked.

'Indeed, James. Mr Ward was a strong advocate on behalf of the vestry, but we eventually managed to find common ground and agree terms.'

Mention of the master of the workhouse had a subtle but noticeable effect on the mood of the group, who all saw him as a necessary evil, providing them with a source of cheap labour but all finding him objectionable when hearing of incidents inside the workhouse. They needed the labour he provided but did not care for stories of cruelty.

'How is the master?' Mark asked.

'He appears to be well,' Brownwigg replied, 'why do you ask?'

'I have heard he is to be found in the Ram most days, which is no crime,' Mark explained, 'but I am told he drinks rather more than one might expect for a man with his responsibilities, and once inebriated, he becomes most generous buying ale and wine for others.'

'I see,' Brownwigg replied.

'One might wonder from where he gets the money to be so generous?' Mark asked, and for a moment the five men pondered the pertinent question.

Brownwigg understood the insinuation; like him the other four paid the master for workhouse labour, trusting him to pass it on to the vestry.

'The temptation for embezzlement must be considerable, requiring moral and ethical fibre,' Mark stated.

All five were sharing the same thoughts, 'Did Daniel Ward instil confidence that he possessed such qualities?' Then the conversation turned to another subject regarding Ward's running of the workhouse.

'I have heard the workhouse has just sold a small boy as an indentured apprentice to a chimney sweep,' James said, adding his voice to the subject of the master. 'People are expressing concern that the boy was too young.'

'My wife spoke to the doctor's wife and there seems to be disquiet over excessive use of the younger children as a source of labour,' Tom said and was met with a serious nodding of heads, as they realised they all might be incriminated as guilty of employing the young. 'We should take care that we are not perceived as the cause of such practices, gentlemen,' he added, mindful of what his wife told him.

'I wonder how much was exchanged for the climbing boy?' Henry Cuthbert asked.

'Hmm, I wonder too,' John Brownwigg finally said, then thinking to himself, 'And I wonder how much of the six pounds five shillings we agreed for Benjamin Squirrell will be passed on to the vestry.' He looked at the others and sought to reassure them. 'Perhaps an audit of the vestry accounts is required, and I shall speak to the doctor and the priest about the use of the youngest workhouse children.'

They all benefited from cheap labour provided by the workhouse but were also aware that they should not threaten this important supply by being greedy. The problem was whether Daniel Ward was of the same mind, or would he go too far in the pursuit of profit for the vestry, or even possibly for himself. It was agreed to leave it to John Brownwigg to investigate, for which he was thanked, and they settled down to enjoy their lunch and a second carafe of claret.

***

It was almost time for supper when Daniel Ward looked up to see Reverend Watson and John Brownwigg appear at the end of the dining room, which struck him as a most unlikely pair. 'What do these two want?' he thought, guessing it was bound to be a problem.

'Good evening, gentlemen,' Ward said aloud, getting his greeting in before them to see how they would respond. 'What brings you to the guildhall at this hour?'

'There is a matter we need to discuss, Mr Ward,' George Watson replied.

Ward could see they were there to discuss something of importance. 'Then let us go to my office,' he said and led them directly to his room without further word. Once inside and the door was closed, he spoke again. 'What is it?'

'We have been discussing the money collected for

inmates' labour, Mr Ward,' John Brownwigg said. 'There appear to be some discrepancies, which we are sure can be explained.'

'Discrepancies. What discrepancies?' Ward's patience was wearing thin and he could not be bothered with wasting words.

George Watson was conscious of the last conversation he had with Ward concerning the apprenticeship of Jamie Bell, in that same room, and it had ended with the master throwing down the purse containing three pounds five shillings and sixpence. 'How much did the chimney sweep pay for the boy?' he thought but would not refer to that matter before speaking to Mr Smogg. If their suspicions were correct there would be other examples of Ward's financial indiscretions. Today he and John Brownwigg would ask about the figures for just a few days or a week for which they could speak of with some accuracy. The problem was the accounts showed the totals paid in each day or week, without detail of the employer. So, if workhouse inmates were employed at several different places, the accounts showed the income as one figure for the day or week. Establishing how much each employer paid would take time. However, a couple of weeks earlier there were few outside jobs, and Brownwigg was one of those employers. He knew how much he paid Ward that week and was curious why the total paid into the vestry account seemed to be lower than expected.

'I was looking at the vestry accounts with Reverend Watson and Dr Parsons. I noticed there was a possible anomaly, Mr Ward.'

'Anomaly? What would that be, Mr Brownwigg?' Ward replied, his displeasure evident by a dark red flush spreading across his face.

'Do you remember when the boy, Benjamin Squirrell, first went to work for me at the mill?'

'Squirrell? Working at the mill? Yes, I remember. What of it?' Ward knew what might be coming; he charged ten pence a day for the boy but paid in eight pence. However, he was ready, as it was paid in with other income.

'That week Benjamin Squirrell was employed at the mill and other inmates were employed elsewhere…'

'Yes, Mr Brownwigg?'

'It was a relatively quiet week for the employment of inmates outside, Mr Ward. I think I may have been the only employer, or perhaps there were one or two others?'

'Yes, and…'

'Well, the amount you paid into the vestry account that week was lower than I would have expected, knowing how much I paid you for workers that week.'

'What were the totals, Mr Brownwigg?'

'I paid you twelve shillings and ten pence and the total you paid in was sixteen shillings and eight pence.'

Ward felt a sense of relief; the amount paid in was more than Brownwigg paid him. He could argue his case with confidence.

'What of it, Mr Brownwigg?'

'These figures suggest the other employers paid only three shillings and ten pence, which seems rather low.'

Ward felt he was offered the upper hand. 'You said yourself it was a quiet week, Mr Brownwigg. It would appear I can do only wrong, as the good reverend and doctor regularly chide me for working the inmates too hard! Perhaps the inmates enjoyed an easier week with less labour.' Ward enjoyed driving home this point in the presence of George Watson.

'But some did work for other employers that week? May I enquire who the other employers were?' John Brownwigg was not quite finished.

Despite irritation at the inference, Ward was enjoying the verbal joust.

'I believe there was only one other employer that week, Mr Brownwigg. Hmm, now who was it? Ah, yes, it was Mr Humphries at Benton End Farm, who must have paid the three shillings and ten pence you mention.' He smiled, satisfied with his answers and explanation.

John Brownwigg and George Watson stood looking at Ward. He seemed to have the answers to their enquiry, so there was no need to stay any longer. 'Perhaps a word with John

Humphries at Benton End Farm was required,' Brownwigg thought, adding, 'Very good, thank you for clearing that up, Mr Ward. We won't keep you from your work. Good evening.'

'Good evening to you, sir, and to you, reverend.'

'Good evening, Mr Ward,' George Watson courteously replied, and with that the two visitors turned and left the master's office.

Ward waited a few minutes, then picked up his cap and went to look for Tess Yates.

'Mistress Yates, I have to go out for a short while.'

'Is there something amiss, Mr Ward,' Tess replied, mindful that the visit of the two vestry members was unusual. She feared it might be regarding the boy, Jamie.

'No, there is nothing to worry about. I just need to speak about a small matter to my cousin, John Humphries.'

***

Returning from Benton End Farm, Daniel Ward was satisfied he had averted the threat to his enterprise presented by the visit of Brownwigg and the priest. His cousin understood what he would say if asked, 'three shillings ten pence was the price I paid the vestry for inmate labour a few weeks earlier.' However, despite the small victory he found himself in bad spirits as he walked along Benton Street.

'Damn these noble men of Hadleigh,' he thought, 'they think to catch me. Perhaps it is time to move on.' He wondered how much they suspected and how deep they would dig? It was a pity if his tenure as master had to come to an end, he had profited from his enterprise, but he could walk away with a tidy sum he had saved and start again in another town. Why not London, the colonies, or even newly independent America. Halfway along Benton Street he passed the Falcon tavern and through an open window he could hear laughter and smell the ale, as men relaxed at the end of a working day. The sounds and smells were irresistible, but he did not leave the road, instead resolving to make his way to the more familiar Ram, just ten minutes away.

'Good evening, Daniel.'

'A pint of ale, Arthur,' Ward replied. Having been

147

greeted on entering the Ram, he saw no reason to waste words on returning the gesture. His mood had lifted since he had set off from the workhouse no more than an hour earlier. At least he had taken the necessary precaution in getting to his cousin, John Humphries, before his fellow vestry members, and now he could relax. However, as he supped that first pint, he still felt a degree of irritation that they strongly suspected him of malpractice. 'Why else would they take the trouble to come to the workhouse?' he thought. 'If they keep digging, they will no doubt discover something. I don't know about the priest and doctor, but Brownwigg is no fool.' He was alone with his thoughts and within fifteen minutes his pewter tankard was empty.

'Another pint, Daniel?'

'Aye, another please, Arthur. Would you like one yourself?'

'That is most kind, Daniel, but I will wait and perhaps join you later.' The landlord had become used to Ward's generosity, observing it grow as the evenings turned to night. Then he would frequently enjoy Ward's bonhomie in the last half hour before closing time.

'Very good, then just a pint for me.'

Enjoying his own company, he returned to his thoughts about his position. 'A change would not be so bad. Time to find new pastures for a man with my talent.' His mood continued to mellow as the second pint was imbibed, irritation being replaced by more philosophical reflection. 'You've done well, Daniel. There must be over ninety pounds in the tin under the bed. Take it and leave, while you can.' He smiled sitting alone in the booth thinking about the money and then his thoughts turned to pleasure. 'I was doing well with the girl, a pity I will not get further with that filly. If this threat had not arisen, I think there could have been further opportunity with her. Perhaps there will be one last chance to enjoy her company before I leave.' Thoughts of Sarah brought him back to the present and he realised he should return to the workhouse, and lifting the pewter tankard to his lips for the last time that evening, he emptied the last mouthful of ale down his throat.

'Thank you, Arthur. Perhaps I shall return tomorrow.'

'I do hope so, Daniel. Good night to you, sir.'

Within a minute he was entering the guildhall through the rear door and walked into the dining room, where the cheerful hubbub of about seventy inmates finishing their supper and clearing up was interrupted by his appearance. Immediately the volume lowered as the diners became aware of his presence and he surveyed the scene.

'Hmm, seems more like a celebration than a workhouse supper,' he said under his breath, but he was feeling more tolerant and amicable than normal. 'If I am to be master for just a few days more, why should I trouble myself?' he thought. 'The damn vestry can find someone else to run this place, applying the discipline and order to avoid mayhem and chaos.' He looked round for Tess, who had handled supper without his assistance, albeit with more noise amongst the inmates than he would have preferred. She was inside the kitchen with Daisy and Evy, tidying a few large pots after feeding three score and ten, and she looked up as his large frame filled the doorway.

'Ah, Mr Ward, you've returned. I trust everything is satisfactory?' she said, not expecting him to provide any detail in front of the two old women.

'Yes, all is well, Mistress Yates. Thank you for asking and I apologise for my absence at supper time, which I know is when you are busy feeding the workhouse.'

Tess was taken aback by the courtesy shown by the master, which whilst being slightly suspicious, was also welcome. Both Daisy and Evy also noticed, having never heard him speak politely, which they showed by glancing at each other without saying a word.

'I saved a plate of mutton stew and bread, not knowing if you had eaten, Mr Ward. Would you care for some?'

'That is most kind, Mistress Yates. Yes, I would appreciate some stew,' he replied, his change of character and manners continuing. Ward took the plate laden with stew and a chunk of bread into the dining room and sat down at one of the tables, which was also something different, as he usually preferred to eat in the privacy of his office and bedroom.

Ward was sitting alone in a space vacated by a few inmates who had finished their supper. Around him other inmates were finishing their meal and gathering the plates to be returned to the kitchen for cleaning. He saw no reason to spoil his good mood by chiding inmates for the quality of their cleaning up. Looking around he could see a number of the younger inmates collecting wooden plates, forks and spoons, and there she was, the girl, Sarah. Like the others, she had seen him sit down at the end of the long table but felt more threatened by his presence in the room. Keeping her head bowed, she stayed at the other end of the room hoping to achieve anonymity. Ben was also helping to clear up and noticed a change in her demeanour. They had sat together at supper and along with some other younger inmates, they had enjoyed the more relaxed atmosphere in the absence of the master, but Ben could see the change in her as soon as Ward appeared. Then as Ward sat down to eat and they were collecting plates, he could see her lowered head and how she kept to one end of the room, furthest from the master of the workhouse.

'Girl! Come here.' Three words struck fear into Sarah's being. There was no mistaking to whom he spoke, as he was facing directly at her, and when she looked up her face was ashen, all colour drained from her cheeks.

Ben stood observing and for the first time he became suspicious. 'She's terrified of him,' he thought, 'but why?' He wanted to interrupt the master's order but knew that probably was not wise. Instead, he watched as Sarah walked with her head bowed to where Ward sat, stopping the other side of the table.

'Sit down, girl.' Sarah moved along the bench and sat down, keeping her head lowered so she was staring at the table. 'Do not be afraid girl, I am not going to hurt you, and certainly not here.' However, his reassurance did nothing to ease Sarah's discomfort. 'I may have to go away for a few days but would like the pleasure of your company before I do, so be prepared to come to my office when called. Do you understand?' There was no reply. 'Girl, look at me. Do you understand?'

he repeated, his voice sterner. Sarah raised her head, a tear appearing in the corner of one eye.

'Yes, sir.'

'Good. Well, off you go and finish clearing up.'

Sarah stood up and resumed her duties. No one else could hear what was said but Ben could see Sarah's pallor, and he wanted to go to her, put his arm around her shoulder, or just hold her hand. Instead, unable to do anything to support Sarah, he was left with sadness, as well as a deepening suspicion of why the master should have such a great effect on her simply through his presence and a few words.

Ben was not the only person to observe the change in Sarah's demeanour brought about by the master. Tess Yates along with Daisy had paused for a minute and watched through the servery. The old woman finally felt she could speak frankly about her concerns with the mistress of the workhouse. As Sarah walked away from the table Daisy moved closer to Tess so she could whisper without fear of being overheard.

'Mistress, may I speak to you privately after we have finished our work?'

Tess Yates looked at Daisy, then glanced over to where Sarah had resumed her collection of plates, forks and spoons. The melancholy state of the girl seemed worse following her brief conversation with Ward and Tess could guess what Daisy might wish to speak of as her own suspicion grew.

'Yes, Daisy, we can talk as soon as we have cleared up.'

Ten minutes later Tess was informed of what Daisy had witnessed in the rope picking room and worse, the incident in his office a few nights ago. Daisy explained she had wanted to tell Tess earlier but concerns about the boy, Jamie, seemed to have taken precedence. But now, seeing the effect of Ward on Sarah confirmed her fears and she had to speak. Tess nodded, acquiescing to suspicions she had held for a long time, suspicions she had managed to avoid addressing. She thought about Lucy's protests some weeks ago before the arrival of Sarah, when Ward put the former in the box. He said it was punishment for her violence towards him, whereas she claimed he molested her. Sarah was more meek than Lucy, perhaps easier to control, but why wouldn't she say something? Without her making a complaint of assault or worse, there was no proof, and the word of two old women as witnesses of seeing his hand on her breast or waist was flimsy against his. A month or week ago, she would not have been moved to do anything; the smooth running of the workhouse and her relationship with the master being more important than the gossip of old inmates. However, her anger and frustration over his handling of Jamie Bell had resulted in her sympathy and support for Daniel Ward dissipating as days passed and there was no word of the boy's wellbeing. Now she could see Daisy's suspicions were not without reason. She realised she would have to persuade the girl to speak openly to confirm their fears.

'Thank you for telling me, Daisy. It is clear something troubles Sarah. I will speak to her.'

'Thank you, mistress,' Daisy said and left the tidied kitchen.

As the sun disappeared in the west the guildhall was covered by shadows cast by St Mary's, the deanery and the large trees that encircled the graveyard. Oil lamps were lit for the last hours before lights out and the end of another day. However, unlike other evenings when once supper had been served and clearing up had been completed, Tess felt she could not relax, as she wanted to address the issue raised by Daisy, and she knew if she did not speak directly to the girl that evening, she would not sleep well.

In the girls' bedroom Sarah had changed into her nightshirt and sat on the edge of her bed still affected by the brief conversation with Ward. Amy sat just across the small space between their beds, looking at her friend who had become an older sister, who seemed unaware of her presence. The little girl felt sad and concerned.

'Sarah, are you well?'

'I am not unwell, Amy,' Sarah replied without looking up.

'Then you are troubled.'

Sarah raised her head, realising her melancholy was affecting the young girl, and she felt guilt. 'Why should others

152

be saddened by my condition,' she thought, chiding herself, and she tried to smile.

'I am sorry, Amy, my thoughts are elsewhere. I miss my family.'

Amy smiled. 'Well, that is understandable, but I can be your family if you like.'

Sarah's guilt grew as she remembered Amy was an orphan with no family to miss.

'Ah, thank you, Amy, we are sisters in here. One day we won't be in here and I want you to become part of my family outside. I think they will like you.' Her smile widened and she reached out with her hands and held Amy's, who returned the smile, relieved to see the improvement in Sarah's countenance.

Just as Sarah started to feel better, a knock on the bedroom door brought a feeling of dread as she feared it would be Ward. The door opened and to her relief it was Tess Yates, who had knocked as a gesture of courtesy and walked over to Amy and Sarah's beds.

'Good evening, girls. Do not be alarmed. Are you ready for bed, Amy?'

'Yes, mistress.'

Good, sleep well, Amy. Sarah, may I speak with you in private for a few minutes?'

'Yes, mistress,' Sarah replied, wondering what was wrong, fearing bad news from home.

'Come to my room, where we can speak.'

Without further word, Tess led Sarah out of the girls' bedroom and along the corridor to her room, where once inside she closed the door behind them.

'Here, sit down young lady,' Tess said gesturing to one of two large, high backed, armchairs as she settled into the other.

'Thank you, mistress, have I done something wrong?' Sarah said nervously, forgetting for a few moments the conversation with Ward, wondering if Tess had a reason to be displeased.

'No, you have done nothing wrong, Sarah, but I

wondered if...' and paused as she sought the right words.

'Yes, mistress...' Sarah was confused and there was another pause.

'You looked troubled earlier and it has been noticed before, Sarah. I wondered if someone has wronged you?' Tess avoided speaking Ward's name. She looked directly at the girl, inviting her to speak openly and immediately a tormented look spread across her face.

'No, mistress.' Just two words and she looked down, avoiding eye contact and Tess became more certain of her suspicion.

'Sarah, I promise you can tell me if someone is hurting or threatening you. I will not betray you and will do all I can to help you. You can trust me.' But she was not certain if Sarah was listening as her head remained lowered. 'Sarah, please look at me.' For a moment there was no response. Then she looked up and tears started to fall.

'I am sorry, mistress. I...' and she was unable to speak as her emotions and fears of the past weeks poured out, her body trembling. Tess did not need to hear anything to confirm her suspicions, that could wait. She got out of her armchair and knelt down in front of Sarah, enveloping her with her arms.

'Here girl, do not be afraid.'

Fifteen minutes later, a calmer Sarah was in bed. Back in her room Tess was not one to drink alone, but she sat back in the armchair with a large glass of port. Sarah had told her everything; the day a few months earlier when he had come to her family cottage, the promise she made to obey him to keep her mother and siblings secure, the incident in the rope picking room, the ordeal in his office, followed by intimidation as witnessed at supper that evening. Her daily existence had become one of constant fear that he would demand more, which she had persuaded herself was something she would endure for her family. Her only defence seemed to be avoiding him and his gaze. Tess realised he had used his position of power to coerce the girl to accept his lustful advances. As she took a mouthful of the dark fortified wine, she felt both ashamed that she had not noticed, or had she chosen to avoid noticing, as well as anger that he should prey on the girl to satisfy his desires. 'Damn you, Daniel Ward,' she said quietly and thought about what to do.

15 Tragedy

John Parsons was in his study when he heard loud banging on the front door, followed a minute later by Caroline appearing in the doorway.

'A boy has come from Kersey and is asking for your help,' Caroline said with a concerned look.

'I see,' the doctor replied and stood up to gather his medical bag and equipment.

'John...' Caroline paused. 'He looks like a climbing boy.' She was well aware of recent events and the apprenticeship of Jamie Bell. John had been clearly affected by the sale of a boy so young and had confided in her his concerns and what he had learnt of the iniquitous trade when he worked and studied under the tutelage of Sir Percival Pott in London. As soon as she saw the boy at the front door, easily recognisable as a member of that trade by his filthy clothes and grimy flesh, she feared the worst. Her concern was immediately shared by her husband.

'Please bring him in.'

Stood in front of the doctor and his wife, the boy was nervous and self-conscious of his condition. He was short, no more than four and a half feet in height, but his face suggested he was at least eleven years of age. His black boots were only just darker than his clothes, which may originally have been lighter in colour but were darkened with dirt and grime. What may have once been trousers were now shorts, torn and ripped just above his knees, which were the darkest part of his skin, encrusted with dirt and a black substance John guessed to be soot. Below his knees his legs were lighter but still darkened. Like his shorts, his shirt could have once been any colour but was now unidentifiable due to the dirt. As with the lower garment the shirt sleeves ended just at his elbows, which matched his knees in colour and texture, his forearms a similar hue to his lower legs. Only his face offered any indication that his skin was once fair, having been wiped clean of discoloration before coming to the doctor's house. However, not all of it could be removed, some remained ingrained in the thin creases and indentations of skin around his eyes and mouth. Like his skin the natural colour of his hair remained a mystery as the thick crop that covered his ears was black.

'Good morning, young man,' Dr Parsons said, attempting to put the boy at ease. 'What is your name and what can I do for you?'

'Good morning, sir, I am Bob Tupp. It is not me that needs your assistance, sir. I have been sent by my master, Mr Smogg. One of the boys needs help.'

Caroline raised her hand to her mouth as if to suppress a gasp and John felt the same sense of alarm.

'Where are Mr Smogg and the boy, Bob? And what is the ailment that requires my attention?'

'They are in a house in Kersey, sir. He's stuck, sir, the boy, he's stuck in the chimney.'

There was a pause as the horror of the image filled John and Caroline's minds, combined with disbelief that it should happen so soon after recent conversations.

'Shall I get help, John?' Caroline asked as he made sure his bag contained anything that might be of assistance.

'Yes, Caroline. Please tell George Watson to come to Kersey with three strong men and tools for dismantling a chimney breast. Which house in Kersey, Bob?'

'I do not know the number, sir, but it is a big house, down the hill from the Bell Inn where the ford crosses the stream.'

'Very well, I will make haste by horse, Bob. How did you get here?'

'I ran, sir.'

'Go with Mrs Parsons to get Reverend Watson and some men. Then bring them to the house.'

'Yes, sir. Thank you, sir.' Bob Tupp looked forlorn but hoped the doctor could save his colleague.

John Parsons walked to the door that led to the hallway, from where he would leave the house and go to the stable just fifty yards away located on the lane between Church Walk and the high street. He would not tarry and once saddled his horse could carry him the two and a half miles to Kersey at a gallop in little more than ten minutes. Before leaving Caroline and the boy in his study, he paused in the doorway and turned.

'What is the boy's name, Bob?

'His name is Jamie, sir. He's a new apprentice, sir.'

'Jamie...Thank you, Bob,' the doctor replied, and as he made his way out he felt a rage rise inside.

The small stable where he kept his family's two horses and pony was always manned by the stable boy, John, or his father Jim, the farrier.

'John, please saddle Jess, I have an emergency to which I must attend with haste.'

'Yes, Doctor Parsons,' the lad replied and jumped up to perform his duty. John Parsons handed him a penny for his speedy work and within minutes was trotting along the dusty lane before turning left onto the high street, where he encouraged Jess to a canter. As she reached the end of the high street and the road forked, the right leading to Whatfield and Stowmarket, Jess was directed to the left passing by vegetable gardens and up Gallows Hill in the direction of Bildeston and Lavenham.

'Get on, Jess,' the rider said as he shook the reins, prompting her to increase her speed from a canter to a purposeful gallop. The road would reach a junction where travellers could choose left to Lavenham or straight on to Bildeston, but about half a mile before that divide, John gave a tug on the left rein and applied some pressure from his right boot to turn Jess left along Mill Lane taking them directly into the village of Kersey.

The parish church shared the same name, St Mary's, as Hadleigh's larger place of worship and from it the road dipped steeply to ford the stream that bisected the village. In winter the little tributary of the River Brett could swell to make the ford difficult for carts and livestock but in the summer months it was no more than a few inches deep. John had slowed Jess to a controlled trot down the steep hill and as she passed through the cooling water, he saw a small crowd gathering outside a large Tudor house with two prominent chimney breasts, rising up at the ends of the house like sentinel towers. He guessed this was his destination and for a moment looked up to admire the intricate brickwork of the two chimneys with identical symmetrical chequered patterns, carefully built two hundred years earlier by skilled craftsmen.

'Here Jess,' John said as he guided her over to the house, where he was recognised by members of the crowd who were his patients.

'Good morning, Doctor Parsons. You are much needed here,' a woman said.

'Hello, Mrs Wright, how is your daughter, Molly?' he asked courteously but not certain of the girl's name. The girl was ill a month earlier, probably with scarlet fever and for a few days her prospects looked bleak, but she pulled through.

'She is well, thank you, doctor.'

'Good.' However, he did not have time to dwell and said no more, passing through the people stood outside the front door of the house. In the hallway stood a smaller group of four, consisting of a woman and three teenage children.

'I am Doctor Parsons.'

'Hello, doctor, I am Ann Atwood and these are my children. We live here. My husband is through there.' Mrs Atwood pointed to the left into a large downstairs living and dining room. The two hearths and chimney breasts kept the large house warm; one serving the room to which John Parsons was directed, the other serving the kitchen and work room the other side of the hallway.

'Thank you, Mrs Atwood.'

At the far end of the room beyond the large dining table, two high backed bench seats had been moved for the purpose of allowing the chimney sweep space to lay grey canvas sheets. Two men and a small boy were unaware of the doctor's entry as they faced the hearth at the base of the chimney.

'I am Doctor Parsons,' John said again.

'Ah, good, thank you for coming so promptly. I am James Atwood,' said one of the two men, who was distinct from the other two being dressed in the clean clothes of a respectable gentleman. The other wore the darkened clothes of his trade and whilst not being covered in the grime and dirt of the boy, who had reported to Church House barely half an hour ago, his skin was permanently stained. 'And this is John Smogg.' The boy was not introduced but it was plain from his clothes and general condition that he was also a climbing boy, just like Bob Tupp. John Parsons paused to look at the master sweep, his attention to the emergency interrupted by a feeling of contempt for a man who would employ boys so young.

'What has happened,' John asked, although he was certain he knew. The master sweep looked sheepish as he looked up.

'A boy has become stuck, doctor. He went up just an hour ago.'

John Parsons' dislike for the master sweep deepened as he guessed it must have been more than an hour. It was unlikely they would have sent the boy on foot immediately.

'Only an hour?'

'Well perhaps a bit longer.'

'The longer he is up there, the less likely he is to survive,' Parsons said.

'How do you know this?' the sweep asked defensively, even though he suspected the same. 'Damn, I should not have sent the new boy up,' he thought, 'but he has to learn. Now they will be looking to blame me.' He remembered Ward's comments about the Hadleigh priest and doctor, and now the latter was standing before him. 'If we do not get him down, they will be crying foul and I will have wasted three pounds and ten shillings. Damn it!' he thought.

'I know this, Mr Smogg, because in London I saw countless cases of boys who died from this very predicament!' Parsons' tone changed, the seriousness of the situation plain. 'We must get him down, or out the side.'

'Do you mean by dismantling my chimney breast?' Atwood asked.

'Yes, if we cannot get him down. If he perishes, we must recover the body.'

'I see.'

'More men are coming with the priest for that purpose, if it is necessary, Mr Atwood.'

'Of course, of course. Is there anything I can do to help, doctor?' and for a few moments the house owner felt guilt that he may have been more concerned about his chimney brickwork than the plight of the boy.

Doctor Parsons leaned forward into the hearth and turned his head sideways to look up into the chimney, but all he could see was darkness.

'What is his name?' John asked, even though he had learnt it earlier from Bob Tupp.

'Jamie,' the small boy said. John Smogg turned and scowled at the boy, angered by his temerity to speak. Parsons did not notice as he was peering up into the darkness but heard the name.

'How old is he?' He was curious to hear the chimney sweep's reply. The boy stayed silent having spoken out of place, not wanting to incur his master's ire.

'He is...erm, he is eight,' Smogg said hesitatingly, as he was well aware of the law. The boy looked down, not wanting to meet anyone's eyes, he knew Jamie's age.

'Eight, you say. Just old enough by law for this trade.'

'Yes, sir,' Smogg replied.

Doctor Parsons stood up in the hearth, his upper body hidden to the others as he raised his head as far up the chimney as he could.

'Jamie! Jamie, can you hear me?' His voiced disappeared up into the darkness, without any immediate reply. 'Jamie!' he shouted, louder. Then, as he paused, a muffled sound could be heard. 'He's alive!' Parsons thought, 'there's still time.' 'Can you move, Jamie?' he shouted. More muffled sounds and Doctor Parsons wondered why the boy could not speak clearly. 'He must be finding it difficult to breathe,' he thought and lowered his body so he could step out of the hearth to speak to the others.

'We must try to get him down now, before he suffocates,' Parsons said to the other three, his knowledge of chimneys offering no solution, hoping they might. Neither John

Smogg nor James Atwood spoke. Smogg knew the chances of survival were slim as the boy had been up there for over an hour, so he had nothing to say that might offer hope.

'Sir, I could go up and try to get Jamie down,' the climbing boy said, and the three men looked down at him.

'That is brave of you, young man. What is your name?' Parsons asked.

'Harry, sir. I am Harry Budd.'

'How will you get him free, Harry?'

'Well, sir, I mean doctor, I would climb up below him and would try to release him from his predicament by pulling his legs downwards. It will cause him some discomfort as his knees will be scraped bare of skin, but it will hopefully free him.' The three men listened, picturing in their minds the small boy stuck in the chimney being pulled from below.

'If you are able to free him, Harry, will you be in danger of injury if he falls onto you?' the doctor asked.

'I will be directly below Jamie, if I can get that far up the chimney to where he is stuck. Jamie is smaller than me, so I may not get that far. If I can loosen him, I shall attempt to support him by seating his legs over my shoulders. He does not weigh much, sir, I can come down bearing his weight on my shoulders.'

Again, the three men tried to imagine the scene of Harry reaching Jamie in the darkness, pulling his legs free and bringing his colleague down on his shoulders. John Parsons felt humbled by the small boy's courage. He looked at Smogg to see if he had anything to add, perhaps some advice for the boy, but the master sweep remained quiet.

'God bless you, Harry Budd. I cannot think of any other options, so please do your best whilst taking care for your own safety,' the doctor said.

'I will, sir, I mean doctor,' and as he spoke Harry Budd leaned down to remove his boots. James Atwood and John Parsons' understanding of the boys' trade was furthered as they realised climbing up into the chimney was easier barefoot, with less likelihood of slipping. Harry's ascent would be achieved with the use of his hands, elbows, knees, feet, and his back, pressing against the soot-blackened brickwork.

'Good lad, Harry, bring him down,' John Smogg said, feeling he should make some contribution.

'Yes, master.'

John Parsons looked at the two members of the same profession and as his contempt for one deepened, his respect for the other grew. Then, without further word, Harry stepped into the hearth and almost effortlessly and silently climbed up into the chimney, leaving the three men to wait. After a minute of silence, Parsons asked Smogg a question.

'How long will it take for Harry to climb to the point where Jamie is stuck?'

'Not long, doctor.'

Parsons' concern grew. The muffled sounds from Jamie were faint, which may have been due to the nature of the blocked chimney, but he could not help thinking it might have been due to be his failing breath. His worry and anxiety was exacerbated by the quiet, then the tense atmosphere was broken by voices in the hallway, and as he looked round he saw a familiar face.

'John, we came as quickly as we could,' a panting George Watson said on seeing his friend. Behind him followed three men; two adults and a younger man, as well as Bob Tupp, the climbing boy. 'We marched and ran from the guildhall.'

'Thank you for getting here so promptly, gentlemen. We will find out very soon whether we will need to dismantle the chimney breast from outside,' the doctor replied.

'How so, John?' George asked.

'A climbing boy called Harry has gone up to see if he can free Jamie.'

'Good, I pray he can. Martin has come along as he has experience of this predicament from when he worked in Ipswich,' George said gesturing to the man holding several tools he brought for the purpose of taking apart the brickwork. Alongside him also holding tools stood Jacob Hicks, who had similar experience of working with brickwork, and Ben Squirrell, who volunteered to help in any way he could.

As the five arrivals moved to join the three stood at the

hearth, quietness descended on the group. There was nothing they could do but listen and for a moment there was excitement as pieces of packed soot fell with a dull thud, but that was all, just some dirt and an accompanying cloud of dust. It was the youngest of the group, Bob Tupp, who took the initiative in stepping into the hearth and peering up into the darkness, trying to hear anything that might indicate how Harry was progressing. Again, nothing, so he joined the others, leaving the hearth clear hoping for the arrival of his two friends.

'How long should it take to climb?' Reverend Watson asked looking at John Smogg, whom he assumed was the master sweep.

'It depends, sir,' Smogg replied, unable to be precise.

'Depends on what?' Martin asked. Because of his status he might have been expected to remain quiet, but he did not care. Stood there in the small group, his gaze had fixed on the man in dirtied clothes, suspecting him of being Jamie's master. 'You bought the boy knowing he must be less than eight years of age,' Martin thought staring at Smogg. He felt a growing anger inside as he waited for a reply, which was not forthcoming.

'It depends on how clear, or blocked, the flue is as it narrows, sir,' a younger voice replied, and Martin's eyes moved from the man who should know to the boy who did. 'There might be bends to navigate, which is why we cannot see light, and also why we cannot hear any sound, sir.'

Bob Tupp spoke to Martin with the same courtesy he would show any adult, which was appreciated by the workhouse inmate and did not escape the notice of the doctor and priest, resulting in further respect for the profession of climbing boys. Martin's feelings towards the man who, along with Ward, was the malefactor in this affair were temporarily interrupted. Once again there was nothing to do but wait and there was quietness as they all listened. Each of them willed for something to happen as they waited in silence and each of them could feel the tension increase as minutes passed. John Smogg found himself at the back of the group having retreated from the workhouse inmate's accusatory stare. He had been in this position before and experience taught him that the longer a boy was stuck, the less likely he was to come down alive. 'Damn it, if the boy doesn't survive, there will be trouble,' he thought, beginning to regret approaching Daniel Ward in the Ram just a week or so ago.

'It feels as if he has been gone hours,' George Watson said.

'It's only been a while since Harry climbed up, George. Perhaps ten minutes or so. More worrying is that Jamie may well have been up there hours,' John replied and could not stop himself from looking at John Smogg, whose discomfort increased.

'Sirs, I think I hear something,' Bob Tupp said hopefully as he moved back into the hearth.

Except for Smogg, the others edged forward towards the hearth, leaving some space for Bob to do anything that might assist Harry, although none of them knew what that might be. More pieces of compressed soot fell onto the tiled base of the hearth, some of it breaking into handful sized lumps, some forming gentle explosions of dusty dirt. Bob stood amongst it, as if it was his natural existence to be struck with missiles formed of soot, breathing naturally the polluted air. He strained his eyes to see through the murk.

'Here they are, sirs,' and he stood up so he could raise his arms to help. 'Harry, it's me, Bob. I'm here, just below you.'

As chimneys broaden at their base, opening wider to accommodate their hearths, the climbing technique of the boys was different to shimmying up and down in the narrower parts of the flues. Descending the last part where it might be four feet or more wide, boys might complete their descent with a controlled fall into the hearth that would have been cleared of any dangerous objects before the climb. Therefore, Bob's offer to Harry was appreciated as it allowed him to lower Jamie down into his friend's arms.

'Thank you, Bob. Here he is.'

Up in the darkness of the flue, Harry manoeuvered Jamie from his shoulders, lowering him down in between his legs which pressed through his feet against the widening flue as his back pressed against the other side. Stood up inside the hearth, Bob could see Harry's legs across the width of the flue and Jamie's dangling legs and feet. He raised his arms up to get hold but could not reach beyond Jamie's ankles and realised Harry had reached the point in the widening flue where they would normally jump the last eight or ten feet.

'Have you got him, Bob?' Harry asked.

'No, just wait,' Bob said and lowered his head so he could be seen by the others. 'Would one of you sirs kindly assist me, please?'

'Here, let me, I'm the tallest,' and the reverend stepped forward understanding the problem. Leaning down to get into the chimney where Bob stood, George stood up and could immediately see the feet and legs of the boy hanging in the dark and four feet higher another boy locked in position where the flue narrowed, holding the same boy by the wrists. Reverend Watson raised his arms and reaching up placed his hands either side of the boy's waist. 'I have him, Harry,' he said.

'Very good, sir, I will release my hold on his arms if you are ready.'

'Yes, well done, Harry.'

As Harry did so the torso of Jamie Bell flopped forward onto George's chest, who put one arm around his shoulders and neck whilst the other folded around the boy's tiny waist. For a moment he held the boy close, just as he might have held his daughter after a mishap like a fall, her needing some comfort. Then he realised Jamie might require the attention of John Parsons, and Harry was waiting to complete his descent, so keeping a firm hold of the small boy he leaned down and stepped out of the hearth, followed by Bob Tupp.

'All clear, Harry,' Bob called, and in an instant the brave boy landed with a thud, causing the eruption of a small cloud of soot.

George was himself covered in patches of soot from standing up in the chimney and holding Jamie, but he was unaware of his appearance and it was only as he carried Jamie from the hearth to lay him on the table that he realized the little boy had not said anything. In fact, he appeared to be unconscious. As he gently laid the blackened body down on the table the others gathered round and John Parsons stepped forward.

'Thank you, George, and well done, Harry, now let me see,' the doctor said moving forward. He stopped as he looked at the limp lifeless body, and without further examination he knew. An initial sense of optimism on seeing George carrying Jamie out of the hearth left him, replaced by a sense of the inevitable, but he had to be certain. He placed the back of his hand close to the boy's nose, then he felt his neck, but there was no sign of breath or pulse. Feeling frustration that it appeared he could do nothing to help, he gripped the blackened shirt at the neck and ripped it apart, revealing a white chest that had not yet been darkened by soot. Lowering his head to Jamie's chest, he placed his ear against the left side where he hoped for some sign from the boy's tiny heart, but there was nothing. Finally, he stood over the body and gently holding the head, he gave the little boy's face a slap, hoping it might waken him from a seizure or coma. Nothing. Jamie Bell's six-year-old blackened corpse covered in no more than filthy rags lay still on the table.

'He is dead,' John Parsons said and gently covered Jamie's chest with the two sides of the torn shirt. 'Was he alive when you reached him, Harry?'

'I am sorry, sir, I cannot say. He was quiet when I spoke to him, so I thought I should get him down as speedily as I could. I hope I did not cause him any harm,' Harry said with a sadness and sincerity that made Parsons wished he had not asked such a question.

'It is I who should apologise, Harry. You did everything you could to rescue Jamie, whilst we were of no use,' the doctor said and looked up at John Smogg, who stood alone at the other end of the table. Once again, the room was quiet as eight men of varying ages stared at the body of Jamie Bell.

'God rest his soul,' George Watson said, adding, 'we shall need a cart to take him back to Hadleigh with some dignity.'

'I will get one, minister,' James Atwood said. 'Shall I do that now?'

'Thank you, sir. That would be most helpful,' George replied. His friend had been in charge whilst it was believed Jamie was alive, but now he was dead, the situation came under his jurisdiction. 'We can return the cart later,' he said as the house owner was turning to leave the room.

'Yes, minister, that can be arranged,' Atwood replied and left the room to contribute as best he could to resolving the tragedy that had occurred in his family house.

'John, I think Jamie deserves a wash, but that would be best done back in Hadleigh. When we leave, could you ride on to tell Mistress Yates, as she will have some ladies who can help her with that task, as well as dressing him in some clean clothes.'

'Yes, George, of course.' As he replied, a thought occurred to the doctor. 'Mr Smogg, Jamie was in your charge for no more than a few days. Are these the clothes he wore when he was handed over to you by Mr Ward?'

John Smogg looked up, startled as his mind was elsewhere. The death of the boy was regrettable, but it was an occupational hazard, and whilst there would be awkward questions asked, he would carry on. He would be a boy light and there was still work to be done, but finding a replacement immediately would be difficult as word of the accident spread. However, he knew memories were short and there would always be poor boys from families and workhouses. 'Perhaps a visit to Ipswich will be called for,' he thought as he was addressed by the doctor.

'The clothes he wore when Mr Ward sold him were exchanged for ones more suitable for this work, doctor.'

'Indeed, Mr Smogg. Perhaps you can return them to the workhouse?'

'Return them?'

'Yes, return them. You had Jamie in your charge for barely a week and he is dead. The least you can do is return the clothes he wore when you received him. Or did the three pounds five shillings and sixpence you paid include ownership

of those clothes and boots, as well as his life?' John Parsons'
bristled, his patience had worn thin, his frustration hidden no
longer.

Smogg was taken aback for a moment. It was a large
room but he felt cornered.

'It is a sad day when a climbing boy dies, doctor, but
you gentlemen go to sleep safe knowing your chimneys are
swept by the likes of us, and it's work that by its nature can
be done only by small children.' Smogg was ready with his
riposte, having expected something approaching blame or
recrimination. These do-gooders were always complaining. But
that was not all, he was irked by the mention of money. 'Three
pounds five shillings and sixpence? You could at least get the
amount right. I paid the master three pounds ten shillings. That
is three pounds ten shillings that takes time for me to earn
through cleaning the chimneys for the likes of you! I wonder
if the vestry might reimburse me some of that three pounds
ten shillings for my losses?' John Smogg was satisfied with his
performance.

'You paid the master of the workhouse for the boy,
Mr Smogg, and as an indentured apprentice, you owned him.
In your care, you have put him to work, as you might a horse,
and he has died. Any loss of income is yours to bear, not the
vestry's, and you would do well to be mindful of the law,
because if he is found to be under the age of eight, a judge may
not look kindly on your part in his death,' John Parsons replied,
his voice rising as his anger grew.

'Few men work their horses to death...' Martin said.
He had listened and like the doctor he felt a rage rising through
his body having seen the small boy laid out on the table. It was
the second time he had witnessed such a fate of a climbing
boy and his grip tightened on the tools he had brought for the
purpose of dismantling the chimney brickwork. His eyes were
again fixed on the master sweep as the muscles in his arms
clenched, ready to pounce and for a moment it seemed there
would be violence.

James Atwood reappeared to break the fraught
atmosphere.

'I have a cart outside and some linen here to cover the boy, minister.'

'Thank you, Mr. Atwood,' George replied, slightly relieved as he could see the tense situation turning violent if they did not get on with the task of taking Jamie back to Hadleigh.

'Could you men help me take Jamie out to the cart in the dignified manner he deserves?'

The five men from Hadleigh carefully lifted Jamie so the large linen cloth could be passed beneath and around his body as a shroud, so that nothing of him was visible. In truth, he was so small it was a task that could have been performed by two or three men, but five of them allowed more care, gently lifting and wrapping him inside the linen with little effort. John and Jacob lifted one side, Martin and Ben the other, and they followed Reverend Watson out of the dining room, through the hallway and out of the house to the waiting cart, which was surrounded by a small crowd.

Before leaving the dining room, George turned to where John Smogg had stayed at one end of the large dining table.

'Good day, Mr. Smogg.'

John Smogg, Bob Tupp and Harry Budd watched them leave. The two boys had kept silent and dared not speak after witnessing the cross words between their master and the doctor. If they said anything at that moment that displeased him, they knew he might later reply with his fists, which they had witnessed on numerous occasions. Instead, they stood quietly with a heavy sadness for the youngest climbing boy in their firm who would not be sleeping alongside them and three others in the same room that night.

Mr Atwood had arranged for a boy from a nearby stable to accompany them, then returning with the horse and cart to Kersey. Jamie was laid with care in the cart, which was led at a slow, respectful pace across the ford and up the hill to Kersey's St Mary's, where they would turn left along Mill Lane, retracing the route they had all taken a short while ago. John climbed up onto Jess and turned to look down at his friend.

'This is a sorry state of affairs, George. I am sorry we did not do more to save him.'

'As am I, John, but we did not kill him, and this matter is not over,' George replied. 'Three pounds ten shillings, Mr Smogg said, unless I misheard.'

'You did not mishear, George. You are correct, the matter is not over. I shall press on to ready Mistress Yates. Thank you, gentlemen,' John replied to George and nodded politely to Martin, Jacob and Ben. Then he turned to look straight along Mill Lane and flicked the reins. 'Get on, Jess.'

As horse and rider pulled away from the cart at a canter that became a gallop, Martin looked over to George Watson. 'You did your best, reverend.'

'Thank you, Martin. I am truly sorry we did not protect him.'

Martin looked over and could see genuine sadness on the minister's face. He noticed the difference of what the doctor said, 'we did not save him,' compared to the minister's 'we did not protect him.' Both good men, both feeling they had failed. Then his thoughts turned to Ward.

Just under an hour later Tess Yates was waiting with Daisy and Evy when the horse and cart came to a halt at the back of the guildhall.

'Here, bring him into the laundry room. Doctor Parsons said the poor mite will need a wash and we've got some clean clothes for him.'

Tess had prepared the bodies of inmates who died on numerous occasions and was always assisted by one or two older women like Daisy and Evy, so she had said similar words before, but this time the circumstances were different. Her greeting to the others hid her feelings, a mix of anguish, sorrow and anger. After being informed by the doctor, she confronted Daniel Ward, who on hearing of events in Kersey shrugged his shoulders. Doctor Parsons said he was concerned inmates in an understandable feeling of anger might resort to disorder, which caused Ward to pause in his laissez-faire attitude. Taking his coat and cap, he left to recruit two constables who would be present throughout the evening until lights out when the inmates could be locked in their bedrooms. Busying herself helped Tess cope with the turmoil flooding her body and mind. 'I told him the boy was too young, but he would not listen, and last night the incident with the girl, Sarah,' she thought. Tess realised this could not carry on; one way or another, Ward would have to go.

The three women were left in the laundry room with the small body inside his linen shroud. Two buckets of warm soapy water were produced and a clean workhouse uniform was put to the side. However, despite being forewarned by the doctor, when they opened the linen sheet they were shocked by the sight before them.

'Dear God,' Evy said raising her hand to her mouth.

Jamie's little blackened body was made worse by the dirty rags he wore, as all three remembered how he looked just a few days earlier. Just a few days climbing chimney flues had soiled his skin, leaving it scraped and cut, particularly at his elbows, knees and feet.

'The master sweep did not wait long to put him to work,' Daisy said sadly, 'I would have thought an apprenticeship might have involved some training before sending him up into a chimney.'

'He must have been so frightened,' Evy said and wiped a tear from the corner of her eye with her forearm.

Tess shared the horror felt by Daisy and Evy but was still mindful of what she could and should say in the presence of inmates. Like Evy, she felt a tear emerging but managed to suppress it.

'Let's wash him and get him dressed,' Tess said and picked up a pair of scissors to carefully cut away the rags that had posed as clothing. With no need to ask again she was joined by the two old inmates in carefully removing the soot and grime that seemed to cover his entire body in varying amounts. The warm soapy water was applied with cloths that had to be continuously rinsed as they turned from white to black and back to a beige as the stains from the soot could not be completely removed. After a few rinses each cloth was replaced with a new one from a small pile by the sink. Jamie's body was beginning to cool but they carried out their task with the gentle hands they might have applied to washing a baby, not wishing to cause an infant discomfort or injury. Working with great diligence soot and grime was removed from every corner and crease of his body, including the small folds of his ears and between his toes. Eventually, after about half an hour, each woman paused to look at his small body cleansed of the world's dirt, satisfied with their efforts to make him look ready for a Christian burial. Finally, they helped each other gently lift Jamie to dress him and Daisy added the last touch by smoothing his wet mop of hair. Their task complete, they left Jamie on the worktable in the laundry room wearing the clean workhouse uniform he would take to his grave.

16 Daniel Ward

'Two constables should be enough,' Daniel Ward thought
as he raised the pewter tankard to his lips. 'If any of them
decide to kick up a fuss, three of us with coshes and a few
cracked heads will soon settle the matter. The bloody doctor
and priest would no doubt start bleating, but they wouldn't
need to know until tomorrow.' He looked around the bar of
the Ram for familiar faces, as some conversation might help
take his mind off more bad news. At the end of the bar stood
three men he thought he recognised and noticed that whilst two
were not facing him, one had fixed his stare directly at him.
Ward nodded, it being too far to say good evening, inviting a
response, but for a moment the man did not, he just maintained
his stare. Then the man relented, nodding in acknowledgement
of Ward's presence, who thought nothing of it and returned to
thinking about the future. 'Perhaps it really is time to move
on.' The option he had considered the previous evening was
becoming more attractive, even before those damn women had
interrupted his pleasure with the girl, Sarah, and then today's
news of Jamie Bell. 'Damn them all!' he muttered to himself
and raised the tankard for another mouthful of ale. He had
turned to face the bottles of wine, port and brandy that lined
the wall behind the bar, so did not notice the approach of the
three men.

'Daniel Ward?' one of them asked, although in truth he
did not need to, as everyone in Hadleigh knew the identity of
the master of the workhouse. Every family feared the prospect
of being housed under his control if they fell upon hard times.

'Aye, that's me,' Ward replied turning to look at the
three men, suddenly sensing menace. He was standing with
his back to the bar as the three men encircled him, so that if
there was a fight and he hit one of them, he would be less able
to defend himself from the blows of the other two. 'What of
it?' he said, realising why the man he thought he knew had not
responded more warmly. Two of them remained either side of
him, while the one who had stared moved closer, creating a

tense atmosphere in the small space the four men inhabited.

'Word spreads in a small town like Hadleigh, Daniel Ward, and word is a small boy who should have been in the workhouse was sold to a master sweep just a few days ago, and now he's dead.' His stare was again fixed on Ward, who looked him up and down. The threat was plain and if it was just the man who spoke Ward would not have been too concerned. His potential opponent was of average build and height, perhaps thirty-five years of age, but Ward could handle himself and was accustomed to the prating of those who disliked his profession. However, he did not fancy a scrap with three men, so he would have to placate them for the time being.

'Indeed, friend, a lad was apprenticed to a local chimney sweep earlier this week, which is common practice placing youngsters in the care of a tradesman,' he replied in a conciliatory tone, offering an explanation. 'They can be trained and learn a trade, enabling them to stand on their own two feet, rather than rely on parish poor relief, at a cost to the ratepayers. Sometimes accidents occur and this is a sad tragedy, so it is.' The usual argument came out easily enough, with Ward adding a tone sympathetic to the fate of the boy, the unfortunate victim of an accident.

'Wealthy ratepayers may be grateful for you putting the inmates to work, Daniel Ward, but ordinary folk are not so impressed as you provide labour to employers for wages a working man cannot compete with,' his opponent said, adding, 'But this isn't about grown men's wages. This is about a young child being set to work and dying, Ward.' He dropped the mister prefix denoting a loss of respect. 'People do not like to think that their own boys, barely six or seven years of age, could be sent up chimneys to die.'

'Listen, friend, I do not set the wages, you should take that up with the employers. My job is to set the inmates to work, and if it can be done providing some income towards the cost of caring for them, then that is what I am required to do.'

'That may be so, Ward, but that should not include small children, and we're no friends of yours.' Ward could see his reasoning was not pacifying his opponent and glancing

175

down he noticed the fists of all three men were clenched, waiting for each other to land the first blow. He steeled himself for the first punch, thinking he could throw at least two punches before he probably went down, but none came as a loud voice from behind the bar pierced the tension.

'You gentlemen seem to be having a serious conversation,' the landlord, Arthur, said bringing his fourteen-inch wooden club down firmly onto the bar with a thud, immediately capturing the attention of the three men encircling Ward, adding, 'I wouldn't want anyone to get hurt in the Ram this evening,' much to Ward's relief. Arthur raised his club so it could be applied in an instant if required. 'You gentlemen should step back a few paces. Perhaps return to the other end of the bar, or even leave,' and without further encouragement the three men backed away. Unable to land the blows they intended, they had to make do with sneers and malevolent looks directed at Ward, resentfully making their way back to the other end of the bar.

'Thank you, Arthur,' Ward said quietly with his back to the bar, sensing the landlord was just behind him whilst maintaining his stare at the three frustrated assailants, lest they had a change of mind.

'You are welcome, Daniel, you are a good customer, but perhaps it would be in your interests to keep your head down for a while,' Arthur whispered leaning forward so no one else could hear.

'Perhaps you are right, Arthur,' he replied and was again left to his thoughts as the landlord moved along the bar towards the three men with the intention of bringing calm to everyone in his inn, the epitome of a responsible landlord. Daniel Ward felt everything was closing in. Questions about money, the doctor and the priest, Tess Yates and her suspicions about the girl, the climbing boy, and now angry locals blaming him for the boy's death. 'Damn them all,' he found himself repeating in his mind, this time with more conviction. Hadleigh was beginning to feel too small for a man of his needs and talents. 'I've had enough of this place.' He emptied the ale from the pewter tankard down his throat and looked over to see the three men were no longer looking in his direction. Before they might notice, he quietly left by the door just ten feet from where he stood and walked briskly the thirty yards or so to the rear entrance of the guildhall, furtively glancing back to ensure he was not being pursued.

Supper was being served and eaten by over seventy inmates, so after the tension and threat inside the Ram, Ward felt some relief to see Robert Cutting and Will Matin. Both were big men, former soldiers with experience of hand-to-hand fighting in the American war. They were recruited by the town to act as constables when there might be the need for increased security, like the summer show when young men might drink too much ale resulting in frayed tempers and fighting. However, inside the guildhall there were no young men emboldened by ale. Neither Robert nor Will needed to wield the cosh each carried, leaving it hidden inside their coats, their presence enough to intimidate the inmates, who walked past the two constables submissively with lowered heads.

Ward stood by the kitchen servery and nodded at the constables, who, unlike the three men in the Ram, responded immediately by returning the gesture. 'This is better,' he thought and felt he could relax, but he was not to be met with warmth or sympathy from everyone. When he looked inside the kitchen he was met with another cold stare, this time from Tess Yates, the disdain on her face suggesting she did not wish to speak to him. 'You too, mistress,' he thought, 'well, you won't have to look at me for much longer.' He walked into the kitchen, picked up a wooden bowl and spoon, then helped himself to mutton stew from the one of the large pots. 'I will be in my room if I am required, mistress, but that should not be necessary with the two constables present until lights out,' he said and left the kitchen without waiting for a reply, which was not forthcoming.

Tess watched Ward leave the eating room with his bowl of stew, noticing him pause to say a few words to Will Matin at the far end before proceeding along the main corridor to his room. 'Good night, Daniel Ward. I hope you are able to sleep tonight,' she said under her breath not thinking anyone could hear, but behind her Daisy had moved close as she collected wooden bowls to be washed.

'I don't think he has a conscience, mistress, so will no doubt sleep well enough,' the elderly inmate said. In a different time, Tess might have chided her for speaking out of place, but not today, not now her estimation of the master had sunk so low. She glanced over her shoulder to see Daisy.

'I fear you are correct, Daisy,' Tess replied and thought about what she could do to be rid of him, unaware of his plans to leave the next morning. Relieved she did not have to speak to him any further that evening, Tess tried to ease the atmosphere by providing the two constables with a large bowl of stew, reassuring them it was unlikely there would be any trouble, particularly as Ward was not present.

The inmates spoke in hushed tones, not wanting to be overheard by the two guards, but their conversations were the same, and by the time supper was over everyone knew of the fate of the boy, Jamie. Martin Lyndon sat across from Ben and Sarah, the girl listening with sadness to their account of what happened in Kersey and found a union with them in despising the master, albeit for different reasons. Whilst her overwhelming emotion was sorrow, Martin's was a seething anger, with Ben's being a combination of theirs.

'I could swing for that bastard,' Martin said quietly, aware that it would not do to announce it but unable to contain himself. 'I see he made off to his room, leaving those two bruisers to keep an eye on us.' His fists clenched tensing the muscles in his arms and Ben was concerned his friend might do something reckless.

'Martin, we all hate him but please don't take matters into your own hands. It would not serve Jamie for any of us to face the gallows,' the young man said with a calm maturity, which continued to impress Sarah, despite having her own reasons for wanting to see the back of Ward. She looked at Ben admiringly, conscious that whilst the man who controlled their lives continued to haunt her, the one alongside her provided some hope, daring to think she might have a future outside the walls of the guildhall. His affection for her was clear, his warm smile being one of the things that made her current life bearable. When allowed some time to think about the future, she wondered if they might one day court, as she knew young men and women did outside the world they inhabited. For the time being, she would have to be patient, wait and hope, and sitting alongside Ben optimism came more easily.

'Aye, you're right, Ben. Don't worry, nothing is likely to happen tonight with those two present in the 'house,' Martin replied, glancing up towards the two constables sitting across the room enjoying Tess Yates' mutton stew. For the time being, Martin would have to wait for justice.

Inside his room, Daniel Ward sat at his desk to eat his supper. Away from everyone he could consider his course of action. He had come to feel comfortable in the room with its small window nine feet up from the floor, allowing some sunlight but preventing prying eyes from outside, just how he liked. His bed, set in an alcove, was hidden by a curtain and a small cupboard contained some clothes and a few worldly goods, most of which would fit into his large canvas bag. Pausing from spooning the stew from the bowl to his mouth, he found himself speaking aloud. 'I know it might be comfortable in this room, Daniel Ward, but they're closing in on you, so you'd better move on.' Listening to his own advice he got up and went over to his bed. It was the same simple frame and straw-filled canvas mattress provided for the seventy-odd inmates, but unlike theirs it had the luxury of a linen feather-filled pillow. Lifting the pillow revealed a small tin, which he picked up and returned with to his desk. Placing it alongside his bowl of stew, he was able to smile to himself. 'You've done well for yourself, Daniel Ward, and here's the proof,' he said, continuing to enjoy conversing with himself. Turning round he took a bottle of port from the shelf and poured a generous measure into a crystal glass, another small luxury in his humble surroundings. Before opening the tin to consider its contents, he moved another spoonful of stew into his mouth. 'No point in letting it get cold,' he muttered through a mouthful of food. Then he took his first draught of port, enjoying the full bodied, slightly sweet, fortified wine, which immediately had a pleasing effect, helping him feel more positive about the evening and the future. 'Right, let us see how much you've got,' and he removed the contents of the tin, placing them down carefully onto his desk. He scooped the last three mouthfuls of stew into his mouth, washed it down with another draught of port and set about counting the money.

Tess Yates filled the bowls of the two constables with second portions of her welcome stew. 'Ah, thank you, mistress Yates,' Will said with a smile, adding, 'You make such work more enjoyable than expected.' The tables had been cleared, the wooden bowls and spoons washed, the inmates had returned to their rooms, which constituted as easy an evening's work as could be hoped for by the two constables.

'You gentlemen are most welcome, I am glad you are here, as trouble would not be in anyone's interest,' Tess said with sincerity, knowing that if there had been violence against Ward, the inmates would pay, and anyway, it would not bring back Jamie. However, that said, she wanted him gone. It was just a matter of how.

'We can stay as long as you require, mistress, but it does not look as if we will be needed. Where is Mr. Ward?' Robert asked.

'He will be eating his supper in his room and will emerge shortly,' Tess replied, uncertain whether that was true, the likelihood being he may fall asleep if he has been imbibing alcohol. However, she hoped he would appear to dismiss the two guards and lock up after lights out. 'You can at least show your face, rather than hiding all night,' she thought, then added after another thought occurred to her, 'Did he pay you for your services this evening?'

'No, mistress, not yet, but that is not an issue, as he can settle with us tomorrow,' Will replied.

'Very well, gentlemen. If Daniel Ward retires early, I can secure the bedrooms after lights out and lock up as you leave.' Tess felt conflicting thoughts; on the one hand she resented his absence, leaving her to do the work, on the other hand glad she did not have to see or listen to him.

'Ninety-six pounds, seven shillings and five pence,'

Ward said to himself. 'A tidy sum of money for any man, so it is, Daniel, enough for a new life in the Americas perhaps,' he continued and leaned back in his chair with a big smile, revealing a line of uneven yellow teeth. 'A tidy sum indeed,' he repeated and rewarded himself with a third glass of port, which following two or three pints of ale earlier in the Ram, served to further anaesthetise his consciousness of the problems of recent days. As the port provided a warm sensation through his body his mind turned to pleasure. 'I can be away before sunrise, borrow a horse from a stable and be in Ipswich in an hour or so. By lunchtime I can be on a packet and sailing for London, or any number of far-off destinations. Hadleigh will not see Daniel Ward again,' he thought. 'Tonight will be the last opportunity to enjoy the company of the girl. She is indeed pleasing on the eye and I would not mind taking her along on a journey,' and he paused to enjoy the thought of having Sarah's company on a sea voyage. 'Perhaps that is not realistic in the circumstances,' he concluded with a smile, returning to what was feasible. 'But I think I might enjoy you tonight, missy,' he said to himself and poured another glass of port.

An hour later, along the corridor the eating room was empty and clean for another day. All of the inmates had been sent to the four large bedrooms, where up to twenty slept each night and time had been allowed for any ablutions. The workhouse settled down to hushed conversations as lights out approached and in the absence of Ward, Tess had told the adult male inmates to ready themselves for bed. This was not an uncommon practice, but what was different was the presence of two constables, which caused some tension amongst a few of the men like Martin and George. They did not take kindly to being guarded, as if prisoners, a further cause of resentment added to the death of the boy. Despite being their match physically, Martin was not likely to take on two big former soldiers armed with coshes and unafraid of using them. Instead, he just stared and scowled, and for a second time that evening he realised his anger would have to wait.

Robert Cutting and Will Matin were feeling relaxed

and happy with an easy job. The workhouse inmates were no bother, helped by them all being sober, which was rarely the case with work outside on Hadleigh's streets, and they had been well fed by Mistress Yates. Payment could wait until tomorrow if Ward was indisposed, which would be no surprise, both were aware of his reputation for enjoying ale, wine and spirits. Standing with Tess on the corridor as the inmates readied themselves for lights out, they were interrupted from their duty by a voice.

'Ah, gentlemen, forgive me for being absent, I needed to rest a while, but I am here now!' and they turned to see the familiar face of the master. As soon as he walked towards them it was apparent to Tess that he had not been sleeping, rather he had eaten his supper and drunk more alcohol. Although he did not stagger, his gait was visibly different. Being less familiar, Robert and Will could not tell, but did notice the friendly tone of his voice.

'Good evening, Mr Ward,' Will replied, followed by Robert joining with a smile and a nod of his head. Tess remained quiet, continuing to weigh him up on the evidence of how he looked and spoke. She had seen him in a variety of inebriated conditions over the last few years and as he stood before them it was not one of the worst, but she had no desire to speak to him unless it was necessary.

'Thank you, gentlemen, for your assistance and diligence this evening,' Ward said, his voice continuing with an affable tone that was beginning to grate on Tess. 'Did Mistress Yates feed you well?' he added, providing further irritation.

'Yes, I did.' She could not bear to listen any longer, adding, 'You need to pay the constables for their services, so they can get home to their beds and we can lock up.'

Checked by the workhouse mistress regarding money, Ward's bonhomie dissipated, not appreciating being told what to do in front of the constables by a female below his station. 'You still harbour animosity towards me, Tess Yates,' he thought as he considered his reply. 'You are quite right, mistress, I have been remiss,' he said with a change in the tone of his voice. 'I shall get the money so you gentlemen can get home. Mistress Yates, I will see to locking up, so you can get yourself to your bed,' he sneered in a patronising tone, telling her to get to bed as he might if she was his wife, daughter, or worse, one of the inmates. Both Robert and Will could sense the change in atmosphere with the master's tone, as a tension appeared between him and the mistress they had not witnessed all evening. In the narrow corridor they felt uncomfortable and would have happily left and waited for payment tomorrow, but that option was removed by Ward exerting his authority. 'Just stay there, you three. I will get your pay and the keys,' and without waiting for a reply he returned to his room, leaving them to wait.

Minutes later the workhouse master handed two shillings to each constable, generous payment for little more than three to four hours in the workhouse, barely worth calling work.

'Thank you, Mister Ward,' Will said.

'Aye, thank you, sir, and thanks also to you Mistress Yates for a generous supper,' Robert added, hoping he might ease the tension at the end of what had been a pleasant job.

'Mistress Yates, why don't you retire for the night, you have toiled enough this evening,' Ward said, his tone less harsh, more considerate, 'I will see the gentlemen to the door and lock up.' He was being more reasonable and in truth Tess was tired.

'Very good, I shall leave you to do that, she said curtly. 'Good night to you both,' she said in a more kindly tone to the constables and turned to make her way to her room at the other end of the corridor.

'Let me just lock this room before you leave, gentlemen,' and whilst they were still there to ensure no late-night uprising, Ward walked twenty-five feet to a door that was closed, placed a key in the lock and turned it firmly, thereby locking up the adult men for the night. From there he escorted the constables to the rear door of the workhouse, bade them good night and secured the 'house from outside intrusion. He had not locked the doors to the other three bedrooms, not wanting to keep Robert and Will waiting, and the inhabitants of those three rooms were no threat. 'I can lock them in shortly,' he thought, 'but it can wait while I have another glass,' and went directly to his room, where he poured more port into the fine crystal glass and sat down to reflect.

'Tess is not going to get over the death of the boy for a while, so if you stay, Daniel Ward, you will face her obstructive prying on a daily basis, as well as the priest and doctor,' he said to himself in an advisory manner. 'Damn it! I will leave at first light. I may be four shillings out of pocket for paying those two, but so be it, I will not tarry another day,' and he paused to take a draught of port, 'but I still have one last night to enjoy the company of the girl.' It was getting dark outside as no light came through the little window and he lit two oil lamps. 'No need to hurry, let the 'house quieten down until everyone has fallen asleep, particularly Tess,' he said to himself, as he settled into his chair with his port and waited. Sitting there in the comfort of his room it occurred to him that he would most likely never see the mistress of the workhouse again, or anyone associated with the place, or Hadleigh for that matter. He resolved to be away before sunrise and on board a ship sailing out of Ipswich by lunchtime. But before getting some sleep, there was Sarah and despite the late hour his desire needed satisfaction.

Taking an oil lamp, he discarded his boots and slipped out of his room, taking care to step carefully and quietly. At the far end of the corridor was Tess Yates' room, with the four inmates' rooms between hers and his room. He only had to pass the men's and boys' rooms to reach the girls' room where Sarah lay. Pausing at the door, which was closed but not locked, he took a deep breath and went in, holding the lamp low so it did not illuminate more of the room than was necessary and he remembered her bed was about halfway along on the right. Just a dozen or so light footsteps down the middle of the room between two lines of beds he arrived at the foot of the bed where she was asleep. Unlike before, he had not told her to come to his room, so he was aware of the threat to his enterprise of waking her suddenly, her taking fright and waking the other fifteen or more girls. Placing the lamp carefully on the floor beside Sarah's bed, it illuminated little more than the floorboards and the space beneath two beds. Moving forward slowly he stood over the girl and could see the shadow cast by her body under the blanket, her head resting on the pillow, her face framed by her fair hair. Feeling aroused, he was drawn towards her, determined as that night would be his last chance to achieve his carnal ambition.

Ward gently but firmly placed his right hand over her mouth, preventing her from calling out. Her eyes opened wide, surprised, shocked. Raising the forefinger of his left hand to his lips he leaned forward until his face was no more than inches from hers, whispering, 'Do not make a sound, missy. You must come to my room.' He kept his hand on her mouth, his face remaining close to hers. 'Do you understand?' She nodded. 'Good, do as you are told.' As he removed his hand from her mouth, it did not occur to Sarah to scream, she was frozen by fear. Instead, she breathed deeply, relieved to be free from suffocation. Within moments of having been asleep she was aware of what was happening and wondered if it was a nightmare, but what informed her that was unlikely was his malodorous alcohol-ridden breath. She closed her eyes, wishing it was a dream, and tears filled her eyes. Ward picked up the lamp and glanced behind to see she had got out of bed, standing in her nightshirt that stopped just at her knees, his desire aroused further. As quietly as he had entered the room, he left with Sarah following close behind and as they passed through the doorway, he paused to close the door. 'This way, missy,' he said quietly and pointed towards his room at the end of the corridor, then followed her so he could admire the curves of her body inside the linen nightshirt, as well as preventing any attempt on her part to turn back. 'My last evening in this place will be pleasurable, after all,' he thought as he followed the girl who would satisfy his desire.

Amy lay awake waiting for them to leave the room, having been woken by the light from the lamp and through almost closed eyes she saw the master lean over and whisper something to Sarah. She did not like the way he placed his hand over her friend's mouth so she could not speak and despite the poor light, she could see Sarah's fear and a tear in her eye. Once they were outside and the door was closed, she waited a minute, then as quietly as she could, she got up and walked to the door. Taking care to open it without sound, she looked right to see if Sarah and Ward were on the corridor, then turned left and walked a dozen footsteps to the women's bedroom to tell Daisy what had happened.

Tears fell as Sarah entered Ward's room and the nightmare of weeks earlier returned. Ward closed the door.

'Here, missy, have a glass of port. You will feel better,' and he walked over to his desk, where he filled the same empty crystal glass he had used. Sarah stood in the middle of the room, trembling with fear, dreading the ordeal she knew was coming. Ward stepped forward so she could again smell his breath, holding the glass up to her mouth.

'Here, drink,' he ordered.

'Sir, I do not wish to drink. Please, I beg you, let me return to my room.'

'Drink!' he said, more forcefully.

Sarah took the glass as there was no escape, lifted it to her mouth and sipped the dark fortified wine.

'Sir, Mistress Yates said…' but before she could say more Ward's face changed to anger and with the back of his hand, he slapped Sarah across the face, also catching her hand that held the glass so it was dashed to the floor, where it shattered, the port splashing across the floorboard. She was stunned by the sharp pain from the blow to her face and tried to get past, but he grabbed her arms, pushing her back towards his desk.

'Mistress Yates might say a lot of things, missy, but have you forgotten who you promised your mother to obey?'

'Sir, please stop!'

'You will pleasure me first, girl,' and he pushed her onto his desk, but as he moved forward to satisfy his desire he was halted by a searing pain in his back. Reaching with his hand he felt blood seeping from the wound and turned to see the old woman.

'You bastard, Ward,' Daisy said and thrust the kitchen

knife deep into his throat. Having turned on unsteady feet after the first thrust, with the second he fell forwards into Daisy, his hands instinctively raised to his throat to stem the blood which flowed with more force than the wound in his back. She was almost knocked to the floor but managed to keep on her feet by stepping to the left whilst pushing his body to the right. So great was the cut his blood gushed out soiling her nightshirt, before pouring onto the floorboards. Laying on the floor, the only sound he made was a desperate choking gasp as blood pumped out of his body, and in less than a minute he was dead.

For a few moments there was quiet as Daisy stood holding the knife, staring in disbelief at what she had done. But there was no regret. She hated him for how he had treated her, even more for what she had learnt about his treatment of Sarah, and the sale of Jamie, so young, to a trade that killed him. Her hatred had intensified over the previous day, so it was without compunction that she took the knife from the kitchen that evening. It was done and if she should go to the gallows, so be it.

Sarah had closed her eyes when she was pushed onto Ward's desk and did not see Daisy enter the room, nor her first thrust of the blade, but his painful groan caused her to witness the second and she saw him fall towards his assailant and bleed out on the floor.

'Daisy!' Sarah exclaimed as the situation changed from her being the victim to something worse. As she spoke the doorway was filled by Gracie Carter and Lucy Draper, with little Amy behind them holding the hand of Evy, who could all immediately see what had unfolded, no need for explanation.

'Let me have that, Daisy,' Gracie said stepping forward, gently taking the knife from the old woman, adding, 'We cannot make this good without the knowledge of the mistress,' knowing that what followed depended on Tess Yates.

'Shall I fetch the mistress?' Evy asked, wanting to help, adding, 'And perhaps I should take Amy back to her bed.'

'Yes, that would be most helpful, Evy,' Gracie replied and they all realised the sight of Ward's body was not one the little girl ought to be exposed to for too long.

'Come Amy, you've been very brave,' Evy said holding her hand and led the little girl out into the corridor.

Within two minutes Tess Yates entered Ward's room wearing her nightshirt and a woollen shawl, with Evy just behind her. 'Dear God, what has happened?' She was shocked by the scene and listened as Sarah and Daisy explained. Like the other five women, Tess paused to think and there was silence in the room as they all pondered what should be done. As she stood thinking it struck Tess that it did not occur to her to blame or raise an alarm. She believed the account of events as told by Sarah and Daisy, his actions no longer shocking or surprising her. 'Damn you, Daniel Ward, you brought this upon yourself,' she thought looking down at his body. The silence was broken by Gracie.

'Mistress, we cannot allow what has happened to become known. We must get his body away from here.'

'Why should we be afraid? He was attacking Sarah and was killed to stop him,' Lucy said.

'It will not be a defence in court, Lucy. The prosecutor will say we could have stopped him without killing him. There were enough of us in this place to overpower him,' Tess said in support of Gracie, as she envisaged how his killing would be viewed by the law.

'When the judge hears of his actions, surely he would show mercy,' Lucy said.

'I doubt it, Lucy. More likely they would see a workhouse master, an important officer of local government, murdered by the inmates. Daisy would be sentenced to death and perhaps we would hang with her as accomplices,' Gracie said.

The others listened carefully, realising Gracie was probably right. Why would a high court judge be merciful? Daisy stood with her arm around Sarah's shoulders, comforting the younger woman who was weeping. The older woman was not afraid, but Sarah's ordeal deepened as she thought of her aged protector going to the gallows. She spoke through tears, her arm around Daisy's waist.

'We must do something.'

'That be right, we need to get his body out of here,' Gracie said, 'there are plenty of folk in Hadleigh who will not be sad at his demise. We could dump him in the Brett and wait for his body to be discovered.' The others nodded in agreement. Why not? It was widely known Ward was said to be too brash with his money recently and the death of Jamie had angered many.

'There would still be an investigation and questions asked,' Tess said. 'Better that he disappeared of his own free will, leaving without notice. People were becoming suspicious, and he faced resentment from all quarters over the death of poor Jamie. There was even talk of a possible prosecution. He might have decided to leave, suddenly, to seek his fortune elsewhere, of which he had spoken more often just recently.'

'Yes, it's true, he might have feared recrimination over the boy,' Gracie said.

'And there was something irregular over money. I overheard the reverend speaking to Mr Brownwigg. Martin has always said Ward had sticky fingers,' Lucy said quietly, glancing over her shoulder lest they too should be overheard, but she need not have worried as Ward's door had been firmly closed by Tess.

'Well, then we just have to put the corpse where it will never be found,' Gracie said, 'perhaps an unmarked grave?'

'That would involve digging a grave and burying him without being noticed, which would not be easy,' Tess said, adding, 'I have an idea, but we may need some help. I do not want to wake all the men, the fewer who know the better. Perhaps Ben could assist us?'

Sarah had stood listening quietly but felt a shudder at hearing his name, fearing his feelings for her might be affected by him becoming aware of what had happened that night and before. How could she expect him to not find out and would she now be considered unfit as a future wife? Along with the trauma of being attacked, she felt ashamed, even though she bore no guilt.

Lucy went to get Ben from the boys' bedroom, who on arriving in the room was, like Tess, shocked by the scene, but his immediate concern was Sarah, whose distressed condition was clear. 'Sarah, are you hurt?' he said looking straight at her without a thought for the body on the floor, wishing he could fold his arms around her, to offer comfort and protection. He had suspected the master's intentions and had been in turmoil over what to do, but now it was solved, and the sight of her distraught melted his heart.

'She is safe, Ben,' Gracie said.

'What can I do to help?' he asked.

'Well, I think Sarah should get back to her room and bed. You too, Daisy, you must be tired. If Evy could clean up the mess, the four of us can take Daniel Ward somewhere I am confident he will not be found,' Tess said and the others all paid attention. Evy took Sarah and Daisy back to their bedrooms, but after a few minutes Daisy returned insisting on helping to clean the mess she had created. They all listened with some incredulity to Tess's plan, but after some brief consideration accepted it was as good as any other option. The first thing they had to do was get into clothes they could wear outside, so quickly went to their rooms to dress, returning with their boots in their hands lest they woke others. Tess took the blanket from his bed and Ward's body was wrapped inside the thick, strong fabric. Then taking a corner each they carefully lifted the heavy package, carrying it into the corridor and along to the back of the building, preceded by Evy who, having been handed the keys by Tess, unlocked the rear door. Outside they could speak in hushed voices in the darkness.

'We will be a while, Evy, but will return before sunrise,' Tess said.

'Shall I lock the door and wait here for your return, mistress?'

'No, that is not necessary, Evy. We can take a chance on no one trying to enter the 'house tonight. Once his room is cleaned of blood, wine and broken glass, you should get some sleep.'

'Thank you, mistress. Good luck,' and with that Evy returned into the building to get water, soap and cloths to set about her task, assisted by her friend, Daisy.

Ben wheeled the workhouse handcart which was kept in the alleyway round to the back door. This night its role was different to its usual purpose of carrying tools for work, cloth for making uniforms, bones for crushing, ingredients for feeding the inmates, and any other necessary transportation. Ward's body was lifted into the cart and with the two long handles, one held by Tess, the other by Ben, it was pushed out onto the road, past the Ram Inn, towards Toppesfield Bridge.

In darkness the road and tracks they would follow could have been hazardous; a broken wheel being the last thing they wanted, but they were fortunate the late summer sky was clear with a full moon and bright stars. The tall wheels turned slowly, the iron rims rattling on the ground, but it was not a noise likely to cause alarm to people in their beds, just a background sound, probably a trader moving his wares.

'How far is it to Polstead following this route, mistress,' Ben asked as they approached the bridge across the River Brett. He was familiar with the route that followed the road north out of Hadleigh, turning west on the Sudbury road for a couple of miles, then south at Hadleigh Heath. However, whilst he was aware there was a more direct south-west route to Polstead, he would not know which farm track and path to follow.

'Perhaps four miles, Ben, but my family farm is closer to Polstead Heath, so only three miles. I have walked the path countless times since I was a girl, so we will not get lost. But be warned, it climbs steeply as we leave Hadleigh, then again near the end.'

'We can share the work, mistress,' Lucy said. She and Gracie were walking either side of the cart and whilst they would normally be asleep at this hour, they were relieved to be outside getting rid of Ward once and for all.

'That will be much appreciated Lucy,' Tess replied, 'you will soon see why.'

Across Toppesfield Bridge they turned left after Tinkers Lane which Ben knew well from his walk to work at the mill. He recognised the road that led directly to Lower Layham but after about 300 yards Tess told them to turn right.

Immediately the smaller track began to climb a hill and Ben ceased to recognise the surroundings, as well as breathing more deeply as he joined Tess in leaning forward to apply more force. As the cart slowed Lucy and Gracie did not need to be asked, joining Ben and Tess at the rear and doubling the force in pushing it up the hill. In the dark they could see a short distance ahead but not the top of their climb.

'Is it a long hill, mistress?' Ben asked, his armpits moist from sweat. As he spoke, he knew the answer, realising they were climbing the hill that was visible looking across the river away from the town.

'There's a farm at the top, Ben. Can you guess its name?' Tess asked, breathing heavily.

'No, mistress.'

'Hill Farm.'

Despite the heavy toil and the serious nature of their endeavour, all four were able to laugh, the levity most welcome, and they applied themselves to getting the cart with its heavy load to the top of the hill with more vigour. After ten minutes or so the ground levelled, to the relief of all four, and they paused to rest for a minute.

'We cannot see it in the dark, but Hill Farm is just over there,' Tess said pointing to the left, and as she did several dogs started barking, alert to the presence of strangers a short distance from the farm and its livestock they guarded through the night. Ben looked nervous, the loud barking sounding closer than he would have liked.

'Do not be afraid, Ben. I know this family and their dogs, but we won't tarry to be discovered with him in the cart,' and they pressed on as the path turned right away from the invisible Hill Farm behind them. The terrain became easier, Lucy and Gracie taking hold of the long handles, pushing the cart, and after several bends they passed another farm.

'Frogg Hall Farm,' Tess said, 'not far to go.' And after a bit further, 'Pott's Farm. Up ahead is the Polstead road, where we turn left. It's just a mile or so from here.' Sure enough, after a while the path ended where it met a wider track. 'Over there to the right is Hadleigh Heath and the Sudbury road,'

Tess said, 'but we are going this way,' leading them to the left. After another ten minutes or so in the dark they could see a collection of buildings to the right. 'Polstead Heath. Nearly there.'

'Finally, here we are, home,' Tess said with a smile as she stopped at a path. 'We can push the cart a bit further, but then we must leave it lest we wake my family.' Arriving at their destination they began to feel nervous about the most critical stage of their endeavour. 'Stop here and lift him out,' Tess instructed and they each grabbed a corner of the blanket, carrying him along the path. A dog growled in the darkness, as was its instinct to guard its masters' property against intruders, causing hesitation amongst three of them, but not Tess. 'Jem, here boy,' she said quietly, causing the barking to stop on recognition of her voice, and a large dog of indistinguishable breed emerged wagging its tail. 'Good boy, Jem,' Tess said as he circled her. Jem sniffed each of the others but was most intrigued by the fifth person carried in the blanket, licking what Ben guessed was blood that had seeped into the fabric. Carrying Ward's corpse wrapped in the blanket, they stopped at a gate, the other side of which they could see the ground change from grass to broken earth, deeply pockmarked so that in winter it would be heavy mud. 'We need to take off his clothes, let's do that here,' Tess whispered. There was no discussion, having come this far, there was no turning back, so placing their package on the ground they unwrapped it, removing his boots and every item of clothing until he lay naked, drawing further attention from the hound. 'Stay, Jem,' Tess said, pushing him away with her leg, before opening the gate. Lifting Ward by each grabbing hold of a wrist or ankle, they carried him into a field with rutted earth. Tess kicked the gate to close it, preventing anything from entering or leaving. 'Bring him over here.' Taking care to not stumble on the uneven ground they carried him twenty yards further into the field. 'Put him down here.' With more care than was necessary for the corpse of a man they all despised, Ward was gently lowered to the ground. Ben peered into the darkness, uncertain of what might happen next and then he heard grunting. 'Elsa!

Over here girl,' Tess said quietly and like Jem minutes earlier, another animal emerged, but this one was much larger. It snorted and lumbered towards the five people in its field, four of whom backed away leaving the fifth prone on the ground. The huge sow sniffed Daniel Ward, rooting around with her long snout, checking if he might move, but he laid still. Watching in horror, they saw her drawn to the blood seeping from his neck, then she opened her jaws and closed them firmly about the deep wound left by the kitchen knife. The effect on the sow was immediate, becoming excited, grunting louder and moving quicker than expected for a beast so large, as if she had to eat quickly before the people withdrew her meal. Then they realised the reason for her haste as more snorting was heard and three more slightly smaller sows appeared from the darkness, competition for Elsa, drawn by the sounds made by their mother. Within seconds the four large pigs were grunting and gnawing at Daniel Ward, chewing his flesh and muscle, crunching through his bones.

'Dear God, look at that!' Gracie said unnecessarily, as all four were transfixed by the sight of a man being consumed by four sows. After some moments, Tess interrupted the spell.

'Well, I thought we could rely on Elsa and her daughters. I think that is the last we, or anyone, will see of Daniel Ward. Let's gather his clothes, boots and blanket and be gone.' Without further word they followed Tess back to the gate, glancing over their shoulders for one last look at the pigs enjoying an unexpected late-night supper, a scene that quickly disappeared in the darkness but could still be heard. Securing the gate, Tess leaned down to Jem, scratching his chin. 'Good boy, Jem. Stay here.' Ward's clothing and boots were wrapped in the blanket carried by Ben and they made their way back to the cart.

An hour later they returned the cart to the alley beside the guildhall and quietly crept back to their rooms and into bed. The last thing Tess did was place the folded blanket and its contents at the bottom of her cupboard until an opportunity would arise for them to be burnt.

17 Disappeared

Looking across the graves occupying the space between the guildhall and St Mary's, despite the bright early morning sunshine, Tess felt there was a distinctly autumnal air. It was cooler and the leaves on the trees over to the left by the deanery were beginning to change colour. Tess had woken early, in fact she was uncertain of how much she slept, the events of the previous twelve hours having filled her mind throughout the night, a good deal of it self-doubt. 'Deary me, Tess Yates, what's done is done, there's no going back,' she said quietly to herself. No one was in sight, the guildhall front door was closed behind her so she would hear if someone came to her from within, where the inmates slept before the morning bell announced the start of another day. Minutes earlier she had walked past Daniel Ward's room quietly, as if he was inside sleeping, but of course he was not. His absence could be ignored for a while, him sleeping off a hangover was not an unknown practice and the two constables could confirm he appeared to have been drinking throughout the previous evening. But she knew that could be used to account for his absence for perhaps the morning, after which his whereabouts would be questioned. The fresh morning air helped clear her head and she thought about what she discussed with the others the previous night. If he fled and made off before sunrise, what would he take? Pausing for a moment to breathe in deeply, she looked around at the gravestones and up at the majestic church. Then she returned through the guildhall door into the workhouse and the masters's room.

Evy and Daisy had swept up the broken glass and washed the floorboards, leaving just a small damp patch. 'If someone saw it, they might become suspicious,' Tess thought. 'Why would he wash the floor before making off?' Looking around she noticed the small rug near the curtain that hid his bed, so she picked it up and laid it over the damp area. Returning to the curtain, she pulled it back to reveal his bed, the sheet was creased and his pillow compressed where his head had rested. It had not been tidied from when he slept there two nights ago, and she made a mental note to replace the missing blanket. In one corner of the room was the cupboard containing his clothes and other worldly goods. Inside, on the shelves were an assortment of clothing items and at the bottom was a large canvas bag, which she opened and filled, leaving the shelves empty. On Ward's desk she noticed a tin, which she recognized as the one he used for storing money. Opening the tin, expecting to see a pile of banknotes, she was taken aback by there being only five pennies. Tess was perplexed. 'Is it possible he hid the money somewhere else?' she thought, but it was not something she could investigate there and then. It was time to get the inmates up and fed, as if it was just another day, so she looked around the room and was satisfied with how it looked. Then she quietly made her way to her own room, where she stored Ward's bag and possessions alongside his blanket and clothes in her cupboard. On the shelf above her bed was a folded spare blanket, so before ringing the bell to wake the inmates, she quickly returned to the master's room, where she let the blanket fall loosely across his bed, pulling back one side so it touched the floor.

Like Tess, her six co-conspirators did not sleep soundly, and were all awake when the bell rang to signal the start of another day. Amy, who had witnessed Ward's body lying on the floor in his room, before being returned to her bed by Evy, was not one of the seven but she was also awake. As sunlight streamed through the small windows high above their beds, she lay on her side facing Sarah just a few feet away, whose eyes were also open.

'Are you afraid, Sarah?' the little girl whispered.

'A little bit. Are you?' the older girl replied.

'Yes, a little,' Amy said, her eyes wide open, uncertain of what happened.

None of the other girls had stirred, or if they had, they were content to doze until the bell ordered them to rise. Seeing Amy was in need of reassurance, Sarah lifted her blanket and smiled, inviting Amy to join her, which was gratefully accepted, and the little girl climbed into the small bed for a comforting hug. It was a small act of affection shared by most of the girls at some time during their lives as inmates, particularly the younger ones who missed a mother's warm embrace. Sarah covered them both with her blanket and folded her arms around Amy, providing warmth and protection.

'Mister Ward has gone, Amy,' Sarah whispered, 'but we must keep what we saw last night a secret.'

'Yes, I understand. Our secret. He hurt you and Daisy. I am glad he has gone,' Amy replied with a whisper and closed her eyes as she snuggled closer to her friend.

In the women's bedroom Daisy and Evy were always awake early, their duties beginning before other inmates, helping Tess prepare the large pots of porridge for breakfast. As well as them, along the two rows of beds on the other side of the women's bedroom, Gracie and Lucy were also both awake and they, like Ben in the boys' bedroom, could not rid from their minds the memory of the four sows devouring the corpse of Daniel Ward. None of them slept much, all uncertain of what would happen next as they waited for the bell to start the day.

If they had been sitting together at breakfast, the six co-conspirators might have been conspicuous by their subdued moods, which contrasted with the other sixty-odd inmates, who after a night's sleep were still pre-occupied with the death of Jamie and for some a growing anger towards the man they held responsible. Martin Lyndon and George Maguire sat facing Ben.

'I see he has not yet shown his face this morning,' George said, the contempt in his voice making it plain to whom he referred.

'Aye, he will do well to keep out of the way,' Martin replied, 'I reckon there are plenty in here who would happily stick a blade in his back.'

Ben looked down, then glanced over to another table, where Sarah sat with Amy and some other girls. Rather than concur with his friend, he felt he ought to recommend discretion.

'Be careful, Martin, lest we are heard.'

'Do not be afraid, Ben, there are none in here who would be sorry to see an end to Ward,' Martin replied, not wanting to unduly worry the young man he had come to like. 'He will most likely appear soon enough, worse for ale or wine, as if nothing untoward had happened in the last day or two,' and with that, Martin scooped two spoonfuls of porridge into his mouth. Before he had the opportunity to say anything further, or continue eating, he and all the inmates facing the far end of the eating room had their attention captured by the appearance of five men who must have entered the workhouse through the guildhall front door. Two were very familiar, Reverend Watson and Doctor Parsons, a third the recognisable John Brownwigg, and the last two being the constables from the previous night. Those inmates not facing the door at the end of the room could see from the looks on those opposite that something unusual had happened or appeared, resulting in about thirty heads turning to see.

'Looks like the constables have returned for a free breakfast, lads,' Martin said with a wry smile, but his levity was lost on Ben, who immediately felt a nervous tension tighten around his stomach.

'Are you unwell, Ben?' George asked, seeing his face turn ashen.

Ben gathered himself and was grateful to see the five men walk directly towards the kitchen, where Tess stood.

'I will be fine, George, thank you. I did not sleep well last night. I think the death of Jamie has affected us all.' He lied convincingly.

'Aye, that's understandable, lad. The sadness of his death will cause sleepless nights for a while to come,' George said sympathetically.

'But not by Ward,' Ben replied, although the ambiguity of his statement could not to be appreciated by George and Martin.

As the five men approached Tess, Ben felt some concern for the workhouse mistress who he had never witnessed mistreating inmates, hoping she would be able to withstand any interrogation. 'Why have they appeared so early?' he thought. 'Perhaps the sows did not eat all of his corpse, leaving parts of him recognisable?' The gory thought was horrifying, but also frightening for what might follow. 'But surely his identity could not be discovered so soon,' and his mind was racing to make sense of why they should be there in the workhouse so early. However, all he could do was watch Tess lead the men out of the eating area towards Ward's room, where he should have been sleeping.

'Mr Ward!' George Watson said loudly, banging his fist against the door, but there was no reply. 'Daniel Ward!' he called his face close to the door. He turned to the other four and Tess, looking for suggestions.

'Here, let me,' John Brownwigg said stepping forward and turning the handle. He had other matters to attend to and as far as he was concerned, Ward was a boil that needed to be lanced. The revelations he had uncovered with the doctor and the priest were illegal, as well as a personal affront. 'How much of my money have you pocketed, Ward?' he had thought the previous night. Without ceremony, Brownwigg led them in.

'He's not here...' John Parsons stated the obvious as they all stood inside Ward's room.

'Was he here last night, mistress Yates?' Brownwigg asked, irritated that he may have wasted his time.

'Yes, sir. He came back from one of the ale houses, probably the Ram. He paid the constables and told me to go to bed as I had served supper without his help, and that he would lock up.' Tess replied and looked at the two constables, Robert and Will, for confirmation.

'Aye, what the mistress says is true, sir' Robert said, adding, 'We were here throughout the evening and Ward arrived during supper. He took a plate of food to his room, emerging later, just before lights out.'

Will decided to contribute, providing further corroboration of Tess's account. 'Mister Ward paid us, sent the mistress to bed and had us wait while he locked one of the inmates' bedrooms, probably the men's. Then he saw us out before locking up for the night.'

'Is something amiss, sir?' Tess asked innocently.

Reverend Watson realised they had caused her alarm through no fault of her own.

'Yes, but please do not worry, mistress, as it is not of your doing,' George said reassuringly, as like the doctor he was aware of her concerns and upset over the fate of Jamie.

As each of them surveyed the room, John Parsons walked over to the cupboard, which upon opening was found to be empty.

'It looks as though Mister Ward has fled,' the doctor said standing back to reveal the empty cupboard.

'What is this?' Brownwigg asked picking up the metal box on the desk.

'That looks like the tin he used for storing money he collected, sir, before paying it over to the vestry,' Tess replied, and they all paused as Brownwigg opened the tin and emptied it of the five pennies.

'Well, I don't know how much was in the tin, but I do know I paid four pounds seven shillings and eight pence this week for workhouse labour. Has he paid over to the vestry any sums of money this week, Reverend Watson?' the businessman asked.

'Only the money he received for selling the boy, Jamie, to the chimney sweep,' George replied.

'Damn him,' Parsons said, 'he's flown the nest, just as we were closing in on him.'

'What do you mean, doctor?' Tess asked.

'The master was embezzling vestry funds, mistress,' Brownwigg said.

'He appears to have been skimming money from the sums collected for workhouse labour. We have suspected this for a week or two but had to investigate monies collected against monies paid to the vestry. It was the employment of the young man, Benjamin Squirrell, at Mr Brownwigg's Toppesfield Mill that first made us suspect something. But it was discovering how much was paid for poor Jamie Bell that made us certain,' John Parsons explained.

'He's a most corrupt, venal, immoral man!' George Watson exclaimed in disgust.

'But where would he go?' Tess asked.

Robert Cutting looked around the room. 'No bag, no clothes, no money, no workhouse master. I suspect he made off in the night, or before dawn.'

'It was a full moon and clear sky last night, so if he left after the 'house was asleep, he could be in Ipswich by now, or even on a packet sailing to London,' Will Matin added to his colleague's investigative reasoning.

'Why would he go there?' Tess asked.

'As the reverend has suggested, his immorality has led him to commit crimes for which the punishment would be severe in a court of law, mistress,' Brownwigg explained. 'Prison or transportation may not suffice for his transgressions, I fancy Mister Ward would likely face the gallows, and he would be aware of that. London, or further afield would be his destination. Somewhere he could find safety through anonymity.'

'Aye, the Americas, or India, would be my guess,' Robert said, his experience as a constable offering further understanding to how a criminal mind might work. His prognosis was met with nods by the others as they considered the evidence as it appeared before them. Tess felt relief, as like Ben she had wondered why the visitors had appeared so early, thankful to hear it was to arrest Ward for his misdemeanours. The conclusions reached by Mister Brownwigg and Constable Cutting were exactly as she might have hoped.

'Unless he reappears, I think our search for Ward is finished here, gentlemen and Mistress Yates,' Brownwigg said. He was a busy man and saw no reason to dwell on the matter. 'He will not show his face again in Suffolk, of that I am certain. Although perhaps the constables could make inquiries in Ipswich?'

'Aye, that we could, sir,' Will Matin replied, 'if the good people of Hadleigh are prepared to pay for our time.' He looked at the three members of the vestry, inviting a reply. Criminals had to be pursued, the law seen to be followed, but if they wanted him and Robert to look for a fugitive, who could be anywhere, they would have to fund such a search.

For a moment there was a quiet pause as Brownwigg, Parsons and Watson considered whether to commission the constables in what was likely to be a fruitless search. Economic reality outweighed the pursuit of justice.

'We could send you on a chase that has no end, as we do not know where he was bound,' George Watson said disappointingly, realising Ward had probably escaped justice and conscious of the cost of two constables looking for him God knows where.

'I fear you are correct, reverend,' Brownwigg said, 'it grates with our conscience that he may not face justice. We could send word to Ipswich, Colchester, other East Anglian towns, and even London. Perhaps a wanted poster and reward. You would be surprised what the offer of money can do to the civic responsibility of the masses.' Again, there was a collective consideration of their options. Tess remained silent, hoping the others would accept the strategy offered by Mister Brownwigg, which gradually came to fruition with further nods of heads and no alternatives.

'Well, there we are. He is gone. We can have a poster drafted offering a reward for information leading to his arrest, with copies taken to those towns and cities you mentioned, Mister Brownwigg. We will also have to find a new master, but can we ask you to manage without for a short while, Mistress Yates?' George Watson said.

'I am sure I can manage, sir.'

'If security and order is a concern, we could have one of the constables assist you,' George added.

'Thank you, sir. It is reassuring to know they are about if required,' Tess replied and thought the presence of Robert or Will would be more welcome company than she had known with Ward, both constables being tall, strong, and pleasing to her eye.

'Ward's work collecting rates and wages paid for workhouse labour might be covered by Mister Grady and Mister Hancock,' John Parsons suggested, and the immediate future running of the workhouse and poor relief provision in Hadleigh seemed to be in order.

'Yes,' George replied, 'we have some tasks to attend to, so perhaps we can adjourn our meeting here.'

'Aye, we all have work to attend to, and there is nothing else we can do here,' Brownwigg said, 'I think Mistress Yates has her hands full and we are in the way, so let us be on our way.'

'Indeed. We are sorry to cause alarm, mistress. Let us know if assistance is required. I can return later,' the doctor said, and he opened the door, inviting them all to leave.

'Thank you, sirs,' Tess replied and led them out.

As the last, Will Matin, left the room Doctor Parsons turned to take one last look at Ward's room, which was easier to survey with the other five out in the corridor. It looked tidy enough, no longer inhabited, and as he was about to turn to join the others, closing the door behind him, he noticed the rug in front of Ward's desk, which struck him as an odd place for it to be located. Looking down at it, he also noticed a partly discoloured patch of floorboard to one side of the rug, so he closed the door quietly and went over to the space in front of the desk. Kneeling down, John Parsons lifted the rug to reveal a large patch of damp floorboard, which he touched with two fingers. 'Hmm, this must have been washed in the last twelve hours, I wonder why?' he said quietly to himself, and as he stood, he turned to see Tess Yates in the doorway.

'Is there a problem, doctor?'

'No, there is nothing to worry about, mistress. Nothing at all. Perhaps Mister Ward spilt some wine last night,' and before he joined the others in the corridor he paused to speak in a hushed voice. 'Do not fear, mistress. Whatever happened here, we are better for seeing the back of that heinous man.'

'Yes, doctor. Thank you,' Tess replied and closed the door.

18 Endings

Ben paused on Toppesfield Bridge, as there were some minutes before he was due to start work at the mill. A gaggle of geese, perhaps twelve in number, squawked loudly as they followed each other from the riverbank into the water, forming a winding line that made its way under the bridge. He was struck by how happy they appeared to be with life, able to co-exist without rancour or cruelty. Finally, he was about to start his apprenticeship to become a miller and would reside outside the workhouse, where he witnessed too many of those human traits that did not appear to afflict the geese. However, even in the workhouse there was hope after the demise of Daniel Ward. Tess Yates was in control of life inside the guildhall, and whilst labour continued to be a daily ritual for the inmates, they faced more benevolent custodians, with Tess supported by Reverend Watson and Doctor Parsons.

Just two days after the disappearance of the master, Watson and Parsons learnt more of the circumstances of Sarah's family and she was immediately returned to the cottage, where her mother was reassured she and her four children would be secure in their tenancy. Poor relief, providing food, clothing and fuel would be maintained, and Sarah was found a position to train as a seamstress to provide some income, for which she was grateful, whilst still harbouring an ambition to become a teacher. 'Why not?' George Watson said when Sarah shared her aspirations and promised he would enquire with trustees of the Ann Beaumont charity that supported education in the town. Before she left, Ben was able to speak to her privately and they were both delighted to hear the other state their hope that they might court once outside the confines of the guildhall. For the past few days that conversation had filled Ben's thoughts, giving him more cause for optimism as he crossed to the other side of the bridge to watch the gaggle wind its way upstream.

'Ben! Benjamin Squirrel!' a voice called from behind, and he turned to see a young woman running towards him along Tinkers Lane. She was laughing as she ran with some difficulty, one hand holding her bonnet in place as strands of fair hair blew free, the other hand attempting to hold her long skirt down for the purpose of modesty, as it bounced against her legs threatening to rise above her knees.

'Sarah!' he exclaimed with excitement and a broad smile appeared across his face. 'What are you doing here?' he asked as she only came to a halt a yard before running into him. Her bonnet safe and skirt in place, her arms could hang to the side as she panted, catching her breath. Her laughter had ceased but she too had a broad smile.

'Well, I thought I would take the morning air and decided to walk along the river by the mill.'

Ben was overjoyed to see her, and in his innocence failed to read between the lines. 'Why would you walk down here? Is it to see the geese?'

'Actually, I wondered if I might see a friend.'

'Oh, a friend. Who...' and the penny dropped. His heart immediately raised a beat or two and he had a warm feeling inside that spread to his head, turning his cheeks red. 'I, I am really very pleased to see you...' and for a moment he was lost for words.

'Benjamin Squirrel, it's you! I came out for a morning stroll hoping I might see you.' Sarah looked into his eyes, then downwards, slightly embarrassed that she might have been too forward, and for a moment there was quiet.

Ben realised Sarah had made an effort to see him to say hello, providing further cause for optimism. Gently taking her hands in his, he wanted to embrace her but was uncertain whether that was the right thing to do on Toppesfield Bridge at about ten minutes to seven in the morning.

'Sarah?'

'Yes, Ben,' she replied looking up at him with less than twelve inches separating them.

'Would it be proper for me to kiss you on the cheek?' he asked, and a smile reappeared on her face.

'If no one is looking, I think that should be acceptable,' and without waiting she leaned forward to kiss Ben on his cheek, which gave him a pleasurable feeling he had never known, then returned the gesture, and again they stood silent for a few seconds, happy with simply being so close to each other.

Ben's thoughts of work had vanished, content to stand with Sarah on the bridge all morning, but she realised that was neither practical or possible and broke the silence.

'Shall I walk with you along to the mill. Then I can carry on up Tinkers Lane to Benton Street? Or would you rather I go the other way?'

The alternative route produced a look of horror on the young man's face.

'No, no, please walk with me,' he replied, delighted they could have a few more minutes together before he entered the mill for the day's work with Steven, Peter and Will. Few words were spoken, each happy to just be alongside the other, until a thought occurred to Sarah.

'Ben, have you heard about Daisy and Evy?'

'No,' he immediately replied stopping to face Sarah, concerned it was bad news, which she could see in his face.

'Oh Ben, I am sorry, I did not mean to alarm you. It is good news. A benefactor has provided them with a small cottage at Benton End, so they will be leaving the workhouse this week.'

Ben's look of concern was replaced by another broad smile. Daisy and Evy had been residents in the workhouse for longer than most could remember, and it seemed they might live out their lives in that place, the only possible alternative being an almshouse, an option that had not been realised.

'This is most wonderful news, Sarah,' and once again he wanted to envelop her in his arms.

'But there is a condition, Ben.'

'What is it, Sarah?' he asked, fearing a financial commitment the two elderly women could not possibly meet.

'They are required to provide a home to at least one, possibly two, orphans,' she said with a smile.

'Oh,' Ben said, wondering who they might house, but he need not have worried.

'They are going to take in Amy!' Sarah exclaimed as St Mary's bell was struck and they were sixty yards short of the mill. 'Oh, Ben, you must not be late, I am sorry if I have got you into trouble.'

'Sarah, seeing you has made me so happy, and I am most grateful for the news of Daisy, Evy and Amy. But you are right, I must hasten to the mill.' He paused. 'Does this mean we are courting?' he asked with a smile.

'I hope so, Benjamin Squirrel. If it would please you,' she replied, with a look of hope for the future that melted his heart.

'That is everything I could wish for,' the young man said.

'Then you had better get to work,' and with that she leaned forward to kiss him again on the cheek. 'Go on, Benjamin Squirrell, don't be late!' she concluded with a smile and watched him run the last stretch of Tinkers Lane to Toppesfield Mill, where he would continue his apprenticeship and make his way in the world.

As Ben disappeared into the tall white building, Sarah resumed her walk along Tinkers Lane past the mill to where it turned left to ford the River Brett, after which it became a short steep climb to Benton Street. Pausing for a moment, her thoughts returned to what she had told Ben about Daisy and Evy's good fortune. Or rather, she thought about what she could not yet share with him. 'He does not need to know Doctor Parsons was the anonymous benefactor who provided the sum of ninety-five pounds for the purpose of purchasing a cottage to house Daisy, Evy and Amy. Nor does he need to be privy to who gave that sum of money to the doctor. Perhaps it is something we can share at a later date,' she thought, pleased with the part she had played. As she arrived at the end of Tinkers Lane a light morning breeze blew along Benton Street, a smile returned to Sarah's face and the future looked much brighter.

***

Richard Leatherton, a successful draper, and four fellow trustees of the Market Feoffment had gathered in the large dining room upstairs at the George tavern to mark the end of Daniel Ward's position as workhouse master. There may have been some reservations over his misdemeanours, particularly embezzling vestry funds, but they had all been indebted to him for his contribution towards keeping down the labour costs they all faced as men of business. However, none felt any strain of conscience, the overall feeling being that those misdemeanours were not their doing as local businessmen and ratepayers. 'The vestry had only itself to blame for not keeping a closer eye on receipts,' had been uttered more than once.

Richard stood up to raise his glass just as dinner was brought into the room by the landlord, Andrew Baines, accompanied by Ruth, a young serving maid who drew admiring glances.

'What dish are we being served this evening, Andrew?'

'Pork, sir. A lovely piece of pork, slaughtered just yesterday, I am assured by the butcher.'

'Very nice, Andrew. Is it locally sourced?'

'Yes, sir. Fresh Suffolk pork, from just up the road at the Yates' Farm in Polstead.'

'Excellent,' Richard said as the large silver plate of sliced pork was placed in the middle of the table, 'Gentlemen, I give you Daniel Ward,' and the five feoffment trustees and local businessmen raised their glasses as one in memory and celebration of the workhouse master.

Further novels by Peter Holland

Peter Holland's first novel, *Barbary Slave*, explores a little-known part of British and Irish history, the white slave trade. The Ottoman Empire had an insatiable appetite for manpower, whether they were from Africa or Europe, and between 1500 and 1800 it is estimated more than 1.25 million Christian Europeans were seized and became slaves.

Barbary Slave is set in 1631, the year of the notorious Sack of Baltimore in Ireland, led by the infamous Murat Reis. All of the other characters in *Barbary Slave* are fictitious but the story of former Spanish Muslims known as Moriscos who became corsairs is true, as is the description of Algiers as a major centre for the holding and trading of white European slaves. The story of Said, Khaled, Callum, Jack, Laura, Mary, Pedro, Oji, Anna, Mehmed and Madeline, is of lives entwined in this tumultuous year.

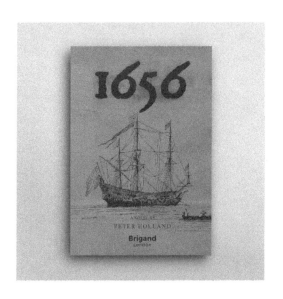

Further novels by Peter Holland

The author's second novel, *1656*, is a sequel to *Barbary Slave*, set twenty-five years after Laura, Callum and Jack were taken captive by Barbary corsairs. England has been through Civil War, a revolution, regicide and significant social change, but the issue of the white slave trade persists. In *1656*, Oliver Cromwell's republic rules through his control of Parliament, and like Charles' earlier government in 1631, the new republic wants to find a solution to the problem of the enslaved in north Africa. Major Adam Pisaner, chosen to find a way of redeeming captives from Algiers, turns to some of the very few people in England with experience of captivity for their advice and help, Laura, Callum and Jack. *1656* tells of their exciting second adventure, during which these ordinary citizens meet the Lord Protector himself.

Further novels by Peter Holland

Peter Holland's third novel, *Susan Bounty*, is set in the same period as his second, but explores different issues that affected everyone living in Britain under the rule of a Puritan Parliament. Between 1648 and 1653 morality laws were passed to make England more godly; adultery, blasphemy, fornication and heresy becoming crimes to be punished severely. Susan Bounty, a young woman from Devon pursued by an amorous married man, was amongst those affected, as were former Parliamentarian soldiers wanting greater political rights and freedom of conscience to worship God as they chose. Oliver Cromwell, a former soldier himself, as well as being the Lord Protector and leader of the country, was placed in a difficult position as many in Parliament demanded transgressors be dealt with by the law. Major Steven Flain, and the scholar, John Milton, were two of the few people he could trust.